Bruce B

Murder at the Meet

A detective novel

LUCiUS

Text copyright 2020 Bruce Beckham

All rights reserved. Bruce Beckham asserts his right always to be identified as the author of this work. No part may be copied or transmitted without written permission from the publisher.

This is a work of fiction. Names, characters, places and incidents either are the product of the author's imagination or are used fictitiously. Any resemblance to actual persons, living or dead, events and locales is entirely coincidental.

Kindle edition first published by Lucius 2020

Paperback edition first published by Lucius 2020

For more details and Rights enquiries contact:
Lucius-ebooks@live.com

Cover design by Moira Kay Nicol

EDITOR'S NOTE

Murder at the Meet is a stand-alone crime mystery, the fourteenth in the series 'Detective Inspector Skelgill Investigates'. It is set primarily in Borrowdale in the English Lake District – a National Park of 885 square miles that lies in the rugged northern county of Cumbria.

BY THE SAME AUTHOR

1. *Murder in Adland*
2. *Murder in School*
3. *Murder on the Edge*
4. *Murder on the Lake*
5. *Murder by Magic*
6. *Murder in the Mind*
7. *Murder at the Wake*
8. *Murder in the Woods*
9. *Murder at the Flood* ✓
10. *Murder at Dead Crags* ✓
11. *Murder Mystery Weekend* ✓
12. *Murder on the Run* ✓
13. *Murder at Shake Holes* – MISSING
14. *Murder at the Meet* ✓
15. *Murder on the Moor* ✓
16. *Murder Unseen* to order ✓

(Above: Detective Inspector Skelgill Investigates)

Murder, Mystery Collection

The Dune

The Sexopaths

Glossary

Some of the Cumbrian dialect words, slang and local usage appearing in *'Murder at the Meet'* are as follows:

Allus – always
Alreet – all right (often a greeting)
Arl – old
Bab'e – baby
Bairn/bairdens – child/kids
Bait – packed lunch/sandwiches
Beck – mountain stream
Bellwether – the leading sheep of a flock
Bleaberry – bilberry
Claggy – mucky
Clout – hit/smack
Cowp – tip over
Crack – chat, gossip
Cuddy wifter – left-handed
Dale – valley
Deek – look/look at
Donnat – idiot
Dub – pool
Fer – for
Foily – smelly
Gannin'/Garn – going
Gill – ravine
Gimmer – young female (lamb)
Girt – great
Guddling – groping
Hause – mountain pass highpoint
Heaf – open land to which a flock becomes attached ('heafed')
Hogg – a lamb that has finished weaning
How – round hillock
In-bye – walled pasture near the farmstead
Int' – in the

Jewkle – dog
Kaylied – inebriated
Kezzick – Keswick
Ken – know
Laddo – lad, boy
Laik – play
Larl – little
Lonnin – lane
Lowp – jump
Lug – ear
Marra – mate (friend)
Mash – brew tea
Mesen – myself
Nicky – rum-flavoured date & ginger tart
Nobbut – only
Nowt – nothing
Offcomer – outsider
Ont' – on the
Oor – our
Ower – over
Owt – anything
Pagger – fight
Pattie – deep-fried mashed potato mixed with, for example, fish or cheese
Pikelet – small thin crumpet
Roding – twilight display flight of woodcock
Scop – throw
Scordy – tea
Scran – food
Skinful – enough alcohol to make one drunk
Tapped – mad (insane)
Tarn – mountain lake
T' – the (often silent)
Tha/thee/thou – you
Theesen – yourself
Thy – your
Tod – fox (also Cockney: alone)

Twat – to hit
Uns – ones
Us – me
While – until
Wukiton – Workington
Yat – gate
Yon – that

PREFACE

The Shepherds' Meet

Stretching back into the mists of time (one Cumbrian year being worth ten in London or New York or Tokyo), shepherds from adjacent dales have informally gathered in advance of November tip lousing to hire out their prize tups and return to their rightful owners those yowes that have strayed during the course of the season. *Tups* are rams and *yowes* are ewes and *tip lousing* is setting the former loose among the latter, so that the hardy lambs are born in April, when the first flush of grass begins to green up the brindled Lakeland fells.

Over the centuries the autumn shepherds' meet has evolved into a more organised annual occasion, with competitions for sheep, dogs, hand clippers, fell runners and stick makers. At the bigger events – called country fairs – there may even be Cumberland wrestling. There are stalls selling traditional delicacies such as gingerbread, rum butter, mint cake and sticky toffee pudding; and artisan pottery, jewellery and knitwear. Shepherds and their kin meet and compete in an atmosphere of friendly rivalry – and retire afterwards to the local inn to celebrate their success or bemoan their bad luck over a pint or two of good cask ale.

The meet unifies what is a disparate community – outwith the village life in the fells can be isolated and lonely. Of course, such congregations bring together not only old friends and relations, but occasionally old enmities too, when ancient clan rivalries long buried resurface for reasons of a modern making. But such is the social significance of the meet to its dale, and neighbouring valleys, that it inexorably casts into close proximity people who might rather avoid one another, and thus calls to mind affairs that might better be forgotten.

PROLOGUE – MARY

Twenty-two years earlier

Cummacatta Wood. Ever since she was a little girl Mary Wilson has been coming here. It is an enchanted place, with its nooks and crags and rocky glades, home to fell sprites that she was sure she glimpsed on more than one occasion as they crept down from their caves to bathe in a slow pool – a *dub* – of the River Derwent, or to glean fallen acorn peduncles to make their pipes. The other kids from Balderthwaite would tease her when she told them, wide eyed with wonder and bursting with the news, a posy of sky blue harebells gripped in her little fist, their fairy-hat blooms trembling with her excitement. They demanded she prove it, show them – but of course, she could not. Jake Dickson was the ringleader – two years older than she – although they were all in the same class at the village school. *Larl donnat*, he used to call her, 'little idiot' in their local twang. And Meg Atkinson was always egging him on, trying to please him, conniving to bring the other lasses in against her. Only Sean Nicolson took with her – but at that time two years of a gap meant he couldn't stand up to Jake in a pagger. In the end she stopped telling; she knew what she saw, and she understood the fell sprites would never show themselves to such spiteful infidels.

On reflection, Cummacatta Wood is not really a wood at all – at least, not this actual spot that is marked out by name, now that the National Trust have put up their signpost. It is more of a rising heath with here and there a cluster of birch or gorse or hawthorn. It is the northern fringe of the Bowder Wood, the great swathe of oaks that cloaks the steep-sided fells at the pinch point, the winding pass into upper Borrowdale, the crags of High Spy rising two thousand feet to the west, the more modest Grange Fell to the east, with its many lumpy prominences, King's How, Jopplety How, Swanesty How. Mary knows these names as well as the townsfolk know their streets. Else how would you find your way about, or give directions to reach a yowe that was cowped?

And down in the Bowder Wood is the Bowder Stone, the colossal tilted boulder the size of a house that, legend has it, dates from the days of the Viking rule, when folk worshipped the Norse god Baldr, brother of Thor and son of Odin and the goddess Frigg. Sitting comfortably in class, Mary loved to hear these tales of 'history'; stories of how the fierce Vikings came and settled as peaceful farmers and brought their Herdwick sheep, and gave names in their colourful language to features of the landscape that folk still use today. Such as their own hamlet of Balderthwaite – *Baldr's meadow* – nestled upon the narrow floodplain that was Bowderwater once, a ribbon lake like Derwentwater and Bassenthwaite Lake further down the dale, until Baldr used his magic to clear the glacial choke and drain the lake, to expose rich and fertile farmland for his flock. Baldr left only the great Bowder Stone, as a reminder and symbol of his power.

Mary Wilson has parked near the Bowder Stone. She could have walked up from the village; she is a fit young woman, only just turned thirty, over the birth and proud of her figure – but the extra mile would waste a quarter of an hour she doesn't have, and the dog can get straight off the lead – although he prefers the open spaces of Cummacatta to the Bowder Wood, rabbits rather than squirrels being more his bag. Not that there aren't plenty of squirrels about as Mary lets the Lakeland Terrier loose; it being September they're caching acorns; overhead there's a telltale rustling in the still-green oaks, and the occasional fruit carelessly dropped, a patter in the crisp leaf litter that has the dog's ears pricking.

Mary thinks it's her favourite time of year, although she wonders if that's because the baby came last September – the twenty-third – "bang on the equinox" someone said, as though it meant something. The weather was as warm as this then, too. She certainly doesn't need the bright pink headscarf she's kept on. It could be a summer's day, no wind – only the sun slanting low through the boughs like it does in spring, illuminating the hover flies, hundreds of tiny golden guardian angels that chart her progress through the great green cathedral. And it's as quiet as a church; the songbirds have finished their business until the days begin to lengthen again.

And unlike in summer she's got the place to herself. The little gravel parking area for the Bowder Stone was deserted. That's also because of the meet. The few holidaymakers that are still kicking about, and everyone who's anyone, are down at the village. The fell runners are due back soon. They say there's a young lad from ower Buttermere who's favourite to win the men's race. Folk'll be jostling to see that, for sure – to watch Jake Dickson put in his place; he still thinks he's God's gift! And any minute now old Walter Dickson and his creepy sidekick, that big oaf Pick Pearson, will be staggering back from the *Twa Tups* with the list of show winners scrawled on a split beermat in his indecipherable writing, leeway to change his mind should someone grease his palm as he passes. Some canny entrants might have put a pint behind the bar for them. She glimpsed them through the snug window when she took a short cut to fetch her car; they looked more interested in their ale and Meg's push-up bra than the judging. And what gives Pick Pearson the right to be understudy to the chief judge? Why Walter chose him to succeed him – well that's a talking point in the *Tups* when neither is there. It's not as though they're related – leastways, not directly that she knows of. And what does Pick ken of sheep – compared to Sean? Quiet, reliable Sean – a man whom contestants would trust to give them a fair crack of the whip. He'd glanced up from his hand clipping demonstration as if he were telepathic; she hadn't needed to slow and feign to retie her loose headscarf. Sean with his sad blue eyes. He's by a head and shoulders the best exhibitor – everyone knows that. So what was that about Pick Pearson sidling up to her stall – saying she could be chosen if she played her cards right? What did that mean? As if she didn't know.

Mary reaches the kissing gate that leads into Cummacatta. Of course, it's not a kissing gate at all – but that's what Jake Dickson wanted her to believe, as if it's got some connection to the

Kissing Cave higher up the fell. And if she's honest there was a little devil in her that wanted her to believe it, too – that summer's night a dozen years back. She'd rowed with Aidan, one of many break-ups and make-ups, out at the back of the *Tups* – she'd stormed off seeing red and before she knew it was following this very path – to her little haven of dusky heath; there were brown owls calling, and Natterer's bats swooping after moths, and woodcock roding.

And then she'd heard the footsteps on the path behind her – and panting – and there came Jake Dickson, jaunty in his flashy trainers. He said Meg had sent him after her to make sure she was alright (she'd doubted that) – it would be getting dark before long, you never knew who might be about – what danger lurked. He'd teased her about the sprites taking her. She'd shrugged off his exhortations to turn and walk back with him – but she hadn't told him to push off when he dogged her heels. Aye – there was a little bit of the devil in her – and, face it, that owl had made her jump, and the bats came too close for her liking; she felt safer with him. Except that wasn't right, was it? When they reached the gate – where she lingers now – he'd darted ahead – gone through and closed it and leaned back over, a smirk in his eyes. It's a kissing gate, he'd said. It's the price to pass. And stupidly – and because she'd had too many vodka-and-blacks – she let herself step too close. Ach! She wants to spit, even now. His tongue, slimy and rough like a sheep's, and his greedy hands running over her. She thought her heart was going to burst out of her chest. Thank heavens the gate was still between them. She'd pushed him off and turned tail. But she'd never have outrun him. He'd almost caught her when there stood Sean, just beside the Bowder Stone, the driver door of his old hand-me-down pick-up swinging open. He never did say if he'd come looking for her – but he'd been in the crowd at the tables out the back of the old inn.

She hadn't stopped to ask questions – she'd just jumped in and slammed the door and slid across into the passenger seat. She saw Sean block the path of Jake. She didn't hear their exchange. But she saw that now – as young men, not schoolboys

11

any more – that Jake might be two years older, but his advantage had passed. Sean was a strapping shepherd – she'd seem him wrestle down a Herdwick and hold it firm while he hand clipped it. Perhaps it suddenly dawned on Jake he could wrestle him down, too – and that wouldn't look good in front of her. Sean told her that Jake wanted to walk back. He said he'd drive her – that Aidan had gone home to his Ma's, and that he'd drop Mary back there – so they could sort things out. And she didn't protest – oh, why didn't she? And so he took her. At the sound of the pick-up's engine, Aidan came to the door to meet her; he wouldn't look Sean in the eye. And Sean went, his face forlorn. And gossip had it that it was the very same night that Sean succumbed to *Jack Daniel's* and Meg's charms; and a wedding followed soon enough after. No shotguns were needed; Sean did his duty. And so Sean was spoken for. Quiet, reliable Sean – what would he do now?

The dog yelps to break her trance and Mary sees he's scrabbling to get under the gate. He must have scented rabbits, or maybe even a tod – but he's got his collar caught on a bent nail. She stoops to release him, and she notices that her cleavage is exposed more than she's realised. She'll have to be careful when she's back at the stall, how she leans over the trestle table to smooth out a shawl for a would-be buyer. She'd chosen the white peasant top so it would go with any of her coloured scarves that she might model – and, truth be told, drawn in at the waist above her tight hipster jeans it shows off her figure, a little act of defiance, and hope. And it flashes through her mind the folk who might have deeked, in envy or admiration as she artlessly showed off her wares, so to speak. And there's a strange frisson that she's not felt for a long time – it even goes back to that feeling of being here at Cummacatta, on her own – when a sprite was about to appear – or that time with Jake Dickson. And she senses a movement – it's on the other side of the gate – but it's no sprite – the shoe she glimpses through the wooden slats is human. And she rises and at the same time tugs down the elasticated hem of her blouse, which has ridden a little above her waist. And she looks up expectantly.

'Oh – it's thee.'

1. THE DIG

Sunday, noon, early September

'Daniel?'

'Aye – Jim. Alreet?'

'I am alright, thank you. You sound as though you are out of doors – although I would expect no less, despite this infernal rain. Bassenthwaite Lake?'

'Actually, I'm on Derwentwater.' Skelgill seems contrite, as if he is taking some kind of easy option. He offers a defence. 'The rain puts the tourists off – it's the best time to come – no folk flailing oars about, bairns scopping stones – whatnot.'

'Aha. Any success?'

'I'm fishing for brownies. Couple. Couple of pound each. They're taking damsel nymphs round the margins. Although I've got a dry on at the moment.'

'Oh, the noble art. I rather wish I were with you. They are so sweet to the taste from Derwentwater.'

'Aye – except I've put them back. Are you looking for your tea?'

The professor – of medieval history, most latterly Durham University, now retired – Jim Hartley catches his breath. With a certain degree of reluctance, he realises he ought to state the purpose of his call.

'You know the archaeological excavation up here at Odinsgill?'

'Above Cummacatta Wood. I thought you'd packed all that in?'

'I am here.' Now it is the professor's turn to sound repentant. 'I was tempted back – purely as an honorary consultant, advisory capacity – no specific time commitment, you understand?'

'It were supposed to be all beer and skittles from now on, Jim.'

The older man chuckles a little uneasily at Skelgill's admonishing idiom. He responds with an aphorism more characteristic of his vocation.

'Ahem – well – wasn't it Prince Hal who said, *if all the year were playing holidays, to sport would be as tedious as to work?*' The professor makes a decent fist of a Shakespearean stage accent.

'I'll have to pass on that one, Jim.' Skelgill rather readily loses concentration – that is to say, a circular ripple that he recognises to be a rise, not an overweight raindrop, close to his home-tied daddy longlegs lure, draws his attention. But the fish eschews his handiwork, and takes a divergent trajectory to sip an alternative hatchling. Skelgill wipes a drip from his nose with the sleeve of his timeworn *Barbour* jacket. 'I thought that were a Viking dig up there?'

'Aha – but the medieval period spans a millennium – or, at least, a thousand years, if I may draw the distinction, roughly speaking five to fifteen hundred AD. The Vikings were slap in the middle – bear in mind the Scots did not see them off until 1263, the Battle of Largs – what, a mere hundred miles from here?'

'Aye, right.'

'However – enough of history – to the present.' He clears his throat, as if to presage news of greater import. 'This morning, in a cave – they have found human remains – more recent. They did not realise at first – they have some undergraduates working for a pittance – and you know what *they* get up to on a Saturday night.'

Skelgill's antennae are pricked and he ignores the potential digression.

'You say recent, Jim – how recent are we talking?'

'Within your lifetime – if not mine.'

Skelgill inhales between bared teeth.

'Have you called the police?'

'Daniel – you are the police.'

There is a moment's pause while Skelgill processes the nuances of his friend's petition.

'You mean you're not sure?'

'Well – it is true. I am a historian, not an archaeologist. But I know old bones and these are not they.'

'But you didn't want a hullaballoo.'

'I shan't be very popular if I become responsible for this dig being suspended.'

'Happen there's no choice about that – if you're right.'

Skelgill glances at the time on his mobile and checks it against his wristwatch. He brings the handset back up.

'Old Herdwick should be out of church by now – he'll be in the *Queen's Arms*. I'll rustle him up. I'll give you a shout – I'll park at the Bowder Stone – I know a shortcut up the fell from there.'

*

There are numerous caves and quarries in and around the Bowder Wood, an area well known to Skelgill, hailing as he does from the adjacent dale, from just over the Honister Pass, from the hamlet of Buttermere. Indeed this was as much his childhood stamping ground as Lorton Vale. If Professor Jim Hartley was his mentor for all things piscine, then the Hope family up at Seathwaite – that limb of Borrowdale that reaches into the Scafell pikes – provided his education upon the fells; gnarled sheep farmer Arthur Hope and son Jud, Skelgill's contemporary, and erstwhile fellow schoolboy adventurer. Thus Skelgill is no stranger to Borrowdale's topography, to its gills and becks and tarns, and its features well publicised or lesser known. In the latter category would be the 'Kissing Cave', as locals call it, up in Odinsgill, a narrow vertical crevice that can only be negotiated in single file. The professor has reminded Skelgill of its name in Viking folklore, *Friggeshol*, a somewhat prurient simile that alludes both to its appearance and its ancient reputation as a place of fertility.

And it is not without some rumbling subconscious reference to his youth that Skelgill awaits news, a disquiet that troubles him, though he rather wishes not to acknowledge it. But it is difficult not to feel melancholy under the prevailing circumstances – not least that an hour earlier he was contentedly fishing just a couple of miles away on Derwentwater. He had allowed himself one last cast, for luck (no luck), shipped anchor, and rowed vigorously if not lung-burstingly to return his borrowed craft to Portinscale, whence he had driven to prise a protesting Dr Herdwick from his favoured hostelry bench; thence still complaining to the Bowder Stone; thence on foot in a near-mutinous state up through steep rain-sodden woodland by a less-than obvious path in borrowed leaky wellingtons to their present location. But such is a pathologist's lot, and though outwardly cantankerous, to his credit the man did not actually waver. And now, while Skelgill awaits his return from the site, he avails himself of the shelter of what is a garden gazebo, erected by the archaeologists, and of their rudimentary but adequate means of making tea. The same level of comfort does not apply to young PC Dodd, a local constable who stands stoically beneath dripping oaks out of Skelgill's line of sight, having been summoned to sentry duty.

This might seem an unnecessary precaution. In such weather conditions ramblers would hardly be expected; those around at this time of year are generally of the genteel, elderly variety, and the location of the archaeological investigation is not on an advertised footpath. But there is another class of possible interference. Skelgill had dismissed the meek-looking crew, who despite the professor's misgivings did not strike him as the hell-raising variety – and indeed isn't there a new wave of students known as *Generation Sensible?* However, there is also 'generation social media' to be contended with – and it will only take one of them to disobey his unenforceable threat not to post online an unauthorised photograph for all manner of ghouls, rubberneckers and press reporters to come swarming like flies to a stinkhorn. Nonetheless, in retrospect he feels a modicum of sympathy for the bedraggled volunteers, rather unceremoniously sent packing having made what ironically may prove to be the most significant find of their entire careers, no matter how long such may henceforth stretch.

Skelgill has taken first look in the cave – considering it to be his duty to witness the scene. In a land that is riddled with holes, hewn in roughly equal measure by Mother Nature and human endeavour, he is no connoisseur of the subterranean, but his training has told him it is safe, and surprisingly dry – a function of its gentle in-to-out declination, and the impervious andesite lava of the surrounding rocks (and, indeed, the Bowder Stone). Knowing its local reputation, he had not been immune from a teenage flashback – not that he ever availed himself of its facilities. Besides, the time team have it well lit with electric lamps powered by lightweight lithium motorcycle batteries that they have shipped up, and its air of the arcane is somewhat diminished. There are other crevices and ledges nearby, but none so deep as this cleft, penetrating a good fifteen feet into the mountain. Elsewhere in the fells sheep would use this place, further eroding its sides with their unrelenting back scratching. They might have served to enlarge it once, but these days the Bowder Wood is enclosed by well-kept walls and the free-roaming local quadrupeds – roe deer, fox and badger – would have little interest in such stony environs.

The students were picking away at a rockfall, thinking there might be a further chamber beyond, when they discovered the human remains. Prior to the professor being called upon, just a few bones were partially exposed. Skelgill has spent only a minute in their company, trying to convince himself that this was a tramp that met with misfortune when the ceiling came down, a person that moved beneath the radar of officialdom and was never known to be missing. Such skeleta must be scattered all over Britain simply because no one knows where to look, folk who creep into a ditch or under a hedge to die just like wild animals – it is only roadkill that ends up on public display. Or possibly it could be a caver or an inquisitive walker, someone from afar – Manchester or Newcastle or Glasgow – who never told their nearest and dearest where they were going (or maybe whose nearest and dearest were content with such an outcome). Moreover, if the remains are at the upper end of the professor's estimated age range, back in the day sightseers travelled to

Keswick by train, and went on by omnibus or on foot to explore the vicinity – there would be no telltale car to set warning bells ringing.

But against this theorising a growing anxiety laps like a flood tide, threatening to drown such ideas before they can bob with buoyant credibility; in his stomach there is a sinking feeling that has little to do with the fact that his packed lunch still nestles in his tackle box in the back of his car; it is a visceral discontent that grips him. Presently, however, there is respite in the imminent return of the two specialists, whom he hopes will disambiguate him of his doubts. He watches with some trepidation as they inexpertly pick their way down the wooded slope; it is uneven under foot, basically a moss-covered scree, and rendered doubly treacherous by the persistent rain, a route barred in places by sprawling ferns and patches of bramble laden with glistening ebony fruits. Beneath his hood the sharp features of the grey-haired professor are animated, his hands move with the practised signing of a lecturer. The pathologist, the bigger, sturdier man, wears an expressionless mask – or, rather, one that is set to his default, dour, disapproving – that Skelgill knows not to take too much to heart. The professor is expounding upon a point.

'The Vikings were not in the habit of performing cave burials. Their modus operandi was to entomb their warrior chiefs with their sword and shield and to raise a prominent mound – a tumulus. In the pagan era they would cremate their proletarian dead and bury the remains in the vicinity; post conversion to Christianity they practised inhumation, and often interred the bodies beneath rudimentary gravestones. However, burial under piles of rocks is also known.'

Skelgill steps out of the shelter of the gazebo – this eavesdropped snippet seems to proffer a straw in the wind. But the more cynical 'doctor' of the pair, he of medicine rather than philosophy is alert to Skelgill's optimism. He clears his throat with an ominous growl.

'I might not be a forensic anthropologist – but I'd wager my roast lamb dinner that she's not been dead above twenty-five years.'

Skelgill is alarmed beyond all expectations.

'*She?*'

'Aye – female of child-bearing age.' The man grimaces, meeting Skelgill's gaze defiantly; the straw is snatched away. 'In fact – as far as the parturition scars on her pelvis can be relied upon – she was probably a young mother.'

2. CASE FILES

Monday morning, Skelgill's office

'Did you know her, Guv?'

Skelgill does not answer. He stands to attention, looking at his map, his back to his colleagues, or at least to the questioner DS Leyton, seated beside the tall grey filing cabinet; DS Jones is at an angle of forty-five degrees, in her regular chair before the window. Beyond, the sky is an amorphous blanket of cloud, paler at the southern horizon. It is no longer raining. Skelgill turns after a while; he eyes his tea and sits and drinks despite that it is steaming; his colleagues' mugs are as yet untouched. Finally he shakes his head.

'I used to knock about with Jud Hope up at Seathwaite. I were barely a teenager. You didn't tend to know folk in their thirties. Besides, we were persona non grata down in Balderthwaite. Bad lads.' He manufactures a grin that seeks to excuse, or at least explain any mischief that it was the boys' duty to perform. 'I took part in the search.'

DS Leyton jerks forward.

'Cor blimey, Guvnor – that's a turn up.'

But Skelgill looks disaffected.

'Every man and his dog were involved – combing the fells for miles around. Arthur Hope organised it for the dale between his farm and Seatoller. It made sense for folk to cover the places they knew best. Make a proper job of it.'

DS Leyton's heavy features strike a look of reproof.

'Unlike the team that searched the wood – the cave.'

But Skelgill seems willing to forgive this oversight.

'It were a massive area. Exhausting work. Try yomping through mature heather or bracken, Leyton. Folk thought they were looking for someone that had turned their ankle walking the dog, someone that were lying injured. There were limited police and no specialist resources – no cave rescue, none of your heat-seeking helicopters, cadaver dogs. The Kissing Cave's just one of half a hundred in Borrowdale. And you're assuming the body was there at the time of the sweep.' This comment causes raised eyebrows among Skelgill's subordinates, but he continues undeterred. 'Besides, I reckon some were going through the motions. The unofficial theory doing the rounds was that she'd been abducted and driven off from near the Bowder Stone.'

Skelgill looks interrogatively at DS Jones, who has a stack of faded manila files perched upon the uppermost of her crossed thighs.

'I've made copies of the final historical report. Also, attached as an appendix, the lab's confirmation this morning that the dental records match.'

She slides a stapled sheaf of papers onto Skelgill's desk, and leans to hand a second set to DS Leyton, who weighs the item and flashes her an impressed glance. Skelgill is not tempted to pick his up; instead he gazes expectantly at DS Jones. She smiles obediently. When she speaks, there is a note of animation in her voice.

'I hadn't realised this was Operation Double Helix, Guv.'

For his part DS Leyton emits a surprised grunt of recognition – and holds out his document with a sudden reverence.

'I remember that being in the news. That was ground breaking.' Then he looks mischievously at DS Jones. 'But you'd have been in kindergarten, girl!'

DS Jones grins a little sheepishly. She glances at Skelgill, to see him apparently pained by her fellow sergeant's observation. She is quick to dispense a palliative.

'It came up at police college.'

Skelgill, however, wrestles the conversation back on track.

'Leyton – it *would* have been ground breaking – if they'd caught someone. If you ask me, it set back DNA testing by a decade – made it look like searching for a needle in a haystack.'

DS Leyton appears unperturbed by his superior's disparaging attitude. A light of fascination burns in his eyes.

'Did they test you, Guv?'

Skelgill turns to his subordinate rather menacingly.

'Are you trying to be funny, Leyton?'

DS Leyton throws up his palms in a gesture of supplication; perhaps now realising he is prodding a nerve more raw than usual.

'Nah, Guv – don't be daft – just curious. These cold cases – it's like they're not real – like something off the telly – but you were *there*, know what I mean?'

This might placate Skelgill to a degree, but it seems he still feels there is defending to do.

'Leyton – as it happens I had a cast-iron alibi. I was with half the blokes in the dale running up and down Scawdale Fell – High Spy, as they like to call it. Besides – I were nobbut a lad – it were adults they cast their net over – driving age and above, as I recall.'

His syntax seems to have dropped down a notch into the vernacular. For a few moments his expression becomes strained, as though he might be remembering these times, mingling with his kinsfolk. Then the trance is broken and he gestures to DS Jones, indicating that she should proceed. She gathers her wits, and bends with alarming suppleness to place the main body of the files on the floor. She picks out a photocopied page.

'Actually, I thought this article from the *Westmorland Gazette* gave the most succinct account of Operation Double Helix.' She glances up to see that her colleagues are nodding in agreement – the exercise was labelled retrospectively for internal police purposes in recognition of its pioneering role, albeit unsuccessful. She scans the document and inhales to speak. 'This piece was written two years ago to mark the twentieth anniversary of Mary Wilson's disappearance, and is entitled *A Killer In Our Midst?* It talks about how it was the first use of mass-DNA testing in a criminal case. When the search drew a blank and Mary Wilson still failed to return, the detectives wrote to every male aged over seventeen who lived or worked in the area asking them to give a blood sample. They set up three testing centres, one in the village hall at Balderthwaite and the others using blood donor vans, at the southern outskirts of Keswick and at Buttermere, routes in and out of Borrowdale. It was a voluntary scheme. A few men initially declined – giving

23

excuses such as they didn't like needles – or didn't like the police!' She looks up with a wry grin. 'But it seems the majority of these bowed to social pressure. Those few that didn't, the investigating team established satisfactorily that they weren't suspects. So the local populace was cleared of possible involvement. The article goes on rather controversially, suggesting this was a convenient outcome – the corollary being that an outsider perpetrated the crime. Also that, given the newness of the technology at the time, and scientific advancements since, ought not the results be independently re-examined?'

Skelgill appears uninspired; instead it is a puzzled-looking DS Leyton that reacts to this suggestion.

'Two questions. Well – two parts of the same question. If there was no trace of the woman, what DNA evidence did they find? And how did they know for sure the offender was male?'

DS Jones is nodding willingly.

'It's a good point. In the executive summary of the police report there is an explicit acknowledgement of these assumptions.' She picks up her own copy and makes to flick through it – but it appears she knows its contents, for she replies without the need of a specific reference. 'Mary Wilson ran a little cottage enterprise – a hobby that grew into a sideline – she knitted scarves and shawls, but she'd also started making small gift items, including a range of key fobs with distinctive sheep motifs. On the day she went missing she had a stall at the local fair – the Balderthwaite shepherds' meet – and had taken a break around lunchtime, it was presumed to exercise her dog, which had been tethered beside her. A key fob – identified by her husband as the same pattern as had been on her car keys – was found at a place she regularly walked the dog, in woods about a mile north of the village. The car was nearby. That key fob was tested. The fabric contained traces of saliva from which a DNA profile was recovered – Y-chromosome. A male. The theory was that she struggled with her assailant – perhaps tried to fend him off with her keys, jabbing at his face – and the woollen fob tore away. The keys were never found.' DS Jones regards DS

Leyton with the hint of a crease forming between her finely curved brows. 'You're right to raise the question. The evidence neither proves that the DNA belonged to her assailant, nor, therefore, that the assailant was a male. They couldn't even be a hundred per cent sure it was her personal key fob. But understandably it was the main tangible lead.'

DS Leyton is looking worried.

'Speaking of leads – what happened to the dog?'

DS Jones smiles generously, despite that she senses Skelgill's disapproval.

'As it happens it forms part of the story. Mary Wilson and her husband Aidan Wilson were lodging with Mary's mother, a Mrs Tyson – she helped look after their child – in the next village, Slatterthwaite. It's under a mile south from Balderthwaite – maybe two miles from the Bowder Stone?' She glances at Skelgill for confirmation; he obliges with a faint nod. 'It seems she was in the habit of spoiling the dog, and in turn it was in the habit of turning up at the back door. When it did so that afternoon she didn't think too much about it. Meanwhile other exhibitors noted that Mary Wilson hadn't returned to her stall – but there was no real cause for concern until it became time to pack up. Mobile phones were rare back then – never mind that you still can't always get a signal in Borrowdale.' (Skelgill makes an ironic scoffing sound but does not otherwise interrupt.) 'Someone was sent along to Slatterthwaite. Aidan Wilson was home from work. Mary Wilson also had a part-time job at the Balderthwaite village inn – the *Twa Tups* – and he suggested that because of the meet she'd been roped in to help behind the bar. But that wasn't the case – and that was when the police were contacted – her husband made the call from the pub.'

DS Leyton is nodding slowly as he processes the unravelling tale.

'What about sightings?'

DS Jones nods as if she expects this question.

'There are several statements to the effect that she was at the Balderthwaite shepherds' meet for the whole of the morning, running her woollens stall. She was seen to leave at about 1pm, taking the dog. The last definite sighting was probably immediately after – she peered into a window of the *Twa Tups* and was positively identified by the barmaid; and the two competition judges who were drinking there at the time also saw her. Mary Wilson used to park at the back of the inn, and the assumption is that she was on her way to collect her car, to exercise the dog near the Bowder Stone – a favourite walk of hers. There were no reported sightings of the car elsewhere – and it was a distinctive battered red *Fiat 500*, so it's probable that she went straight there. The parking area isn't visible from the road, and the car wasn't found until just after 7pm – so the investigating officers defined a six-hour window in which something could have happened to her.'

Now DS Jones looks at Skelgill anxiously. It is plain she seeks his approval to speculate. He recognises her appeal and nods brusquely.

'Well – of course, one lesser theory was that she drowned in the River Derwent and her body was swept into the lake – but it was a dry year and water levels were low. Another was that she had basically run away – with a lover – and there is some evidence that we can consider in that regard. Except now we know she *didn't* run away; most likely she was murdered in the vicinity. The caveat being the PM.' Her colleagues are nodding grimly – they none of them expect any other outcome from the detailed forensic examination that is in progress. 'And think about it – never mind that she had a child, more pressing was her stall and all the stock, on which she depended for pin money – perhaps even to make ends meet. Surely she would have intended to be absent for at most an hour? That would suggest that whatever befell her had occurred by two o'clock. And as such it would make a significant difference to an investigation. The angle you would take with witnesses – it would be more focused – and, well, frankly more accusative.'

Skelgill is watching DS Jones intensely. He raises an eyebrow but it might be with approval as much as alarm. To treat witnesses as suspects might contradict protocol, but it is uncannily consistent with his gut feel. DS Leyton, however, seeks additional reassurance.

'What makes you so convinced about that, girl?'

DS Jones taps with a toe the files at her feet.

'The basis of this investigation was that Mary Wilson was a random victim of an outsider, that she'd been abducted by a stranger. We can rule out abduction. As for the stranger – yes, that remains perfectly possible. But if we were called fresh to a case like this – given the knowledge that she may have been attacked within minutes of reaching a secluded spot she was known to frequent – we wouldn't give up so easily on the idea that she was killed, as most female murder victims are, by someone whom she knew. Maybe by someone she went to meet?'

3. THE BOWDER STONE

Monday, late morning

'Reckon those nippers are safe up there, Guv? I'd be having kittens if they were my lot.'

Skelgill seems indifferent to the danger that faces the clambering children – he is wondering why they aren't at school – until he hears a shout, *"Maxime, Mathilde – faites attention!"* and realises they must be the offspring of foreign visitors. Besides, he subscribes to the principle of fledglings being encouraged to spread their wings – despite that a test flight from the top of the towering rock would not be in the best interests of any of those present, including himself and his colleagues.

'The Victorians used to charge folk to climb the ladder – they advertised it as the biggest rock fragment in the world. I expect the women were blowing off it all the time, those dresses they wore.'

DS Jones is reading an information board.

'It says it weighs 1,253 metric tonnes.'

Skelgill frowns.

'Call that two thousand in proper money.' He squints at the giant boulder, tilting his head. 'The weight of fifty thousand yowes, Arthur Hope used to reckon.'

DS Leyton puffs out his cheeks.

'Cor blimey, Guv – imagine the wallop when that came crashing down. You wouldn't have wanted your motor parked here.'

Skelgill looks at his subordinate with some dismay.

'Leyton – it was during the Ice Age.'

DS Leyton grins sheepishly.

'Chariot, then, Guv.'

Skelgill shakes his head despairingly. He turns and begins to move away. As he does so he checks his wristwatch.

'Come on. Let's time this walk.'

The Bowder Stone occupies a clearing – it has been compared to a ship marooned on its keel – and Skelgill leads his colleagues astern in a northerly direction to a point where a footpath disappears into the surrounding vegetation. While September is considered to be an autumn month, and certainly berries are plentiful and some birches are beginning to turn, the ancient oaks of Borrowdale will resolutely cling onto their leaves well into November. Thus, under today's leaden skies, beneath the dense green canopy there is a preternatural twilight. Accordingly, it seems, Skelgill proceeds cautiously – when he might be expected to stride out, requiring his companions to hop and skip to keep up. In fact his measured approach reflects that he wrestles with the notion that dog walkers have as many speeds as there are dogs. His practice is to set his own pace and emit the occasional whistle. But plenty of times he sees folk dawdling – patiently waiting, even, while their pet inspects every vertical target or plunges off-path to forage for pheasants.

'What's that there, Guv?'

Skelgill's musings are interrupted by DS Leyton's inquiry. His sergeant's voice a hint tremulous, he refers to a fenced off area to their right, with a latched gate on which is strung a warning sign, *Dangerous Cliff.*

'It's an abseiling anchor point – above an old quarry. The adventure companies use it for their outward-bound courses. We use it for training sometimes.' Skelgill is referring to his role in the local mountain rescue team. 'It's only a hundred foot or so.'

'Whoa! A hundred too many for me, Guv.' DS Leyton is tentatively peering over the fence. 'I ain't got no head for heights. I'd rather paddle out on the lake on a homemade raft than go over that flippin' edge. Cor – look at it – I'm getting vertigo just thinking about it!'

'Mind the ground don't give way, Leyton.'

DS Leyton almost jumps away from the fence, and quickly gets back into step with his colleagues. He resumes his monologue.

29

'I remember seeing that film about that geezer who fell down a crevasse. Broke his leg. Got out and survived somehow. *Touching the Cloth*, it were called, I reckon.'

DS Jones emits an involuntary laugh, but Skelgill is more taciturn – but he seems to be suppressing a grin.

'Aye, sommat like that, Leyton. I'll pass it on to our operations manager – he'll like that. Name our next big exercise after it.'

They might pursue the subject further, but Skelgill's chosen 'average' pace now brings them – in six minutes – to the gate that marks the boundary of the Bowder Wood; beyond lies the more open heathland of Cummacatta.

'So it were here, aye?'

He addresses his question to DS Jones. She nods.

'According to the description, yes. Although reading between the lines "beside the stile" was an approximation. There were about a hundred searchers working over a period of several days. People drop things all the time – and when you think of how many walkers come here. Across the dale they picked up scores of objects – gloves, scarves, hats and suchlike. Each group of searchers had evidence bags and they marked them with a description of the location and the map reference if they knew how to record it.'

Skelgill is nodding broodingly; now he remembers this. His own party, under the stewardship of Arthur Hope collected a dozen miscellaneous items, in various states of decay. Jud Hope had found a wallet with £50 in it that months later came back to him unclaimed as the finder.

'So you see, Guv – it was only later when they enlisted Aidan Wilson to look at a selection of the more promising finds that he identified the key fob. There was a delay before its significance was recognised; this spot wasn't treated as a possible crime scene.'

Skelgill has a supplementary question.

'What was their explanation for it being here?'

'That she was accosted at this point – and forced against her will to a vehicle – either back at the Bowder Stone or on the north side of Cummacatta Wood where there's another small parking area.'

'What did she weigh?'

'Forty-seven kilos – seven-and-a-half stones, if you prefer.' DS Jones regards her superior with a flash of insouciance – that he should presume she has command of such detail – which of course she does. 'That was based on her six-month post-natal medical – the birth of her child was actually a year previously.'

Skelgill does not react directly to this information; indeed he seems to digress.

'There's one or two popular dog-walking spots that I know. When folk find a glove they tend to stick it on the end of a twig. A scarf they'll tie to a branch. Over a period of a few days things move about. Other folk look at them – maybe to see if there's a name tag. Put them somewhere else more obvious – a stile or a gate – where's there's traffic. Then things get picked up and dropped again by the dogs and other animals. I was clearing salmonberry last year, in a copse beside Bass Lake – it's an invasive shrub; you have to hack it up by the roots. I didn't finish the job so rather than carry the mattock to and fro I buried it with my rigger gloves under the leaf litter. I came the next day – one of the gloves was gone. I found it a few weeks later near the shore, a quarter of a mile away.'

He glares at his colleagues. DS Leyton obliges with a suitable prompt.

'So how did that happen, Guv – a cheeky little squirrel, digging for its nuts?'

'Tod, like as not, Leyton – a fox.'

'*Ha* – a foxglove, Guv!'

Skelgill gives a sarcastic laugh.

'There's a few times I've had stuff disappear from the back door – if you've left claggy shoes on the step – owt that's foily, they've got an instinct to scavenge. Work out later whether they can eat it. Cubs – they'll take it just to worry at it.'

His graphic tale seems to have a moral – for his sergeants are nodding in synchrony: they should only set limited store by the particular locus. And yet, as if by design, there is the sudden clink of the latch of the gate at its centre. They swing around in unison.

'Ahoy there! Are we on course for the Bowder Stone?'

It is a couple, middle-aged, clad in smart county attire, well groomed and noticeably suntanned. The woman, a honey blonde with a stiff-looking bonnet of hair, is surely fresh from the services of a cosmetologist. The detectives make way, stepping to one side of the woodland path. Skelgill assumes responsibility for mustering a reply.

'Aye – just stick to this path – six minutes and you'll be there.'

'My good fellow – that is jolly precise.'

Skelgill sees the man examining them. While he rarely looks out of place in the countryside (if not so elsewhere), his colleagues are more conspicuous. DS Leyton is wearing a suit, and wellingtons are his only concession to the outdoors; DS Jones has the look of a student, in a college sweatshirt, jeans and trainers, albeit of the trail variety. But Skelgill is not about to explain their presence, nor the reason he knows the exact timing. He tilts his head to one side.

'Happen it's the correct answer.'

The man hesitates, as though his curiosity is piqued and he wants to know more. Then he seems to think the better of it.

'Excellent – I shall wish you good morrow. Onward, Margery.'

He pushes off from a brass-topped cane, while the woman nods in a regal manner, as though she anticipates a bow and a curtsey and is rather premature with her acknowledgement. The detectives watch with a certain bemusement until the visitors disappear from sight, the man marching with a military bearing, his wife trailing a waft of expensive perfume in her glamorous wake. But now they turn to spy a slim young woman of medium height approaching the other side of the gate – in fact she is a teenager, attractive and sultry beyond her years, with long smooth dark hair, brown pools for eyes and crescent brows that are surely artificially enhanced. She appears suitably bored for one of her generation, but is taking a selfie nonetheless, and is plugged in to her mobile via white earphones. He notices that she clasps in her hand behind her phone a few sprigs of late-flowering enchanter's nightshade. She does not make eye contact with either of the males, just DS Jones – whom she takes in with a sweeping glance, one of interest rather than condescension, and she smiles engagingly and DS Jones reciprocates. Again they watch – now just the slender figure, in no hurry, though perhaps on reflection maintaining a sanitary distance between herself and what must be her parents. Though it is unlikely she can hear him, DS Leyton mutters under his breath.

'That don't feel too clever to me, Guv.'

Skelgill is scowling. But he does not answer, so it is left to DS Jones to request clarification.

'What do you mean?'

'Well – if it was right here that Mary Wilson was accosted, attacked – whatever. Makes you realise – a girl on her own – about that size – your size, Emma – bit of a sitting duck – lonely spot like this.'

DS Jones looks tempted to demonstrate a karate move, but restrains herself. There is a combative glint in her eyes. DS Leyton emits a growl of frustration and appeals directly to Skelgill.

'It ain't right, is it?'

'That's why we do the job, Leyton.' Skelgill punches his left fist into the opposite palm. 'Come on – we'll walk up through Cummacatta – it's the most obvious route to the cave from here.'

They pass in single file through the gate and Skelgill leads them out into a more open area, skirting clumps of trees and patches of deep bracken, finding ground underfoot where there is shorter grass by means of a succession of traverses, drawing the sting out of the gradient, while all the time broadly veering to his right as they ascend the steepening flank of Grange Fell. Eventually they swing back one final time towards the woodland fringe and their path becomes more level. Unlike before, Skelgill has not spared the gas, and DS Leyton is panting heavily. From a little behind, he calls out.

'Flippin' heck, Guv – if this is the obvious route I shouldn't like to try and find the difficult one.'

Skelgill stops dead in his tracks and turns. DS Jones is right on his heels and has to put out a hand against his shoulder to avoid a minor collision.

'Think about what you just said, Leyton.'

DS Leyton seems more inclined to deal with his oxygen debt – but he gamely contrives a response from limited resources.

'I see where you're coming from, Guv.' He buys a second or two while he mops his brow with a handkerchief. 'Local knowledge, you're talking about – right?'

Skelgill nods gravely.

'The Bowder Stone's a proper tourist attraction – like you just witnessed. Notice there's no signpost to the Kissing Cave. It's not on the map and it's nowt to look at – there's dozens of formations more spectacular. And it's hard to reach even if you know where it is.' Now he regards DS Jones with a rather peculiar expression – his gaze seems to address her midriff. 'But if I were carting you up here, this is the way I'd come. Even then it would be no picnic – but that's what I mean by the obvious route.'

While DS Leyton seems content with this assessment DS Jones nods more reluctantly. There is a spark of defiance in her response.

'Or, if I knew the way, you could just let me walk, Guv.'

Skelgill stares at her for moment. The purpose of their visit is to get the lie of the land, not to firm up hypotheses – which was surely the failing of the original investigation. Accordingly, he raises a hand and turns, and leads them, in the manner of an Indian scout, back into the shade of the oaks. A couple of minutes more brings them to the minor ravine that is Odinsgill, complete with its eponymous beck, and a cordon of police tape confirms they have reached their destination. They have a brief encounter with a prowling PC Dodd, who appears to be patrolling the perimeter in order to keep himself occupied. The forensic team has made the archaeologists' gazebo its base; conveniently they have similar methods, if not motives.

Following a confab with the senior investigator, the three detectives move up to the mouth of the Kissing Cave. DS Jones and DS Leyton carry white high-density polyethylene suits and overshoes; Skelgill has decided he need not enter for a second time. They reach the rock face, an almost vertical section on the steeper southern side of the ravine, with clumps of ferns and sedges springing from ledges. Skelgill indicates what is, at a glance, an inconspicuous crevice, a narrow rippling slit in the rock that begins about two feet from the ground and extends to a height of maybe seven feet – it looks impenetrable and indeed DS Leyton reacts with apparent disbelief.

'In there?'

DS Jones is adroitly donning her overalls, wasting no time. DS Leyton, however, remains rooted to the spot.

'I ain't gonna fit, Guv – you could end up with another corpse on your hands.'

'Leyton – it's wider once you're past the opening – I'll give you a shove.'

DS Leyton looks with alarm from one colleague to the other.

'I'm happy for Emma to report back.' He mops his brow again. Then a note of rising hysteria seems to grip his voice. 'You know me and caves, Guv?'

Skelgill is unsympathetic.

'Come off it, Leyton. Water, heights – now it's caves. At this rate you'll run out of things to be allergic to.'

But DS Jones is staring at her fellow sergeant with sudden concern – for she is remembering tell of an episode of which her colleague does not speak – yet could rightly boast – for he received one of the highest orders of bravery that can be bestowed in peacetime. It concerned a case of fire on the London Underground. Now she guesses it is resurfacing as a case of PTSD.

'Guv – let me go – there's probably not much to see – I'll take photos if need be. It'll save time if there's just the one of us.'

There is something about her tone that attracts Skelgill's attention – although his expression remains sceptical as he

35

considers her request. Whether the penny has dropped is not clear – and DS Jones does not wish to embarrass her colleague by explaining her reasoning. Before Skelgill can react, she darts towards him and feigns a lunge with puckered lips.

'Kiss me luck!'

And she has turned and gone, disappearing with alacrity into the fissure.

There ensues a brief silence. A look of relief spreads across DS Leyton's strained countenance, and he makes a double-clicking sound with his tongue against the roof of his mouth.

'She's got the bit between her teeth on this one, Guv.'

Skelgill is staring at the rocky cleft. He appears to ignore his subordinate's observation.

'What did she just say?'

'What, Guv? Er – wish me luck, wasn't it?'

4. MRS TYSON

Monday, midday

'I'm glad we've not had to tell her, Guv. I reckon that's the worst blinkin' part of the job, breaking bad news to bereaved families.'

Skelgill is staring solemnly ahead. He has pulled up beside a small marked squad car on a patch of roadside gravel. There is a hand-painted sign, flaking and askew affixed to a weathered farm gate, that may once have stated, "Private Parking" – something of a necessity during the summer months in particular, when Slatterthwaite, in common with many Lakeland hamlets, becomes a depository for the vehicles of inconsiderate trippers that disgorge their oft-unruly occupants to fan out across the fells, with limited regard for the Countryside Code.

But September is somewhat different. All but the elite private schools are back and the visitor profile therefore shifts along the social spectrum to well-heeled empty nesters, dedicated to making the most of their golden years, coming to explore and tramp while there is still sap in the veins and warmth in the air; it is a time when late rooms in Cumbria's myriad gourmet hotels become as rare as hens' teeth. As such, the hamlet of Slatterthwaite – the last settlement on a dead-end B-road – is something of a time capsule, since it has been spared the scourge of holiday homes and B&Bs, and has no ancient inn to serve up langoustines and quinoa, there is no talk of Marx and nuclear fission; indeed it offers the quality of entering a farmyard as much as a village.

Mrs Jean Tyson's is the end cottage of a row, a low stone-built slate-roofed terrace that fronts directly onto the single-track lane, and behind which there is space only for truncated rear gardens where runner beans strain before the parabola of the post-glacial dale curves skywards, a looming feature that eats into the light of the winter afternoons and above which the silhouette of a buzzard seems permanently to hang like a child's tethered kite. There is a side fence of wooden palings, rather rickety, and a gate – ajar – from which three red hens now explode like a crackling firework, pursued by a young Lakeland Terrier – and it is apparent that the back door of the property has been opened and a uniformed WPC whom they recognise reverses out, evidently concluding a conversation and making consolatory hand gestures. An elderly lady becomes partially visible on the threshold. The detectives emerge from the car and are noticed – and there now ensues what could look like a choreographed handover.   DS Jones intercepts the WPC and exchanges information. Skelgill intercepts the big-pawed pup and wrestles with it playfully.   DS Leyton intercepts the householder and chaperones her back inside, shortly to be joined by his colleagues – and the pup, which has not had enough, and persists in sallying at Skelgill's shins. They have entered a low-ceilinged 1970's-style dining kitchen with a formica-topped table and matching chrome-framed chairs. The woman seats her new visitors and shoos the dog outside, and a renewed bout of clucking reaches them through the open top section of the stable-style door. Then she sets about putting on the kettle and pulling down mugs from a shelf. She speaks without turning her head.

'I didn't expect you this quick. I shouldn't have thought there were no rush.'

Her words are surprisingly matter of fact. She is a small woman of just over five feet, with a helmet of short grey hair. She has a stocky masculinity, and fair skin that looks like it might be mottled with a heat rash. They know from their files her age to be seventy-two, but there is nothing creaky about her deliberate movements. She wears a pale-blue short-sleeved overall in keeping with the canteen-like impression of the spick-and-span kitchen. Skelgill is wondering if her busy, offhand manner is a reaction to the news she has received – a sort of displacement activity to keep at bay the shock. He is also thinking that 'no rush' was part of the problem twenty-two years ago. He realises his subordinates are waiting for him to reply when Jean Tyson speaks again.

'Thoo's one of Minnie Graham's lads, int' thee?'

Though she intones it as a question it is clear she knows it to be a fact. Skelgill clears his throat self-consciously.

'That's right, Mrs Tyson. You know her, aye?'

'I see your Ma on her bike – sometimes when I'm down at t' Post Office in Balderthwaite. Then she pedals back over t' Honister.' She seems to snort. 'You're tapped, you lot are.'

Skelgill raises an eyebrow.

'You're not the first to say it.'

The woman has filled a teapot and brings a tray to the table.

'And you're the lad that won t' fell race the year oor Mary disappeared. That set t' cat amongst pigeons.'

Skelgill is caught out by this remark. It is plain to see he is conflicted. When he might bask in the unexpected ray of glory, there seems to be a reprimand, a sting in the tail – as though he were responsible for something of which he is unaware. He senses his colleagues are staring at him – perhaps they are surprised he eschewed the opportunity to allude to his fell-running prowess earlier. He is further confused that Jean Tyson has conflated mention of her daughter with reference to himself. He nods accommodatingly, not knowing what he is accommodating. But the woman settles at the end of the table. There is milk already in the mugs and she pours tea without a further word and divvies out the strong brew. Skelgill avails himself of sugar and then realises Jean Tyson is waiting her turn. He watches her stir in two heaped spoonfuls. He has seen photographs of Mary Wilson in the files, but in her mother he does not recognise anything of the fine featured brunette, with the exception perhaps of the high cheekbones that in the older woman are cancelled by a belligerent jaw; there is a tight-lipped narrow mouth where the daughter's was full and voluptuous; the eyes are small grey gimlets versus generous lanceolate emeralds. He wonders what her father looked like – a man who had not been on the scene since her childhood and now known to be deceased.

Skelgill's lack of response – his distraction by talk of the fell race, and his mind thus caused to wander – sees DS Jones begin to extract her prepared notes from her shoulder bag. But before

39

the detective sergeant can initiate what might be considered formal proceedings Jean Tyson makes a stolid pronouncement.

'I allus knew she were close by. She wouldn't have left t' bairn – not after all them years tryin' for one.'

At this, Skelgill seems to snap out of his reverie.

'What did you think happened to her, Jean?'

His tone is conservational, and that he has switched to use her Christian name seems in keeping with the familiarity she has demonstrated with his own antecedent. However, when she faces him there is a distinct hardness in her eyes – albeit difficult to read; is she bottling up her emotions, or simply inured by the passing of two decades to the reality that has finally become manifest?

'Tha don't get buried under a pile of rocks int' cave without being murdered.'

That she evidently regards the new information to be consistent with her original belief does not prompt Skelgill to contest this view – although murder has a strict technical definition of which they cannot yet be certain; thus he is obliged to offer a partial caveat.

'Obviously, we're waiting for some tests to come back. But – aye.'

The woman regards him unblinkingly, and compresses the small straight line of her mouth.

'Will thee catch him, this time round?'

Skelgill wrestles with the muscles of his face that might betray the practical doubts that writhe beneath. He takes a pull at his tea and observes her over the rim of the mug. An outsider listening in might have heard a cynical note in the woman's voice: that she has not the least expectation of what she asks, and is disparaging of officialdom and all that it cares for her. But Skelgill detects an entirely different aspiration in her harsh inflection. Fell folk like Jean Tyson do not wear their heart on their sleeve. As if hewn from the very rock beneath their feet, their character shaped by the rugged landscape and the inclement weather and the economic hardship, such people have their own special code for sentiment. So what Skelgill hears is not a dismissal of his predecessors' ineffectual efforts and distrust in the lip service his new generation of coppers will pay, but an appeal that taps his provenance. He maintains eye contact and, once more conscious of the gaze of his subordinates upon him, he nods gravely.

'Who would have murdered her, Jean?'

For split second there is a reaction – an involuntary, almost furtive glance at the green fellside framed in the open half-door – that makes Skelgill in the instant think that she expects to see a face there. But his perception is infinitesimal, and when the woman replies her answer dispels his fleeting fantasy.

'Who would do sommat like that? A young mother int' prime of her life.'

Skelgill waits, but she has nothing to add.

'I realise that if anything specific had come up – some event, something said that triggered an idea – you would have got straight in touch. But is there a more general feeling, an impression you've formed over time?'

'Like, someone's tried to make amends – or who still can't look us in the eye?'

Skelgill snatches a sidelong glance at his colleagues. This is far more explicit a response than he has dared to expect. She has cut through the well-meant flimflam and has called a spade a spade. She stares grimly into her tea, stirring methodically.

'When you've had sommat like this happen, you think everyone's acting strange towards you.' She looks up, again betraying little emotion. 'And they probably are.'

Skelgill pauses for thought. He can see that DS Jones is poised with her list of prepared questions. But it is dawning upon him that it is his instinct to treat the death of Mary Wilson as though it were a current event. Rather than pass the baton to his sergeant he raises both palms with spread fingers to indicate their surroundings.

'What were Mary's circumstances, prior to her disappearance?'

Jean Tyson seems unperturbed that he has changed the subject.

'She liked it here – but that Aidan, he didn't. But beggars can't be choosers. And I were around to look after t' bairn when they weren't.'

'What brought them to stay here?'

The corners of the woman's mouth seem to twitch with disapproval.

'Aidan lost his job at Wukiton – he were some kind of draughtsman in the office at the steelworks. They couldn't manage their rent – and Mary seven months wi' child and not being able to work towards the end.'

'But, Aidan Wilson, he got another job?' Skelgill glances at DS Jones, who gives a barely perceptible nod.

'Aye – he got work as a sales rep – but it didn't pay as much. And Mary were just getting back on her feet – with her own work. He didn't pull his weight.'

It is not Skelgill's inclination to take sides. Of course, he has sympathy for this woman, dour and painfully unemotional though she may be – but there is the other's perspective. He is guessing that the tiny property has only one additional room downstairs, at the front, and two small bedrooms in the half-attic floor above. It would have been cramped – something he knows all about – but it does not escape him that living with the mother-in-law is a different species of cramped. Moreover, the bereaved husband would have been investigated as a possible suspect. There should be nothing read into such – it is basic police procedure to eliminate close acquaintances, a circle from which the perpetrator can oft be drawn. But for Aidan Wilson – knowing his mother-in-law will have been questioned about his whereabouts, his relationship with her daughter, his habits and behaviour – there would have been a lasting discomfort. Though cleared by the DNA sweep, when the process failed it damned everyone, as DS Jones's article opined. It cannot have been easy to live both under the same roof *and* under suspicion.

Jean Tyson may almost be reading his thoughts.

'Afterwards – after Mary disappeared – he got himself out soon enough. And it weren't long before he were going wi' his landlady. And that never lasted.'

Skelgill is pondering which of several avenues that are opening up to take. The original police investigation was not designed to chronicle the subsequent life histories of the actors – and yet, if there is to be a solution it may lie in occurrences since. Certainly any attempt simply to re-navigate the inquiry of twenty-two years ago is likely to wash up on the same old rocks, tarnished by time and tide and holed by the absence of participants who may have passed on or drifted away. Yet there is something in what DS Leyton said – that, yes, he was there. He was *here*. Naïve maybe, green, teenage – nonetheless those events form part of the continuum for which he has an unbroken affinity. The same cannot be said of the now-retired DI who was in charge of the case, a well-respected detective, but a man that hailed from urban Newcastle and was every inch Skelgill's opposite.

Just as his colleagues must be thinking he has lost his train of thought, Skelgill responds, if a little obliquely, to Jean Tyson's remarks.

'But Mary and Aidan Wilson had been together for a good time, aye?'

The woman seems to take pride in this point, shifting into a more upright position and pulling back her shoulders.

'Since oor Mary were fifteen.'

Skelgill inclines his head. That is half of the lifetime that was cut short.

'Aidan Wilson was older than Mary, am I right?'

Jean Tyson nods decisively, as though this were the righteous state of affairs.

'They were wed when oor Mary were eighteen. He were twenty-four.'

'So he'd have been, what – twenty-one when they started seeing each other?'

'There weren't many lasses that could say they'd got a boyfriend with his own motor car. When they were courtin' he took her on trips to Windermere, Whitehaven – and Blackpool once.'

There is an almost wistful look in her eyes – it seems she is recalling her impressions from that time – perhaps her boasts to other mothers whose daughters had not achieved the same success. It seems the bachelor Aidan Wilson held out prospects that did not come to fruition as a son-in-law.

'Where did they live, after they were married?'

'At Aidan's Ma's place at Balderthwaite. She were an invalid – she suffered MS. She died of her illness after a couple of years – and they took over the lease of the cottage.' Jean Tyson frowns introspectively. 'I'd allus said they could come to mine – and they did in the end.'

'And what was their relationship like – during the time they lived here?'

The woman looks momentarily puzzled – as though the idea that there is some volition over such a thing is a revelation.

'I don't suppose it were any different to most married couples.'

'Were they the sort to have rows?'

She shakes her head, but with some indecision.

'Not rows, so much.' (Skelgill waits patiently and in time she supplies more detail.) 'Mary knew her own mind. Happen she thought sometimes Aidan were holding her back – he weren't the ambitious sort. But if she snapped at him he'd like as not go out wi' dog. He weren't what you'd call confrontational. I never saw him lay a hand on her – if that's what you're getting at.'

Skelgill shrugs noncommittally.

'And after Mary disappeared – what happened?'

'I'd been minding the bairn, anyway – a lot of the time. I just carried on. Aidan had his job – he had to keep that up.'

She looks at Skelgill, beseechingly, he thinks, from beneath the austere exterior – as if she seeks his approbation for the turn that domestic events must have taken. But his analysis is merely what he regards as common sense: why would you live with your mother-in-law? What, for instance, if one day you wanted to bring home a female friend?

'Jean, you mentioned that he moved out – how soon after was that?'

She thinks for a few moments.

'Six months, maybe nine. Any road, it were before the bairn were two – I remember Aidan were supposed to come for his second birthday – and he forgot – or he made up some excuse that he'd been called away.'

There is news in this to Skelgill.

'Are you saying the child remained with you?'

She looks at him as though she is surprised that he asks; and that she is irked that he might think otherwise.

'I've brought him up like I was his Ma.'

For his part Skelgill remains perplexed. It is an unexpected turn of events.

'So – Aidan Wilson didn't have the boy living with him – not part-time – weekends or whatever?'

The woman shakes her head, her expression somewhat blank.

'What'd have been the point? His cot were here – and all his things. This were his home. Besides, Aidan wouldn't have known how to look after him – changing nappies, making up bottles. Never mind that the place he moved to – he took lodgings in a B&B down at Grange – he only had a bedroom there, leastways at first.'

She ends the sentence with a disdainful "tch".

Skelgill takes it as an invitation to probe further.

'You mentioned that relationship didn't continue.'

'He moved to Keswick within the year. Then the less he had to do wi' bairn – the less he knew what to do wi' him. And t' bairn weren't fussed about seeing him. They'd never what they call bonded. Oor Nick grew up – made his own friends hereabouts – he were more interested in laikin' with them.'

'Nick – that's the name of your grandson?'

'Aye. Mary were particular about that – not Nicholas – just Nick.'

'He's not here now – I mean, he doesn't stay with you?'

Skelgill casts about in a guileless fashion, as if looking for some sign like a pair of men's boots or empty beer bottles; but the woman nevertheless seems a little defensive.

'He'll be twenty-three this month.'

'Where is he living?'

'He's a mechanic at Dickson's garage – he's got free use of a caravan there – they've three static vans out t' back – they let them to holidaymakers. It were right for him to have his independence.' She frowns introspectively. 'He still comes round of a morning, mind – for his bait, like?'

'Dickson's – that's Balderthwaite – down Beck Lonnin.'

Skelgill says this to be conversational – the garage has been trading for donkey's years, so long that it was once a traditional cartwright's, and everyone knows of it. But she seems to read into his statement some intent. Now there is perhaps a hint of anxiety in the small grey eyes, and she clutches her mug to her chest with both hands.

'I said to your uniformed lass I ought to be the one as tells him.'

Skelgill glances at DS Jones, who gives a confirmatory nod – this must be a point that was conveyed to her by their colleague upon arrival. Jean Tyson however moves to pre-empt any new objections.

'He never knew his Ma. You have to remember that. He were nobbut a bab'e when she disappeared. There's no cause for him to be upset.' She hesitates – and only after a moment's indecision does she appear to yield to one side of some internal conflict: she blurts out a supplementary justification. 'He's got a learning difficulty – you have to know how to speak wi' him.'

Skelgill regards her implacably, such that his response, when it comes, might be unexpected.

'Jean – that's no problem. You do it in your own good time. Like you say – he were a babe in arms. Whatever happened to your lass, he's the one person we can be sure weren't mixed up in it.'

The woman's features remain conflicted; there might be a silver lining, but her repressed emotions hang heavy, an immovable bank of dark clouds. As if to distract herself she reaches for the teapot, presumably knowing it is empty – but she appears bewildered by the fact and rises automatically from her chair.

'I should tell him soonest – before he hears it ont' wireless. He listens t' local radio while he works. I'll be garn along when you've done wi' us. I'll make a fresh mash.'

Skelgill judges her words to be a polite invitation both to stay and to leave. He glances at his colleagues – who indicate via body language that they are replete – but his own response to the sound of water filling a kettle is entirely Pavlovian, and he does not try to dissuade the woman. Besides, there is more to discuss. He begins by adding a qualification to his concession.

'We'll make sure there's nothing released to the media before tomorrow morning. They don't like it when they've got a sniff of something – which no doubt they have – but they realise we have to contact the next of kin before they can go public.' He inhales between clenched teeth, as if to add emphasis to what he is about to say. 'Jean, you have to expect the presence of news reporters and film crews in the area – at least for the first day or two when the story breaks. Folk are sick to the back teeth of moaning politicians – so an unsolved murder, a historical case like this – it will attract attention.'

Jean Tyson returns to the table with the recharged teapot. She puts it down with an excess of care that suggests she is containing her frustration. And yet her next question is pragmatic.

'Does that include Aidan? As next of kin?'

Skelgill glances sharply at DS Jones – but for once here is a detail of which she is uncertain. In the limited time during which she has familiarised herself with the case, the present address – indeed the status – of Aidan Wilson has not yet been established. Of course they intend to see him, but that is a plan to be made. DS Jones, however, at least knows her law.

'To be frank, Mrs Tyson, there's no legal definition. Next of kin is any person you nominate in the event you suffer a sudden illness or an accident. They have no powers or rights. We use it as a more general term to refer to the close family. So whether Mr Wilson remarried or not wouldn't make any difference. We naturally came to you first. No one can be closer than a mother.'

47

The woman seems pleased by what DS Jones has said, and she regards her confidingly.

'He don't have hardly any contact wi' oor Nick – sends him a text on his birthday and at Christmas. But I don't reckon he's remarried. Happen he'd have told him that much.'

Jean Tyson now moves to pour out more tea. DS Jones and DS Leyton tactfully decline. As she is filling his mug, Skelgill rather absently poses what is of course a particularly salient question.

'Jean, did Mary know about the Kissing Cave? Up in the woods.'

Jean Tyson seems to hesitate in her movement – the heavy clay teapot held motionless between Skelgill's mug and her own. Her grip trembles a little as she commences to pour.

'All t' folk int' dale know about t' Kissing Cave – it's been known for generations. Least, up until recently. Once in a while we'd laik up there as bairns.' She flashes a self-conscious glance, almost coy. 'Teenagers an' all.' But her thoughts are evidently jerked back to the issue at hand, to the horror of what the place now represents. Her voice becomes strained. 'But Mary wouldn't have walked t' dog up there – she'd have stuck to t' path along t' bottom.'

'What kind of dog were it, Jean?'

'Jewk? Same as I've got now. That Archie out there – he's us third Lakeland since Jewk died. There were Tupper, but he got run down by Pick Pearson's tractor. Then the last one were named Cur – he lived till he were twelve. I've had Archie just above a year.'

Skelgill nods encouragingly.

'On the day Mary went missing – what time did the dog – Jewk – come back here?'

The woman looks troubled by the effort of recall.

'I can't rightly mind. It were afore Aidan got back from his work – and that were normally about five. It were maybe threeish.'

Skelgill is thinking it is probably documented in the case notes. This question must have been asked at the time, and the answer would have been fresh in the memory.

'And he were in the habit of doing that – you didn't think owt were amiss?'

She shakes her head.

'Afore they moved in I used to keep him if they went away for the night. And Mary'd often walk him along – it's no distance from where she were living at Balderthwaite – there's a path beside Slatterdale Beck, so she could let him off t' leash. Jewk knew his way well enough, and he'd turn up here – especially evenings when Mary were at work and he'd bin left wi' Aidan.'

She seems to display a measure of satisfaction in regard to the creature's allegiance.

'You kept the dog – after Aidan Wilson moved out?'

'Aye – he were a marra for oor Nick when he were growing up.' She lapses into thought, and begins to shake her head ruefully. 'If only dogs could talk, eh?'

Skelgill nods pensively – although there are various explanations for the dog's behaviour. Often enough he encounters owners whose pets have become separated for reasons of their own making – lured by the hot whiff of a fox, spooked by another bigger dog, or they've tagged along with a commercial dog-walker's pack to scrounge treats – and it is not uncommon to find the miscreant skulking back at the car park, while the owner whistles in the wind. The dog Jewk may not have been a silent witness to Mary Wilson's fate.

'Was Mary in the habit of meeting anyone – when she took the dog, I mean? Another dog walker? A friend? It's what a lot of folk seem to do.'

But Jean Tyson shakes her head.

'Most folk back then had proper working dogs, hounds, sheepdogs, ratters. It weren't a big thing like it is now – all these fancy mongrels – and t' dog-walkers' vans you see about the place. Mary just used to like that she'd get a break – some peace when the bairn were sleeping. She'd come back and say she'd had this or that new idea – for her woollens, or for how she was going to make more of a business of it. And she liked the exercise – she had a lovely figure, did oor Mary, and she soon got that back, what wi' all her walking. No, she preferred to go alone. And that were her downfall, weren't it?'

It is not easy for her audience to divine the nuances of the elderly woman's sentiments; such is her bleak and cheerless delivery. But Skelgill's assessment is that her tone implies sadness rather than rancour.

'She were only doing what thousands of other folk do, Jean. You can't be expected not to go for a country walk, for fear of something happening to you.'

She looks at him directly.

'Aye – except folk kept their bairns away from t' Bowder Stone after oor Mary's car were found there. And from t' woods all down t' dale. The Bowder Wood, Cummacatta, right past Grange down t' Girt Wood.' She pauses reflectively. 'T'aint much of an issue nowadays, though. You hardly see bairns at all – they're too busy with their computer games and mobile phones.'

Skelgill is nodding. What she says is probably true, even in these relatively isolated villages. Kids just don't laik about – play out – like they used to, even in his day, when the first curling tendrils of digital technology were beginning to take their insidious grip on society. It has struck him on his two brief visits to the Kissing Cave – *Friggeshol,* as the professor would have it – that the vicinity is overgrown and appears unvisited. And both of the routes he has forged, on Sunday the more direct ascent from the Bowder Stone, and today the traversing zigzags from Cummacatta, required old memories of the lie of the land; there was no actual worn path in either case. His musings are interrupted by Jean Tyson's determined voice.

'Course – I never let oor Nick out on his own – not down there. Not till he were a big lad. I could never have lived with mesen if lightning had struck twice.'

Despite the implied improbability of the idiom, Skelgill can't help thinking that, when he narrowly misses a take, the first thing he does is cast back to the exact spot. The woman has a point; and now she raises another depressing aspect of their mutual business.

'Happen I'll be able to start preparations for t' funeral.' Her voice becomes weak and plaintive. 'To lay Mary to rest – proper like.'

There is the rather uncomfortable truth that her daughter has been buried; but she seems phlegmatic, sustained by what for bereaved relatives is surely only a meagre crumb of comfort, when human remains are located.

'Jean – it could be a few days before the Coroner will be able to give the go ahead. You understand it's something we need to get right – in case we miss a vital clue.'

The elderly woman looks tired; she acquiesces.

'I've waited nigh on twenty-two years. A mother can bide her time.'

Skelgill is about to commend her stoicism when there is a sudden clamour, a renewed commotion from out of doors. It is the hens and what sounds like a vagrant goose that has entered the fray, to throw in its weight on the avian side of the equation. The dog is yapping spiritedly. Skelgill rises.

'I'll go and referee.' He reaches and places a palm briefly on the woman's shoulder. 'My colleagues will just take a few technical details that we'll need. And we'll be back in touch as soon as we have some information for you about timings and suchlike.'

The woman forces a grin of sorts.

'Aye – that's alreet, love. You tell yer Ma I were askin' forra.'

Skelgill bows and steps away. He turns on the threshold to address his subordinates.

'Just top line. I think Mrs Tyson's helped us enough for one day.'

DS Jones nods amenably, though she may be disappointed that her preparation has not yet been put to good use. DS Leyton turns a new leaf of his pocket notebook.

When the two sergeants emerge they find Skelgill reading a photocopied hand-drawn bill that has been tied to a wooden

51

telegraph pole inside an inverted punched plastic sleeve (though the Cumbrian damp has still got at it). They amble across – there is something in his body language that suggests he is waiting for them to do just that.

'Look at this.'

He steps back.

DS Leyton squints. He clears his throat. Beneath an illustrated Herdwick sheep is a paragraph of flowery text that he now reads aloud.

'"Balderthwaite Shepherds' Meet – Wednesday 23rd September. More than two centuries of tradition, not to be missed. Over 40 classes for Herdwick and Swaledale sheep. Working shepherds' dogs. Fell race. Hand clipping. Shepherds' working sticks. New this year, Yat Lowpin! Categories fer bairdens an' fer arl uns. Scordy an' scran served in the *Twa Tups* public house. Music afterwards. All welcome – even offcomers frey Kezzick. Entrance free."'

'Cor blimey, Guvnor – some geezer's havin' a larf. What the flippin' heck's Yat Lowpin when it's at home?'

Skelgill grins. He gives a gentle nudge with his elbow to DS Jones, who stands at his side.

'You're a local lass. Translate Cumbrian to Cockney for him.'

DS Jones takes a deep breath – it suggests she is not entirely confident.

'Well – a yat's a gate. And to lowp means to jump. So I guess if you put the two together, you get the idea. Bairdens are young people, and arl means old.' She looks at Skelgill impishly. 'It doesn't say where the cut-off is. Maybe you can make a glorious return, Guv?'

Skelgill grins sardonically. But it seems his cheeks begin to flush and he turns and heads back towards his car.

'Aye, very funny, Jones.'

But he *is* thinking of making a glorious return, just not of the manner about which DS Jones teases him. They join him in the car; he reverses and they pull away in silence, each to their own thoughts. With a practised knack Skelgill jack-knifes the vehicle around a tight angle between jutting barns built from tightly stacked slate. As the long brown shooting brake disappears from sight of the cottage, Jean Tyson emerges from the back door. She has exchanged her blue overall for a tan raincoat, and she is fastening a multi-coloured knitted headscarf beneath her chin, the determined squareness of her jaw exaggerated by the action. She calls the terrier, Archie, and threads a length of twine through his collar, and together they set off walking; almost immediately they turn off the narrow lane onto a track that leads to the old stone footbridge over Slatterdale Beck, and beyond the footpath that faithfully follows its course.

5. SCORDY AN' SCRAN

Monday afternoon

'*What?*'

Skelgill is responding to the looks of his subordinates as he approaches them. Under protest they have yielded to his impulsive demand to stop – having driven hardly three minutes – at a signposted farm shop and café; it has a secluded outdoor area, a handful of rustic benches and tables surrounded by lush ornamental foliage and a view over a pasture grazed by good-sized black Herdwick lambs and scruffy shorn ewes. Now he is met with faces that speak of his incorrigibility, since he has procured unasked not just teas but also three mountainous fruit scones made up with dollops of homemade jam and cream. *Scordy an' scran,* as the whimsical author of the poster phrased it.

'Look – it's on me – what's the problem?' In rather rebellious fashion he drops the tray on the warped oak-planked picnic table and takes a seat between his colleagues. 'If you can't finish yours, I will. You have to support local businesses. I know Debs in there – it's bad enough she's given us a discount.'

It seems DS Leyton has quickly resigned himself to the situation.

'What are they, Guv – Bowder Scones? They ought to be, the size of 'em.'

Skelgill is obviously ravenous, for he is already tucking in, spilling crumbs onto his lap and beyond, and a raiding party of waiting house sparrows moves in. He shows his approval of DS Leyton's quip with a raising of his eyebrows.

'You're on fire today, Leyton – you should be in advertising. I'll tell her that.'

DS Leyton seems pleased by the unaccustomed praise. He gazes rather wistfully at their surroundings.

'I suppose it's inspiring being out here, Guv.'

'Leyton – that's exactly why I want a chat now. Before we get swamped by what everyone else thought. While all this is fresh in our minds.'

Skelgill waves his part-consumed scone, making a circle in the air, sending an arc of crumbs across the lawn and precipitating a splinter movement from the main flock of passerines. His colleagues follow his indication to the horizon. Directly before them are the hills that all but close off Borrowdale; Grange Fell, wooded with oaks and birches, and the imposing ridge of High Spy, Scawdale Fell as Skelgill was taught to call it and as it appears on his precious antiquarian map of Cumberland. But this lofty raised skyline sweeps around to encircle them. The impression is less of a dale and more of a great wild amphitheatre with no easy way out; and it was thus a century ago, before the motor car and tarmacadam, when a visit to market in Keswick was a day's expedition; for the superstitious or faint of heart there were the dark woods, the supernatural – and wild animals and human vagrants and vagabonds; this mountain enclave a stage where modest rural lives were lived out largely in isolation, and it is a phenomenon that has not entirely changed.

DS Jones has brought her notebook that contains the questions she had prepared for earlier. She does not open it, but she lays a palm on the cover as a precursor to her contribution.

'Are you thinking it was a local man, Guv?'

Skelgill could toss in a handful of caveats – woman, accomplices, conspirators – but it would be pedantic, for they all know this; the operative word is *local*.

'That's what she reckons – Mary's Ma, aye?'

There is no obvious reason that Skelgill should believe this – there was no clinching fact – he gave Jean Tyson ample opportunity to point the finger; yet even the widower Aidan Wilson whom she had some cause to resent largely escaped her disapprobation. So he seems to be going by gut feel – the principle that what has been absorbed by the senses is translated by the mind but not always fed back to the conscious brain. Skelgill knows this – his subordinates know it of him – until some unexpected catalyst sparks a revelation it is a case of the proverbial 'unknown unknowns'. And it is not a process that can be artificially hastened. Besides, there is the small matter that they cannot properly pursue the 'crime' until they know what it is. Mary Wilson may have died from natural causes and the only offence the concealment of her body. But while Skelgill is evidently content with the spontaneous nature of the interview, and now his eyes track a couple of feisty lambs that suddenly decide to go head to head, DS Jones indicates that she is more comfortable dealing in tangibles.

'Guv – among other things, I've set the team onto reviewing all similar 'lone female' cases in the north of England in the past twenty-five years. First to see if there's any pattern that has emerged since, and then to identify whether known perpetrators could have been contenders in Mary Wilson's death – specifically their whereabouts at the time. I've requested that the original DNA sample be re-tested.'

Though he is still watching the jousting lambs, Skelgill nods bleakly. However, DS Jones is ready to voice what may be his unspoken objection.

'Guv – I realise no match has ever come to light – but I don't think we should risk being accused of leaving such an obvious stone unturned.'

Her metaphor is perhaps a little unfortunate – but that she would go to such lengths of diligence is commendable – despite that she has already picked a hole in the process that she proposes. DNA analysis was in its infancy at the time of Mary Wilson's disappearance; the criminal database expanded rapidly thereafter, effectively turning the future process on its head. Where the Cumbrian police were obliged to build their own database, wastefully trawling through hundreds of entirely innocent civilians in the surrounding area, today there are six million records on file of people who have actually been cautioned; many continue to reoffend. That a match from the unknown DNA found at the 'crime scene' at Cummacatta has never been thrown up is potentially significant. It allows the tentative hypothesis that the perpetrator was probably neither a serial killer nor even a career criminal; sooner or later such fugitives make a mistake. It is another leap altogether, however, to conclude that Mary Wilson's murderer came from the local community.

DS Leyton shifts uncomfortably on the bench and rubs a hand through his tousle of dark hair. Then he makes a sudden lunge for his scone and takes a greedy bite.

'Flippin' heck – I'm comfort eating!' He emits an exasperated splutter before composing himself. 'Reckon it's a red herring, Guv – this DNA malarkey?'

Skelgill's response is characteristically cryptic.

'Happen it made them take their eye off the ball. Thinking that would sort it. Then a month's gone by and they were back to square one.'

'We could be at blinkin' ground zero, Guv.'

Skelgill demurs.

'We've got a lot more evidence than they had, Leyton.'

He means there is a body – and rather like the *Three Wise Monkeys* the detectives ranged along the bench nod in unison. Skelgill despatches the last of his snack and sucks a thumb and a forefinger and rubs his hand on his thigh. He glances speculatively at DS Jones's as yet untouched scone. But the sugar boost seems to have kicked in and he pronounces with more gusto.

'What do you reckon about what old Ma Tyson had to say?'

DS Jones leans forward to glance around Skelgill at DS Leyton – but he is contentedly chewing and inclines his head to suggest she should answer.

'Being brutal about it, Guv – if you take the relationship between Mary and Aidan Wilson, there wasn't much to give cause for alarm. I guess most mothers-in-law would have a few complaints about their daughter's husband.'

Skelgill turns sharply to DS Leyton, who plainly feels suddenly conspicuous. He makes a 'guilty as charged' face. However, Skelgill seeks an opinion of a different nature from his male colleague.

'Slinging his hook – I get that. But what about leaving the bairn?'

DS Leyton's thick-necked head seems to sink deeper into his broad shoulders. He nods pensively.

'Can't imagine it myself, Guv – but it ain't unheard of – how many thousands of deadbeat dads are there? And maybe the geezer thought, I'm only down the road.' He cocks a thumb to indicate the short distance they have travelled. 'If the old girl weren't too keen on him, maybe she was quite happy. Having the kid must have been a big comfort for her – gave her something to do, a purpose. Maybe she didn't go out of her way to keep Aidan Wilson involved. I suppose we'll find out his side of the story.'

Skelgill is nodding reflectively as his sergeant continues.

'But I reckon it's right what she said about Mary Wilson and her dog. Having traipsed up there, I can't see she would have climbed to that cave. And, like Emma says, she had her stall to get back to.'

Skelgill looks less convinced by this argument. He turns to DS Jones.

'But you also pointed out the easiest way to get her body there was to let her walk. It's not called the Kissing Cave without reason.'

DS Jones regards Skelgill rather guilelessly; perhaps now her cheeks begin to colour a little – she makes a dart for her notebook and quickly opens it to one of a series of pages marked with indexed yellow stickers.

'That she had a rendezvous – naturally it was one of the theories they investigated. Several of the interviewees – those with closer connections to her – were probed about this. In one of the decision reports the officer wrote that it could have been a possibility, but nobody was prepared to go out on a limb and state that they knew she was having an affair.'

Skelgill is frowning.

'Little community like this – everyone knows everyone else's business. It's not something folk are usually slow in coming forward about.'

'Unless they've got something to hide, Guv.' It is DS Leyton who chips in.

There is a short pause before DS Jones speaks again.

'What you asked Jean Tyson about Mary meeting another dog walker or a friend, Guv? If you did want to meet a person that you weren't supposed to – then by doing something that's part of your regular routine – it wouldn't arouse suspicion. And if you were seen it could appear like a coincidence.'

Skelgill rather suspects he sometimes witnesses such a scenario – when one dog walker arrives at a parking spot, and another jumps out of a waiting car. There might as well be a winged cupid hovering above them as they head into the woods, so obvious is the affected 'normal' body language. DS Leyton puts it another way.

'Like they say – in plain sight?'

DS Jones nods.

'Well – kind of. I mean – it would be out of sight in those secluded woods and easy to avoid what few people were about. But no one would be suspicious of Mary Wilson setting out with the dog – like her husband, or mother, or other people in the village who might disapprove, or who might gossip if they found out.'

DS Leyton grins.

'So we need a list of former dog owners!'

DS Jones frowns, although her suntanned forehead is smooth and just a crinkle forms between her eyebrows.

'I suppose it would depend on whether the other person needed an excuse or not.'

She glances at Skelgill and sees that he is scowling, staring fiercely into the middle distance across the pasture, his eyes unblinking, and his gaze fixed and unseeing. She recognises there comes a point when too much speculation discomfits him; and, frankly, at this juncture they could weave a web of possibilities that could render them tangled and immobile. She makes an effort to draw back the wayward threads.

'Nowadays – with all these dating apps – a woman like her could hook up with anyone from miles around. But you'd think, back then – a little place like this – if there were a person, they would have been swept into the inquiry.'

Skelgill snaps out of his trance. For a moment he appears disconcerted by some aspect of her suggestion – but then he speaks evenly.

'Remind me of the folk that saw her leaving.'

DS Jones locates the corresponding page in her notebook.

'There were eleven formal statements – and notes of approximately a hundred short interviews. That covers everyone who lived in the immediate vicinity, and visitors who got in touch when they heard the appeal for information. Obviously there are detailed statements from Jean Tyson and Aidan Wilson. There were four positive eyewitnesses to her leaving the shepherds' meet. First, Sean Nicolson, then aged thirty, a local shepherd. He'd been at school with Mary Wilson, and he also supplied her with wool – so he must have known her quite well. He was considered to be the main reliable witness to her leaving the actual event – he saw her walk out with her dog on its lead at shortly before one o'clock. Then she went across to the pub where her car was parked – and that was where the other three saw her through the window. There was Megan Nicolson, also thirty, wife of Sean, and also a former schoolmate; she worked with her as a barmaid. Then there were the two competition judges who had retired to the bar to make their decisions. That was Walter Dickson, described as a mechanic, aged seventy-two, and Patrick Pearson, fifty, a tenant farmer from up beyond Slatterthwaite – I wonder if he's the same person that Jean Tyson referred to when she spoke of her dog being run over – she called him 'Pick'?'

Skelgill is nodding.

'Aye, I've heard of him. I'm sure he still judges now. I reckon the other feller might be dead. It was the Dicksons that had the garage – it must be one of the sons now. I might ask me Ma.'

DS Leyton, however, appears perplexed.

'If they all knew one another you'd think more people would have noticed.'

But Skelgill has his doubts.

'It's not like the Cumberland Show, Leyton. There's half a dozen tents and stalls, and most folk are crowding around getting a look at the sheep. Or they might be watching the runners going along the ridge. Folk that had stalls were probably busy selling to tourists. Those showing sheep would've had their hands full with them and their dogs. Meantime all she needed were thirty seconds to walk from her stall across to the pub and round the back.'

DS Leyton remains discontented on this point.

'What about beyond the shepherds' meet – were there no other sightings of her? At the Bowder Stone, or whatever.'

Perhaps to his and Skelgill's surprise DS Jones nods in the affirmative. She picks out an indexed section in her notebook.

'Yes, there was one probable sighting. A touring cyclist who was heading down Borrowdale came forward to say he had been, in his words,' (she refers directly to the page) '"dangerously overtaken by a small red car that was travelling too fast". He pinpointed the spot to a sharp bend about a quarter of a mile from where Mary Wilson would have turned off to park for the Bowder Stone. He didn't know the exact time, but based on his overall day's journey it was estimated at around 1pm.'

DS Leyton is listening attentively.

'Did he get a look at the driver? Any passengers?'

DS Jones shakes her head.

'I think he nearly came off the bike – and the car was around the bend before he knew it.'

'So, she was in a hurry.'

DS Jones nods at her colleague.

'She was known to be a cautious driver – never had any points on her licence. Apparently she would often walk to the woods from the village. The suggestion was that she took the car so she wouldn't be away for long.'

Skelgill is brooding, thinking about why he often drives too fast.

'Or she was late for an appointment.'

It is a reminder that there will always be an alternative explanation, and for the time being a silence descends upon the trio. DS Jones puts down her notebook and tests her tea from the artisan mug that bears the name of the village and indeed has its provenance in the local pottery. With dexterity she slices her scone into six segments and watched by an increasingly anxious Skelgill proceeds to eat them one at a time, displaying an unsuspected turn of speed, belied by impeccable manners. But when there are two pieces left she suddenly hands him her plate.

'I'm full, Guv. These *are* Bowder Scones!'

Skelgill looks relieved. He makes an unconvincing attempt to offer a portion to his other sergeant.

'Leyton?'

'Nah, you're alright, Guv – I'm stuffed an' all.' He leans to glance around at his fellow sergeant. 'Surprised you managed so much, Emma – slip of a thing like you. Didn't realise you liked cakes. Always assumed – you know – you're watching your figure – how you go to the gym, an' all that.'

DS Jones looks amused.

'My mum bakes almost every day – I have to save myself for teatime to keep her happy. I could eat cakes for England!'

There ensues more pensive silence – DS Jones's revelation has set her colleagues thinking. In time it is DS Leyton who ends the little hiatus – and certainly it appears that his thoughts have drifted from the case. He indicates their 'Balderthwaite' mugs ranged on the table before them.

'Everywhere you go round here, Guv, these villages are called this thwaite or that thwaite. What's all that about?'

Skelgill starts as though his mind is still occupied elsewhere.

'What?' Then he casts a hand somewhat absently at the sheep-flecked pasture beyond the café garden. 'Field – near as dammit.'

'Oh.'

DS Leyton sounds disappointed. But before he can respond Skelgill continues.

'Cumbria were just one great forest once, Leyton. What you see now – the bare fells, the walled enclosures – everything up to seventeen, eighteen hundred foot, that were solid trees. Obviously – not during the Ice Age. I'm talking after that. Then along came farming tribes that hacked out clearings – starting in the valley bottoms where the land was most fertile. Called their settlements after one thing or another.'

DS Leyton purses his lips.

'So, what's Balderthwaite, then – boulder field?'

Skelgill guesses DS Jones probably knows this – but he was once taught it, too. It just takes a greater effort to prise the fact from his memory.

'Something to do with a god.'

He detects that DS Jones is nodding – and he turns to her with a raised eyebrow that invites her input.

'We did a project on it when I was at primary school. *The Vicious Vikings*. Although most of their settlements' names are quite innocuous. Applethwaite, Brackenthwaite, Crosthwaite – quite often you can work it out.'

DS Leyton looks rather bemused.

'So, what – did they speak English?'

DS Jones giggles as though she thinks he must be joking. But then she responds. 'No – we speak Old Norse!'

Skelgill is nodding contemplatively.

'Here's one for the pair of you – Slatterthwaite.'

Each of his subordinates make as if to speak – and each realises they cannot conjure an educated guess. Skelgill provides a hint.

'I'll give you a clue – happen it was where they had the local abattoir.'

6. PRESS CONFERENCE

Tuesday 11 am

'Just a few days short of twenty-two years ago Mary Wilson left her woollens stall at Balderthwaite shepherds' meet in order to walk her Lakeland Terrier. When she did not reappear at the close of the event informal inquiries began to be made concerning her whereabouts. It was established that she had neither returned to her mother's cottage at the nearby hamlet of Slatterthwaite where she lived with her husband and their baby son, nor had she gone directly to her part-time job at the *Twa Tups* public house in Balderthwaite. The police were notified and her car was located at approximately 7pm near the tourist attraction known as the Bowder Stone, a place she regularly exercised the dog. It emerged that the animal had returned home of its own accord during the middle of the afternoon, although this was a common occurrence, and had not alarmed Mary's mother, Mrs Jean Tyson.

'Mary did not come home. In the ensuing days a major search took place of the surrounding countryside, but only one small possible trace of her was found – a woollen key fob of the type she knitted, which was identified by her husband to have the same pattern as that she used on her own bunch of keys. This was discovered in the woods a short distance from the car. The item was sent for forensic testing and a male DNA profile was recovered from traces of saliva. At that time DNA profiling was in its infancy.'

'Haha – like you, eh, darling?'

Skelgill, by the wonders of modern technology, is silently watching the media briefing on the screen in his office, in company with DS Leyton; now the latter detects telltale signs of his superior inwardly bristling. DS Jones, however, ignores the intervention.

'There was no national DNA database against which to compare the sample. Cumbria police took the unprecedented step of testing all males aged over seventeen who lived or worked in the district of Borrowdale. This was a voluntary programme, to which most consented. A handful that did not were eliminated by other means. The scheme did not produce a match. This line of investigation was based on the theory that Mary Wilson had tried to fend off an assailant, perhaps using her keys as a weapon, and the fob became detached in the struggle. However, not only was there no local match, in the intervening years there has been no profile added to the national database that has corresponded to the sample. Mary Wilson's disappearance has remained a mystery.

'A mystery that is until Sunday, two days ago. A research group from Durham University working in a wooded ravine known as Odinsgill discovered human remains beneath rocks in a narrow fissure. The archaeologists refer to the cave by its Viking name, *Friggeshol*.'

In avoiding the colloquial epithet it is DS Jones's intention to diminish the potential for sensationalism. But the graphic Old Norse alternative triggers a ripple of sniggers; these journalists, in the main older males, are long in the tooth and set like concrete in their undesirable ways. But she continues unperturbed; she knows she is in possession of facts they covet.

'The remains were identified by means of dental records as those of Mary Wilson. A preliminary autopsy has concluded that the cause of death was by strangulation. Further, a forensic geologist has determined that the nature of the concealment of the body was not by a natural rockfall. We have therefore formally opened a murder investigation.'

DS Jones pauses, and takes a sip from her bottle of mineral water – but, apart perhaps from one pair of keen eyes that are upon her, these hoary hacks are reluctant to concede much in the way of enthusiasm to the fresh-faced female detective. She glances tentatively at her notes.

'Further detailed forensic tests are underway to recover any available evidence from the site. We would request that members of the public please keep away from the area.'

Now she puts her papers aside and casts about in a manner that invites questions.

'Surely we are talking local knowledge?'

It is the bright-eyed young man who wastes no time, Kendall Minto of the *Westmorland Gazette*. His question is incisive, and he knows it. He is none other than the author of the controversial article to which DS Jones has drawn her colleagues' attention. She finds herself backpedalling.

'It is correct to say it is not a publicised landmark. But there are many quarries and caves and even small crevices throughout the area – literally hundreds across Borrowdale. If you were searching for somewhere to conceal a body, you would sooner or later come across such a place.'

'It's a long way up the hillside to lug a corpse.' Kendall Minto's tone is guileless, but his argument is persuasive.

'Mary Wilson's dog was a breed that would readily follow the scent of a fox. It is quite possible that it strayed to the vicinity of the cave. If it had a fox at bay she would have needed to go and pull it away.'

'And there just happened to be a madman hanging about?'

This is the cynical drawl of one of the other journalists.

'More likely she was followed from her car.'

The audience might appear indifferent but they have a nose for obfuscation. If they sense there is something the police do not want to admit, they will home in on it. Another now pipes up.

'How did they miss the body?'

Evidently he refers to the original unproductive search.

'They had to cover almost twenty thousand acres. Much of the terrain could be described as hostile. The area of Odinsgill comprises steep-sided moss-encrusted scree, cliffs and gullies swathed in dense woodland and tangled undergrowth. With limited resources it would be physically impossible to explore every square inch.'

DS Jones's response brings some disgruntled murmurs. But there is at least a tacit understanding that she is obliged to make unsatisfactory excuses for the failings of her predecessors.

'Was it a sexual assault?'

DS Jones fixes her steady gaze on the questioner.

'There are no such indications. The forensic examination has identified remnants of material that match the outfit she wore on the day she disappeared. Therefore the initial opinion is that she was buried fully clothed. It is considered unlikely that any DNA of the nature of which you speak will have survived.'

'Why do you think she was strangled?'

'There is a fracture of the hyoid bone – it is consistent with fatal strangulation – found in a third of adult cases.'

The questioner tries again; he seeks a motive rather than a diagnosis.

'Why would anyone do that?'

'There was nothing that came to light in the original inquiry that suggested Mary Wilson was the subject of some grudge or dispute. She was thirty, and had been married since the age of eighteen, and a year earlier the couple had had their first child. Their financial situation was stable, if somewhat restricted.'

That she parries the second thrust seems to prompt a sudden flurry of questions.

'Who's the prime suspect – they must have had someone in the frame?'

'Do you still think it was a serial killer?'

'How about the husband – are you going to be arresting him, now?'

'Was she having an affair?'

At this DS Jones holds up her palms to quell the disorder. That there are four questions rather than one in fact enables her to answer none.

'I have told you as much as we know – and we will keep you abreast of developments. I would ask you not to speculate. The obvious lines of inquiry were thoroughly investigated – an accident, for instance that she had drowned in the River Derwent; that she had been abducted from the district; that she had eloped. Please remember that Mary Wilson's mother is still alive, and so of course is her son – who was only a year old at the time – and consider their feelings at this moment.'

There crystallises a just-tangible aura, a collective sense of sheepishness, at being ticked off by the young detective sergeant. Having gained sway, DS Jones presses home her advantage.

'You could help them – and us – by emphasising the crux of this case. After almost twenty-two years we know of Mary Wilson's fate. Perhaps that knowledge will now make sense to someone who did not previously realise it. Indeed, her killer may no longer be alive – which might make it possible for someone to come forward who formerly felt constrained.'

This profound appeal maintains the silence – and DS Jones senses it is the note on which she ought to conclude. She closes the file on her tablet, screws the top on her water bottle and gathers up her notes and rises, thanking the journalists for their attendance. The main group seem to have had their fill – besides, opening hour beckons – but Kendall Minto hangs back. As a high school contemporary DS Jones finds tiresome his brazen self-confidence. But he is sharp witted, and she rates his commitment to his job, and in the past he has proved himself to be insightful; and so she gives him the time of day.

'Detective Sergeant Jones.'

That he uses her title – half fawning, half mocking in his insouciant, chatting-up manner – warns her of what might be coming. He gives a flick of his swept-back hair; with his boyish good looks and his leather jacket there is something of a latter-day Billy Fury in his demeanour; and he is evidently undeterred by previous rejections.

'Wait.'

DS Jones switches off the lights and ushers him out of the interview room, out of earshot of the microphone. He contrives casually to occupy the centre ground of the corridor.

'I'm pretty certain I still owe you a drink.'

'Then you would know I'm not able to drink on duty.'

She raises her water bottle.

'It doesn't have to be alcoholic. Albeit that's half the fun.'

DS Jones squeezes past him.

'And I'm sure I don't have to tell you how busy we are with this case.'

He regards her quizzically, as though he thinks she is simply stalling. But then he makes a sudden pronouncement.

'There must be a flaw in the DNA process. You realise that?'

DS Jones stops and turns – she holds his gaze, her hazel eyes unblinking and clear.

'Naturally, we're getting that aspect reviewed.'

'That cave – *Friggeshol* – it's known to locals as the Kissing Cave. Am I right?'

It is not like Kendall Minto to eschew the opportunity for innuendo – but no trace of it has entered his voice. DS Jones gives a shake of her naturally streaked blonde hair; but she does not gainsay his suggestion. Instead she begins to move away. Kendall Minto persists.

'Listen, I can be an extra pair of eyes and ears. People tell reporters things they won't say to the police.'

'Do they?'

But this might almost be a little trap. He produces a smug grin.

'I thought you would know that.'

DS Jones looks like she might be about to object. But again it is the young journalist that speaks first.

'Look – my final offer – coffee and cake. Who could possibly resist?'

They have reached a security door marked 'exit'. DS Jones presses the release button and holds it open for him to go out.

'We'll see.'

Through the glass she watches his jaunty departure; there is a decided spring of conquest in his step.

That Skelgill and DS Leyton have observed the media briefing by CCTV reflects the former's thinking to present their message as a low-key affair. However, there is a certain *Catch 22* at play here, for he desires to achieve maximum reach for their appeal. But he does not want the area flooded with reporters, getting under their feet and interviewing local people before they do. By delegating the task to a lower rank, and indeed excluding the Chief when she might legitimately have been present, he has run the risk of throwing DS Jones to the wolves of the press pack. And he has bridled at times at the chauvinistic undercurrent of disrespect. Though he has to admit that his female deputy handled the press conference with greater aplomb than he would have. That said, when DS Jones returns it is her fellow sergeant that congratulates her.

'Nice one, Emma.'

She shrugs modestly, and glances apprehensively at Skelgill – but he has his nose in a mug and the look he flashes her is hard to read. She takes her seat by the window and composes herself. It is DS Leyton that comments again, his tone buoyant.

'Who knows, girl – like you just said – maybe some geezer's been stewing all these years with the key to the mystery. When they read it in their paper it'll prick their conscience. This time tomorrow we could be sitting pretty.'

But Skelgill seems set on a more fatalistic note. He addresses the room but his remark must surely be directed at DS Jones.

'Just watch what you say to that Minto character. We know the tricks he can get up to. I don't want him putting ideas into folk's heads.'

If the remark were intended as bait, then DS Jones rises to it.

'But, Guv – he did write that article – and he may be proved correct. I think he'll want the right outcome. I do believe he is committed to the local community. He's an intelligent guy and he could have left for a bigger job in London long ago.'

Skelgill is glowering, perhaps unreasonably now.

'Name me a journalist that's not out for themselves. Besides, he's nailed his colours to the mast. You say he wants the right outcome – but what is that?'

It is unclear whether Skelgill expects a response or if his demand is rhetorical. But his assertion of neutrality is a stance that does not entirely hold firm. And he knows this, too – for the interim forensic report that has reached them this morning – an abridged version of which DS Jones has relayed at the press conference – supports the theory that Mary Wilson was murdered and her body meticulously concealed. It is the conclusion of the forensic geologist that the stones used to create the impression of a rockfall inside the Kissing Cave were gathered from perhaps ten distinct sources, not just from the fractured mouth of the cave itself. This shows an appreciation that such a visible disturbance would draw attention. In all, an estimated seven hundredweights of rubble had been ferried to conceal the body – an act that likely took several hours, and quite possibly required more than one visit to the cave. This is further suggestive of a person that lived or at least was staying locally – certainly it is not the typical behaviour of a transient serial killer who would strike and promptly leave both the scene and the district. Moreover, that significant remnants of clothing have been recovered lessen the likelihood of a sexual motive – again the most statistically probable cause of an impulsive, opportunistic attack. Expert opinion is that Mary Wilson was interred fully clothed in the outfit for which there is a reliable description of what she wore on the day of the shepherds' meet. Only a magenta headscarf has not been identified – but wool is most prone to rapid biological decay, and a scarf the one item likely to have become separated in a scuffle.

Like it or not, these straws in the wind are indicative of the putative verdict that the precocious local reporter has championed. Accordingly, for Skelgill, the sense of spinning out of control has him instinctively applying the brakes. At such times his colleagues must endure the frustration of his apparent death wish to thwart their progress. Of the pair, DS Leyton is the more likely to acquiesce to his superior's foibles. Having worked with Skelgill the longer, he has honed non-confrontational tactics for seeding ideas that he knows will otherwise rub against the grain. Typically he will enter throwaway remarks that can surely only be meant in jest – as indeed he has already voiced more than once in this embryonic investigation. For he has learnt that, though Skelgill might be a recalcitrant git, he is capricious, too – and this latter quality is a redeeming feature. He absorbs what might seem to pass him by, and has the ability to perform an audacious volte-face on the strength of information that he has previously denied.

DS Jones, on the other hand, is more straightforward. A quick and rational thinker, she is prone to counter Skelgill's arguments with her own, and confront head on his unmindful riding roughshod over their points of view. It is in her nature to pursue a hot trail, and to follow it at a canter. In the case of Mary Wilson, she has initiated activity to re-examine the outsider-cum-serial-killer theory, and has balanced this with the opinion that the local community should have been treated with greater significance in the initial investigation. This latter point is reflected now in her response.

'Guv – the team are still trying to make contact with Aidan Wilson – but they've arranged for us to see Nick Wilson today in his lunch break – at one o'clock.'

Skelgill checks his watch and scowls, as if he might have other plans. It is now approaching noon, and to get back up into Borrowdale is a good forty minutes. DS Jones takes advantage of his hesitation.

'I was wondering, Guv – if what Jean Tyson said about him is correct – that he is a bit awkward. What if initially I saw him on my own – maybe that would be less intimidating?'

But Skelgill harbours misgivings.

'Aye – but what if he's awkward with lasses? That's most likely. Look – I'm on a level with these country folk. Leyton can take notes.'

'But, Guv –'

Skelgill cuts her off.

'Jones – the serial killer – this DNA business – we need it knocked on the head one way or another. You stay on top of that – get it sorted – today if possible. Then we can focus on Borrowdale.'

DS Jones fleetingly bites at her lower lip – perhaps in annoyance that her superior seems to be applying a double standard to his ranking of these respective lines of inquiry. But she swallows her disappointment.

'Sure – leave it with me.' She looks downcast as Skelgill rises and pulls his jacket from its fish-hook peg. Via a jerk of the head he gestures to DS Leyton, who gets up with a groan and flashes a clandestine face of apology at his counterpart. DS Jones endeavours to sound agreeable. 'When will you be back?'

'Maybe three – depends if Debs' place is open.'

They turn in opposite directions from Skelgill's door, he and DS Leyton heading for the rear exit and the car park, DS Jones towards the open plan. As she reaches her desk the screen on her mobile lights up with a text. She bends over to see an abbreviated location and an imminent time – and emojis of an Americano and a cupcake. She glances up at the clock on the wall – and then at the stack of files in her tray marked 'action'. Like Skelgill a moment earlier, she reaches for her jacket.

7. NICK WILSON

Tuesday 1pm

'What's *lonnin*, then, Guv? I get the *beck* part.'

DS Leyton refers to the council-issue street sign, behind which is fixed a more rudimentary notice on plywood, hand-lettered and merely stating, 'Garage – Repair's – MOT's'.

'Lane.'

Skelgill's reply is terse – but when he offers nothing further his colleague persists.

'Well – there you go. One of my old aunts used to live down a street called Water Lane – Canning Town, near the River Lea, she was.'

Skelgill seems unimpressed – but in fact he is thinking he read only recently in *Angling Times* of some monster chub fished out of the lesser-known London flower. Equally, it might appear to his colleague that he is simply concentrating upon navigating the narrow passage that is Beck Lonnin, barely a car's width between high stone walls. Indeed DS Leyton comments accordingly.

'You need the old cat's whiskers for this one, Guv.'

Skelgill makes a grunt of acknowledgement – and then a more encouraging growl of triumph, for as they swing around a sharp bend they see their destination ahead, the gable end of an elongated stone barn, its entrance doors and lintel high enough to admit carriages of yore. It is effectively the end of the lane, and to continue would see them driving directly into the garage, were it not for a line of vehicles that disappear into the gloom. There is a peeling fascia that announces, 'Walter Dickson & Co, Motor Mechanics' and a dated MOT sign, three fused white triangles reversed out of royal blue, that Skelgill sees as the face of a wolf, and which looks like it once took a peppering from a shotgun.

Skelgill parks a couple of yards short of the entrance, and he and DS Leyton squeeze down the side of the first car, a pre-1963 *Morris Minor* that has its bonnet raised to reveal an engine the size of a peanut. To their right they pass a poky office with no door and standing room only, its walls plastered with grubby certificates, invoices, raunchy calendars and miscellaneous hand-scrawled notes stained by greasy fingers. The main body of the long byre is dimly lit by a couple of inadequate strip lights; there is the impression of a hunter-gatherer's cave, with tools on wall hooks and engine parts and wheels in stacks, and everything coated in a primordial patina of axle grease and iron filings. There is no sign, however, of an incumbent troglodyte until a sudden metallic clunk and a violent curse (as if someone forcing a wrench has shot the thread and skinned a knuckle) can be traced to a pit beneath the third vehicle, an original *Land Rover* that Skelgill thinks he recognises – though of the same colour and model he knows it cannot belong to Arthur Hope, for he does all his own repairs.

'Mr Wilson?'

What has evolved into a rendition of oaths is curtailed. There comes a man's voice, a strong local accent.

'Who wants him?'

Skelgill edges forward – now he can see the whites of eyes from a blackened face like a coal miner's – there is lank black hair – and scowling up at them a man perhaps in his early fifties.

'DI Skelgill, DS Leyton – Cumbria CID.'

Suspicion fades slightly.

'About his Ma, aye?'

'We've made an appointment.'

'He's in his van – having his bait. Thoo'll need to gan around t' side – out t' front, to your right – where it says 'Caravan Park'. Number three.'

Skelgill hesitates. He stares at the man, wondering what each of them must be thinking – or feeling, more like. But the man's face is hidden behind its oily mask – and Skelgill must only be a dark silhouette against the fluorescent lamp above his head.

'Cheers.'

Skelgill follows DS Leyton back the way they entered. As they disappear around the corner the man hauls himself out of the inspection pit and pads noiselessly after them on rubber

75

soles. Blinking in the daylight he spends a few moments staring at Skelgill's car – then he retreats into the semi-darkness and picks his way to the far end of the building where a crate is placed beneath an arrow-slit window. He steps up on the crate, stretching on tiptoes with his palms spread against the stones of the wall, and peers through the gap.

But an onlooker will see only innocuous behaviour from the two detectives. As they pass the end of the barn and through an open gate they must experience the anti-climax of many an expectant visitor. The less-than-salubrious 'Caravan Park' can only be a disappointment, set in such an idyllic village and spectacular dale. The environs might be an overgrown orchard, although none of the gnarled and tangled trees long past recovery-pruning bear any late fruit. Underfoot the grass is uncut and damp, while irregular stepping-stones run past three static caravans of increasing age, like sarcophagi of successive generations. There are no immediate signs of occupation – Skelgill finds it hard to believe these vans are ever let, despite the popularity of the Lakes; it is easy to envisage trippers turning up in hope and turning around in dismay, and making an angry beeline for the tourist office at Keswick. He feels a nudge from his sergeant, who indicates a dilapidated shed between vans 1 and 2 with the letters 'W.C.' painted on the planked door. A standpipe has its tap dripping into a drain concreted at its base.

'Outside karsey, Guv – that takes me back – me old nan's place had one of them – you could see a person's feet dangling under the door – torn-up squares of *News of the World* hanging on a nail.'

'Leyton, you were lucky to have *News of the World*.'

The third caravan is a model that could date from the 1960s, puce in colour and shorter than its neighbours, and rounded, as though streamlining were significant in those days. Despite its vintage it is in smart condition and looks to be the recipient of diligent husbandry. The windows are polished and the exterior is free of the prolific algae that streak the first two mobile homes. The door is at the far end and there is a black japanned step and integral handrail on which respectively are arranged steel-toe-capped work boots and a navy blue boiler suit. As the detectives approach they must be spotted for there is the hollow resonance of footfall keeping pace and the door opens as they reach it.

It is not Skelgill's habit to envisage what someone he has not met might look like, but had he done so Nick Wilson would have matched closely his expectation. And thus he feels a curious sense of acquaintance as he sets eyes upon the tall, well-built young man who appears in the doorway in stockinged feet and wearing blue jeans and a black t-shirt with some kind of musical motif; though it is not the outfit that rings true – more so the broad, honest face, rather nondescript in its features – a smallish nose and mouth and pale brows to go with a blond crewcut – and most distinctly pale blue eyes that are totally and entirely ingenuous. Such is the impression of instinctive familiarity that Skelgill is left wondering if he might be related to this lad – and the sentiment perhaps informs his salutation.

'Nick – we're from the police – it's about your Ma – one of my colleagues has been in touch, aye?'

'I was expecting you.'

The young man is quietly spoken, in the local brogue though with the absence of dialect. There is no surprise in his cool gaze; nor hostility, probably the most common reaction encountered by a policeman. Shy, he certainly appears, and he seems uncertain of how to deal with the protocol of their entrance. He glances fleetingly at their wet footwear but then pulls his eyes away and retires to the far end of the caravan where there is an orange cushioned bench seat either side of a prop-up table raised before the bay window. He attends to a *Tupperware* box, pressing back on the lid with dexterity for such large and unexpectedly clean hands, and screws the top on a flask, although he leaves the cup because it still holds some tea or coffee. Unsure of himself, he slips back into the seated position from where he must have been able to observe their approach. It seems he expects his visitors to settle opposite, and they duly oblige.

'We saw Mrs Tyson – your grandmother – she's talked to you about what we told her?'

His gaze is now lowered meekly – an unknowing observer might suspect he is the accused in this situation. He nods, but does not tender a response.

'Nick – how are you feeling – now you've had chance to sleep on it?'

He looks up sharply, as if these were not the words he expected Skelgill to use (and DS Leyton might indeed be thinking along similar lines: that it is an un-Skelgill-like question).

But now the young man answers.

'If the police couldn't find him then – why is it any different now? They say there's no chance of catching him.'

Skelgill regards him quizzically. It is too soon for the story to have broken – they listened to the local radio station on their journey up into Borrowdale, and there was no mention in the news bulletin.

'Who's *they*, Nick?'

The young man looks anxiously from one policeman to the other – as though he were about to be required to betray some confidence.

'I were talking to the Gaffer about it.'

'The Gaffer?'

Nick Wilson glances in what is the approximate direction of the workshop.

'Me boss – Mr Dickson.'

His rising inflection suggests some concern, perhaps that they have not consulted his employer en route; Skelgill puts two and two together.

'He were under a *Land Rover* – in the inspection pit.'

A light seems to come on in the pale eyes.

'We've had to drop the gearbox. The clutch is slipping when it's on a steep incline.'

'Not so handy, hereabouts.'

'Thing is, the clutch disc doesn't look worn. And the diaphragm spring's working.'

'One of those mysteries, eh?'

'Happen when we put it back together it might be alright.'

'That's my number one method – failing that, a good clout.'

Nick Wilson looks at Skelgill with a flicker of interest. He seems a little less restrained now, but is clearly not comfortable initiating a conversation himself. He waits for Skelgill to speak.

'How long have you worked here, Nick?'

'Full time, since I left school. Before that I had a Saturday job. It started out just cleaning up – but the Gaffer saw I were interested in being a mechanic and when I were sixteen he set me on as an apprentice.'

'You did well to get a decent job. If you're not in agriculture or hospitality, there's not a lot round here.' Skelgill turns somewhat disparagingly to DS Leyton. 'Unless you want to end up as a copper.'

DS Leyton accommodates his superior with a self-conscious chuckle. In turn the young man reveals the hint of a smile.

'Growing up, what did you know about your Ma – what you thought had happened to her?'

Nick Wilson regards Skelgill with candid sincerity.

'Gran told me from the start – there were no point not knowing – someone in the village would have said something soon enough.'

'Were there theories – rumours?'

The young man shakes his head.

'Gran said that she'd been taken. She knew in her bones – that Ma weren't alive. That she wouldn't have left me.'

Skelgill respects this reply with a suitably reverential pause.

'What about your pals? What did they think? Kids can be cruel to one another.'

Perhaps Skelgill asks the question because adults gossip and children eavesdrop, and it is a shortcut to knowing what opinions are being voiced, rather like the picnic litter strewn at beauty spots that tells which youth alcohol brand is currently in vogue.

The young man's tone is flat, his demeanour somewhat reflective.

'They never really spoke about Ma. I suppose there were a time they used to rib us about living with Gran. At school they'd joke more about me being thick. I weren't ever much good at writing and that.'

He looks at Skelgill apologetically – his response recalls the remark made by Jean Tyson that the boy has a "learning difficulty" – and the discussion with DS Jones about who should see him. Skelgill realises he had fallen into thinking that he probably suffered from some personality disorder – when in fact all he sees before him is an obviously intelligent lad who is merely shy, and untutored in social situations. As for struggling with "writing and that" – tell him about it!

Apparently unconcernedly, Skelgill casts about the interior of the caravan, which is clean, tidy and austere. He notices there are certainly no books or writing paraphernalia, and on a shelf just a small collection of Ordnance Survey maps neatly stacked spine-outward and in numerical order. Rather curiously there is no television – unless it is in the bedroom at the far end — and then it strikes Skelgill that there is probably no mains electricity, for the lights are the old-fashioned type, gas taps with fragile incandescent mantles. The cooker is also gas, just a couple of rings and a grill beneath. Next to that is a stainless steel drainer and sink with a single pump-action tap that he can see is connected via a jubilee clip to a length of clear hose that dips into a free-standing aluminium churn. There is no refrigerator – the sole electrical item that is visible is a battery radio on a small built-in sideboard, against which is propped an acoustic guitar – a possession with which Skelgill long ago had a love-hate relationship, terminated by mutual agreement – although he remembers sufficient to note it is strung left-handed.

'You play guitar, Nick?'

The young man looks surprised that Skelgill might be interested.

'Aye – I've played since I were a bairn.' But now a remembrance clouds his eyes. 'That were me dad's. He gave it me – one Christmas.'

There is something poignant about his qualification, the pathos of orphanhood.

'You're a cuddy wifter.'

Skelgill grins at his own quip, and Nick Wilson appears to understand that he is taking the mickey.

'I had to re-string it. I were much better after that.'

Skelgill seems to suppress the beginnings of a hysterical laugh.

'Do you sing?'

'I just do instrumental.'

He lowers his eyes, perhaps concerned that he might be asked to perform. Skelgill, however, seems momentarily distracted; DS Leyton may suspect that his superior does not think they are getting a great deal out of their visit. Indeed Skelgill indicates the food container and shifts in his seat as though he might be about to rise.

'We're interrupting your dinner.'

The young man looks up, suddenly alarmed. Skelgill, poker faced, is in fact thinking his little ploy might have worked.

'Was there something you wanted to ask?'

Nick Wilson begins to shake his head; it seems to be a default reaction.

'I were – I were thinking I'd like to go up – to where they found Ma.' He hesitates, but then hurriedly qualifies his statement. 'Just to be at the place – not inside the cave or owt.'

Skelgill is nodding amenably.

'Aye – I'll take you.'

A frown creases the young man's broad brow.

'I thought I might just like to do it – on my own, like.'

Skelgill appears unruffled. He dips into a side pocket of his jacket and produces a rather dog-eared calling card – and then gestures to DS Leyton, demanding a pen. His sergeant produces a biro. Skelgill scrawls on the back of the card and signs it. He passes it over.

'There'll be a police guard on the site for the next couple of days. Most likely PC Dodd – you'll have seen him about. Show him that.'

His expression still apprehensive, Nick Wilson is staring rather helplessly at the card, tiny in his expansive palm.

'You know the best way, aye?'

'I think so.'

Nick Wilson glances at the maps on the shelf – and Skelgill needs no further encouragement to demonstrate his prowess.

There is nothing like giving directions to boost the male ego; it panders to some primeval tribal inheritance. He slides from the seat and deftly selects a map from the collection. He raps the cover with his knuckles.

'I've got the same edition as this. They're good, these two-and-a-half inchers.'

With practised aplomb he unfolds, partially refolds and lays the map the table surface. He stands over it at the head of the table.

'The cave's not marked on – so if you're not sure the safest bet is to find where Odin's Beck comes down into the Derwent.' He indicates with a finger. 'There – just downstream of the Bowder Stone – see?'

The young man is nodding. But Skelgill suddenly seems to stiffen, and his voice sounds distant as he issues his next instruction.

'Follow the beck up into the woods.'

And now he jerks his finger a few inches, just over a mile to the west, and taps the sheet urgently.

'See that – High Spy? You know the old folk call it Scawdale Fell? *Scawdel*, they'd say.'

Nick Wilson's gaze has been drawn to the spot where Skelgill's finger insistently taps. He appears bemused, not understanding the significance of this abrupt change of subject. But Skelgill is determined.

'I've got an old map in the car.' Now he reaches and pats DS Leyton on the shoulder. 'Leyton – do us a favour – nip and get it for us. It's in the glove box.'

DS Leyton looks even more perplexed than the boy – but he knows Skelgill well enough not to question his order; somewhat inelegantly he shuffles from his seat.

'Righto, Guv – won't be two ticks.'

Skelgill calls after him.

'There's half a dozen. Bring the lot, Leyton – save getting the wrong one and having to go back.'

In fact it takes DS Leyton barely a minute to reach the car and return with a wad of maps – he finds in progress some small talk about haystacks. Skelgill has folded away Nick Wilson's map and now he slides this to the far end of the table. From the selection retrieved by DS Leyton he chooses a much older specimen, small and printed on fraying cloth, with a Prussian blue cover and the word 'Cumberland' prominent in orange. It is perfectly distinctive and DS Leyton is sure he could easily have identified it. However, with some reverence Skelgill now lays it out.

'Family heirloom, this. Printed in 1920 – but the survey was done between 1897 and 1903. A masterpiece, aye? And they hadn't even invented flying.'

He turns the pastel coloured square of cloth so that it is angled towards Nick Wilson, and points triumphantly to a chocolate brown smudge in the dun contoured terrain to the south-west of the turquoise diamond that is Derwentwater.

'It's tiny print – it's two miles to the inch – but you'll have good eyes.'

Nick Wilson cranes over, his face close to the page. He seems to have no difficulty with the short focal length that is required. And yet he appears confounded.

'What does it say?'

Skelgill has no need to read the legend; he knows it.

'Scawdale Fell, 2143. No trace of High Spy. Where did that name spring from?'

DS Leyton seems to share the boy's misgivings.

'Sounds like something dreamed up by a marketing executive, Guv. High Spy with my little eye – *hah!*'

Skelgill makes a disparaging tut and, looking at the boy, jerks his head towards his sergeant.

'He's missed his vocation. He wants to be a copywriter.'

The young man glances at DS Leyton – it seems to ascertain if Skelgill is being serious; the sergeant, standing a little behind his superior, makes a face of affable resignation.

Skelgill carefully gathers up and folds away his antique map. Nick Wilson remains seated; he seems uncertain of quite what is going on – perhaps wondering if he has not done very well in some obscure test. And there ensues another left-of-field demand from Skelgill.

'Any chance you could stick on a mash? I'm parched.'

Nick Wilson regards Skelgill rather blankly – but after a moment's hesitation he begins to prise his long limbs out of the seating arrangement.

'Aye. But I've only got powdered milk.'

He crosses over to the kitchenette section. With his back to the detectives he lifts a kettle from the gas hob and pumps vigorously at the tap – a procedure that intrigues DS Leyton who therefore does not notice Skelgill extract an Ordnance Survey map from his own pile and slide it into the shelf, and tuck the one from the table under his arm with the rest. Then there is a sudden change in his demeanour.

'Tell you what, Nick – second thoughts, don't bother. Finish your bait – your Gaffer'll be wanting you back on that clutch. We can go round to the farm café.'

The young man stops what he is doing. Again he is unsure of how to react, but Skelgill steps over to the door.

'You've got my number – otherwise, we'll keep you posted.'

A trace of anxiety seems to have crept into Nick Wilson's pale eyes. Skelgill endeavours to be reassuring.

'And don't believe everything *they* say, right?'

The boy is still nodding dutifully as DS Leyton pulls shut the door. They hear his steps; the hollow caravan like a great bass sound box – and they might assume he is coming to the bay window to observe their departure. But then music strikes up – it could be the transistor radio had they not seen the guitar. The notes seem jumbled at first, almost experimental, but they coalesce into a discernable structure and there is a surge in tempo. To Skelgill's dismay, his none-too-nimble colleague breaks into a 'Cockney Walk' – a mini pantomime of four or five swanky steps, as though he is powerless in responding to the energy of the tune. Skelgill is equally powerless in letting loose a phrase of Anglo-Saxon origin.

Unfazed by the adverse nature of such critical acclaim, DS Leyton concludes his performance with a click of his heels and falls in alongside his superior.

'Django Rheinhart.'

'Come again, Leyton?'

'It's jazz, Guv – *I'll See You In My Dreams* by Django Rheinhart.'

They round the end of van number 2 and the melody fades.

'Are you taking the you-know-what, Leyton?'

'Straight up, Guv. I had an uncle used to play in *Ronnie Scott's* back in the day – trumpeter, he was. Kenny, his name. Used to dodge over to our gaff on a Sunday for his dinner with his missus. I was given some of his record collection when he popped his clogs.'

Skelgill is silent as they pass in Indian file down the side of the workshop and split to reach their respective doors of his car.

'So, he knows what he's doing.'

'Sounded like it to me, Guv – jazz guitar takes a lot of practice.'

There is a brief hiatus as they clamber into the long brown shooting brake that had attracted the attention of the proprietor. Skelgill makes an observation, his tone introspective.

'I didn't see a telly. Nor any books.'

DS Leyton detects some unease in his superior's manner. He contrives to sound at once chiding and admiring.

'That card you gave him, Guv – you flippin' signed it *DI Odinsgill!*'

'Hark at Sherlock Holmes.' Skelgill forces a grimace. He starts the engine and begins to reverse using his mirrors, back towards a gateway where he can perform a turn. 'It's got my name on the front, Leyton. No need to give away my signature. If Dodd's not sure he can phone me.'

He pulls the car deep into the opening, out of sight of the garage. He yanks on the handbrake. On his lap he has the wad of maps.

'Leyton – in the glove box – are there any poly bags?'

'Yeah, I noticed some, Guv.'

He leans forward with a grunt and pulls down the flap.

'Chuck us one over.'

DS Leyton does as bidden – he extracts a clear plastic evidence bag. Skelgill exchanges it for the pack of maps, first retaining that which refers to their locality. He puts the bag momentarily aside and pulls open the map like a concertina.

'Look at this.'

DS Leyton gazes somewhat cluelessly at the sheet. Skelgill jabs a finger, but without actually touching the paper.

'There – that's where the Kissing Cave is.'

'Like you showed him, Guv.'

Skelgill has used up his day's quota of patience with the boy.

'Look harder, you donnat! Oily fingerprint – bang on the spot.'

DS Leyton still does not quite get it. He frowns and stares even harder, like a schoolboy confounded by the Pythagorean theorem. Skelgill spells it out.

'Leyton – I switched the maps. *This is his.* Mine's on his shelf.'

Now the penny drops. DS Leyton stares at the smudge and then casts about the corrugated sheet, as if to satisfy himself that this is not a widespread phenomenon. The map is aged; its white background is slightly faded, but generally clean. There can be no doubt that someone has pressed a finger onto the precise location of Friggeshol.

'Cor blimey – so he knows something, Guv?'

Skelgill inhales forebodingly. This is a step too far. He carefully refolds the map and slips it into the evidence bag.

'Here – stick that away. Like I said, I'm parched.'

They have only to drive a couple of hundred yards to reach the tiny rural emporium, farm shop and café of Skelgill's acquaintance, 'Debs'. Rain is beginning to fall from an enigmatic sky, so Skelgill opts to dine inside; though a windowless barn conversion, it is a surprisingly bright and cheerful space, its slate walls hung with engaging Herdwick caricatures, the labours of a local watercolourist. Beside the counter a refrigerator retails homespun produce, bleaberry jam and heather honey, and various vacuum-packed cuts of lamb. But Skelgill has his eye on the hot counter, and is decisive in ordering tea and a Cumberland sausage bloomer; DS Leyton follows suit for convenience.

'There you go, Leyton.'

Skelgill gestures to a glass display cabinet. Between 'Sticky Toffee Pudding' and 'Ginger & Rum Nicky' are boldly labelled, 'Bowder Scones'.

'Ah.' DS Leyton looks pleased with himself. 'All they need now are some Scafell Pikelets, Guv.'

'Don't push it, Leyton.'

Skelgill leads the way to a secluded table tucked in what would have been a cattle stall beneath a hayloft – although at this juncture they are the only patrons. The elderly lady who took their order, whom Skelgill does not know is prompt in serving their lunch. He immediately tucks in, pre-empting any discussion of their findings. So it is after a suitable period of consumption that DS Leyton judges he can tentatively venture a question.

'Reckon it's a coincidence – that fingerprint?'

After a long pause Skelgill replies.

'Probably.'

Then after an even longer pause he qualifies his answer.

'Possibly.'

DS Leyton is nodding. He wonders if he waits long enough will Skelgill graduate to something even more definite – but when no further adjustment is forthcoming he makes a light-hearted quip.

'Maybe's he's a bit of a psychic, an' all, Guv.'

Curiously, Skelgill does not baulk at this; whether it is the boy's unforeseen musical talent that lends some credibility to the improbable suggestion, or that Skelgill draws upon his own experiences that certain places in the fells send an inexplicable shiver down his spine, and he has more than once wondered if some momentous fate befell an ancestor there. On the journey from Penrith they had heard on the radio of the latest attempt to corner Nessie – by sampling the free-floating DNA in the great Caledonian loch. It had concluded the 'monster' is in fact a giant eel. Skelgill's ears had pricked up for more reasons than one –

not least that he fishes, and that DNA is prominent in their present enquiry. Though he had listened to the piece without comment, he was struck by the futility of the quest – why would they think science could solve a conundrum that is plainly supernatural?

Engrossed in such thoughts – and there also being competition for his faculties in the deconstruction of his sausage sandwich – it is left to his partner to progress the conversation.

'Queer set up, that, eh? Living like a monk in a caravan when his old granny's got a half-decent cottage a mile down the road. I reckon she'd be happy to be looking after him.'

Skelgill is chewing vigorously, but his face manages to suggest disagreement. As an outdoorsman ascetic self-sufficiency harbours a certain appeal – and, he must confess, for him the "queer set up" conjured a pang of nostalgia. The only childhood holidays his parents could afford were to a caravan at Silloth, overlooking the bleak Solway, accommodation only slightly less primitive than that he has just visited. It had recalled the soporific hiss of the gaslights and the cosy thrum of rain upon the aluminium roof. And, despite the overcrowding and the fug, a curious sense of family harmony, of collaborative board games and jigsaws, gin rummy and knockout whist with no punches thrown – until, of course, cabin fever, insidious, surreptitiously began to take a grip. Thus four Skelgill brothers were booted out to wreak havoc upon the surrounding district.

'Like the old lady said – he probably needed his independence.'

'I suppose that's how he's so good on the guitar, Guv – ain't got much else to do.'

Skelgill shrugs.

'He probably works long hours in that sweatshop.'

DS Leyton nods.

'That cove Walter Dickson's not exactly laying out the red carpet for his holidaymakers, neither.'

'Walter Dickson's dead, Leyton. I spoke to me Ma last night. That was Jake Dickson – a nephew. Seems he runs the show now.' Skelgill squints reflectively, his mind's eye focused upon some distant object. 'He were a half-decent fell runner in his day. Until I beat –'

But Skelgill's revelation will have to wait. It is the arrival of an effusive Debs bearing dessert, on the house: Bowder Scones, no less – in celebration that she has sold two dozen since rebranding them. DS Leyton remarks that they are selling like hotcakes, but the lady's favouritism seems to lie with Skelgill. Indeed, during the course of the ensuing exchange he gets the distinct idea that Skelgill has claimed the credit – and unashamedly makes no attempt to introduce his subordinate as the creative genius behind the name. But such is the life of a sidekick, and when the young woman departs he gets on with the job of his unfinished Cumberland sausage bloomer.

'I'm stuffed, Guv – reckon I'll need a doggy bag for that scone.'

Skelgill's wolfish surveillance of the table is an indication that he will be prepared to attempt to clear it. DS Leyton digs in his heels.

'I might take it back for Emma. She weren't half tucking in yesterday – I nearly asked her if she were eating for two.' He sees the look of alarm in Skelgill's eyes, and launches into something of a monologue. 'Joking, like, Guv. I remember the missus had a craving for chocolate cake her first time. Mind you, that's nothing – there was a woman in her maternity group who was chomping through a packet of *Kleenex* every couple of days.'

This unlikely claim penetrates Skelgill's disquiet.

'What – eating them?'

'Yeah – her GP had to contact the manufacturer to make sure they weren't harmful. Pink, she preferred.'

Skelgill ponders the fact.

'Tissue paper – it's mainly wood.'

'High fibre diet, Guv.'

Their conversation tails off, and in due course they depart; it is later than Skelgill had casually predicted in response to DS Jones's query about their return; now he feels a sense of urgency to get back. As such he is driving rather too fast, an act incompatible with the winding lane and his compulsion to survey

89

the River Derwent; as it skirts Cummacatta Wood it belies its title as one of Europe's fastest rivers – instead, crystal clear and serene, it holds trout that burgle chironomids from the taut meniscus and have Skelgill twitching to suppress an involuntary casting reflex.

'That was that geezer Minto's car, Guv.'

'What?'

Skelgill's wandering gaze is jolted back to the road – and just as well, for it requires a rapid adjustment of the steering wheel to avoid a curving verge. His eyes flash to the rear-view mirror, but he is too late.

'Are you sure?'

'Reckon so – fancy red convertible, letters "KM" in the reg.'

Skelgill makes a resigned hissing sound. He knows there is little they can do to prevent the media poking about. He is secretly hoping for torrential rain, as at least that might put off some of the less hardy hacks. But Minto is a tenacious little blighter, although those are not the generous terms in which Skelgill now thinks of him.

'One interview and the jungle drums will be thumping all round the dale.' Skelgill makes a growl of frustration. 'Happen we should have got Jones to make more of the serial killer angle.'

DS Leyton, who has been watching the road for his own safety, glances across at his superior, whose suggestion contradicts his attitude hitherto.

'You mean to put the journos off the scent, Guv?'

But Skelgill seems distracted; his reply is unconvincing.

'Aye – something like that.'

DS Leyton sinks back in his seat and folds his arms pensively.

'We could get DS Jones to issue an update, Guv – say a new lead has come up.'

This time Skelgill does not answer at all – but his colleague's words prove prophetic, for when they reach headquarters he notices that DS Jones's car, parked close to his when they left, is no longer in the constabulary lot. Moreover there is a terse note on his desk that castigates him for failing to respond to mobile communications and summons him to an audience with the Chief.

When Skelgill returns he routes through the open plan offices and is conscious of eyes upon him; those surreptitious looks that try to read the emotions of one who may have suffered some trauma. For his part, his features are implacable (a clue in itself) and his eyes staring, as he accosts DS Leyton and peremptorily interrupts his conversation with a young detective constable. Back in Skelgill's office DS Leyton finds his superior nursing a face like thunder.

'Careful what you wish for, Leyton.'

DS Leyton senses he is getting the blame for something *he* hasn't actually wished for, and beneath his peaceable exterior he is scrabbling to gird his loins. He is wondering to which aspect of their earlier conversation Skelgill may refer. All he knows is where his boss has just been, that sparks can fly in such encounters, and that the Chief doesn't do coming off second best.

'Don't tell me she's pulled the inquiry, Guv?'

'It's worse than that, Leyton – there's been a confession. To the murder of Mary Wilson.'

DS Leyton is momentarily dumbstruck.

'What! *Who*, Guv?'

Skelgill's skin seems unnaturally white, his features strained. When he answers, his voice is distant.

'Some no-mark lifer in Strangeways.'

'The old nick – HMP Manchester?'

Skelgill nods grimly.

'Jones has been sent to take a statement. She drove to Penrith station about half an hour ago.'

DS Leyton looks perplexed.

'Why only DS Jones, Guv? Why not wait for you to get back?'

'Because DI Smart just happens to be working down there.'

8. AIDAN WILSON

Wednesday morning, Keswick

Whereas his estranged twenty-two-year-old son seemed intensely conscious of his awkwardness in company, fifty-eight-year-old Aidan Wilson exhibits no such self-awareness. This is manifest not just in his manner, but also in his appearance. While it is hard to appraise his clothing (he wears the staff overalls and protective footwear of the supermarket in whose fast-food franchise they now interview him), his looks invite speculation. He is a substantially smaller man than Nick Wilson, around average height – an inch or two taller than DS Leyton, Skelgill had noted when they rose to greet him – there is a gaunt frame and a physiognomy of weak chin, a pointed nose, small dark eyes with pared eyebrows, a mole on each cheek (rather disturbingly almost but not quite symmetrically placed) and a schoolboy helmet of mousy hair; collar length at the back it covers his ears and there is a long uneven fringe. Thus while his outfit is tidy and in keeping with the bright polished environs, the head that tops it is a misfit – to Skelgill's eye it could be the head of a man he might see smoking outside a betting shop or a public bar during the daytime, the head of a man who has not changed with the times, but is unaware that in these subtleties he does not look like anyone else around him.

They are seated at a table, the detectives with their backs to floor-to-ceiling windows that give on to the sparsely populated car park; more immediately there is a jam of shopping trolleys awaiting use. They have no food or drinks, which is a challenge for Skelgill as a trickle of customers leaves the counter with laden trays that pique his curiosity. A survey of potential eavesdroppers gives him no cause for concern. Nearby a well-groomed elderly man toys with the *Telegraph* crossword; he seems out of place. A young peroxide blonde inaccurately spoon-feeds chocolate yoghurt from a six-pack onto the face of an infant while engrossed in her social media. Across the floor a trendily dressed couple of about his own age who look like they are not married to one another each pay detailed attention to what their companion has to say; it seems early in the day for a clandestine meeting. Now DS Leyton clears his throat purposefully. In the absence of the prodigiously literate DS Jones, he has spent the preceding evening swotting up on the statements and reports in the files that concern Aidan Wilson.

'Mr Wilson, you've heard from one of our colleagues about the discovery and identification of your wife Mary's remains.' He pauses to allow for the man's reaction, but little is forthcoming beyond a slight swaying of his torso. 'Inspector Skelgill and I wanted to see you in person. Just to make sure –'

The man interjects.

'What are you hoping to achieve?'

His accent is local but not thick. He has the throaty voice of an asthmatic deprived of the full power of his lungs. His tone is cynical, his question curt.

DS Leyton gives him the benefit of the doubt, and replies amenably.

'We have good reason to believe your wife was murdered. That was never previously established. We have a duty now to investigate the possible crime. I expect you're glad to hear that.'

Aidan Wilson shows no emotion.

'You know it weren't a local man.'

DS Leyton glances at Skelgill. Quite likely at this very moment DS Jones is taking a statement inside the Victorian walls of HMP Manchester. Their agreed strategy in this regard is that, until there is proof positive, the 'confession' should be disregarded. Not only is it rare for a convicted killer to own up to additional murders, but also *false* admissions of guilt (perhaps from the criminally insane) are not unusual. Moreover, there is the absence of the vital fact that would have emerged long ago – that there is no DNA match between the 'Cummacatta sample' and the prisoner that has laid claim to the slaying of Mary Wilson.

But there is a further paradox in this regard, and it is raised by Aidan Wilson's assertion. And DS Leyton hesitates; perhaps he is minded to spell out the flaw in the logic. The alien DNA found on Mary Wilson's woollen key fob apparently did not belong to a local man. But that is all. It is not as though the key fob were the murder weapon. Therefore the facts do not preclude the possibility that a local man killed her.

Skelgill and DS Leyton have speculated en route about the concealment of guilt. How would a man behave, after many years of thinking he has evaded justice, when confronted by the prospect of being found out? It is something of which they have experience, in crimes ranging from petty to heinous – although they have concluded there is a spectrum that extends from the dour and downright uncooperative to the gushingly compliant. But, meeting a person for the first time, it is never easy to judge how out-of-character is such behaviour, which might be tainted by genuine shock or subverted by duress. Or it might be distorted because a person has something else to hide – an unrelated skeleton rattling in their closet. Such reasons and more can insert an extra variable that confounds what ought to be a linear equation.

There is also the issue that a good detective will approach a situation with an open mind, not seeking culpability – but simply truth and facts. On this basis, there is an argument that an investigator should discount a suspect's conduct entirely. It is not the form of the exchange that matters, but the content. Skelgill may have his failings, but he is quite competent in this regard. Perhaps it is something he takes from the hard-learned lessons of fishing, when to strike too early is usually counterproductive.

But it is to be human to be influenced by another, if only subliminally. And there is an accumulating pattern of first impressions that are contrary to the expected optimism. Not even Mary Wilson's mother's response could be described in such terms. True, Skelgill detected a controlled reserve – the will *not* to build up hope, despite that it was surely bursting inside her. In Nick Wilson it was a case of bewilderment – as if he had suddenly awakened on stage in the midst of a production he knew nothing about. And now Aidan Wilson – the overarching sentiment is of bitter detachment. Skelgill is questioning whether that can just be his nature. For a man to have his wife snatched away would surely leave at very least a burning sense of injustice, if not inerasable vengeance. Yet he does not even express his wish that they will now catch the culprit, never mind couch it in the unprintable terms that Skelgill would wholeheartedly endorse. He wonders if Aidan Wilson is ashamed – that his experience at the time was of emasculation – or perhaps guilt, that he was not there to protect his family. The latter, at least, he could understand. Does he therefore hide his shame beneath feigned indifference? But, Skelgill is fighting a losing battle in trying to convince himself of these worthy excuses. Truth be told he wants to grab Aidan Wilson by the collar and give him a good shake. Perhaps the man gets a whiff of something, for he looks suddenly fearful. Skelgill turns to DS Leyton and gives a jerk of his head, indicating he should continue.

'Mr Wilson, we would have met you sooner – but we had a little difficulty tracing you.' Aidan Wilson is watchful now, his dark eyes narrowed beneath the fringe. 'We've spoken to both Mrs Tyson and your son, Nick. It's our role to inform close family in such circumstances. As I said, after that, we have to consider if this new intelligence casts previous knowledge in a different light. Someone who knew Mary may be in possession of facts that now make sense.'

DS Leyton's wording is not the most succinct. It seems that he is treading on eggshells in order not to antagonise his subject – but the man exhibits a casual wiliness that this does not get past.

'Has the old crone been giving us the evil eye? I shouldn't be surprised if she still blames me.'

His lips curl to reveal irregular yellowed teeth in the silent snarl of a cornered dog that is beaten but still has some vain fight.

DS Leyton looks a little disconcerted – perhaps that Aidan Wilson has leapt to this conclusion. The man seems to read his reaction, for he offers a qualification.

'I don't mean for killing her.' He grins humourlessly.

DS Leyton takes a moment to gather his thoughts.

'In what respect would Mrs Tyson blame you, sir?'

Aidan Wilson shrugs as if the reasons the woman would propose are manifold.

'That woollens business, for a start. I tried to get it into Mary's head – she'd have needed to charge ten times the price for the labour that went into those scarves and shawls. And who would pay that around here? Even the tourists are not so tapped. If she'd got them listed in *Harrods*, maybe.'

DS Leyton is looking perplexed.

'Sir – I still don't quite see the connection – to what you say about your wife's mother?'

Aidan Wilson looks like he regrets mentioning the idea.

'She should have stuck to her job in the pub – put in more hours. She were paid a pittance, but at least it were guaranteed.'

There seem to DS Leyton to be contradictions in what the man says – as if money were somehow at the root of the problem and yet he is disparaging towards his wife's enterprise. There is an iota of practical logic in that had she not been running her stall she may not have gone to Cummacatta Wood – but even that is not necessarily the case. He discerns no urge from Skelgill to untangle this particular issue, and it strikes him that the antagonistic relationship between son-in-law and mother-in-law feels like a sideshow to the main event, by which they could unnecessarily become distracted. Accordingly, he shifts the emphasis of his questioning.

'What do you recall of your wife's state of mind around that time, sir? Had there been anything in her behaviour that was unusual?'

'Why would it make any difference?'

DS Leyton is still a good way from end of his tether; but he senses it is probably just as well that Skelgill is not doing the questioning; he accurately suspects his boss would have Aidan Wilson pinned up against the windows by now. Looking down at his notes, he continues patiently.

'Given what we now know, sir. She left her stall unattended. She drove to the nearby woods. Almost certainly she was murdered there. We have to look more closely at the idea that she went to meet someone.'

The sergeant glances inquiringly upon the interviewee; but the man merely sneers.

'You mean what if she were having an affair, more like.' He does not pose these words as a question.

Still DS Leyton takes the rejoinder in his stride.

'Could she have been, sir?'

The man seems to be leering.

'Your lot went all through this at the time. You must know that. Nowt came of it.'

Though technically accurate, in some respects this can be judged an evasive retort. DS Leyton wonders whether Skelgill is thinking along the same lines and, if so, what he would say next. But before he can even guess, the answer is forthcoming, from Skelgill's very lips. His superior's tone is uncompromising.

'Mr Wilson – on the day your wife disappeared – did *you* meet her at Cummacatta Wood?'

To a fly on the wall Skelgill's intervention might seem to be a classic case of 'good cop, bad cop' – except there is nothing premeditated about it. While it is in DS Leyton's temperament to be amenable, Skelgill, having exceeded his threshold of forbearance, has simply fired from the hip.

The man's reaction – as they may reflect upon in due course – is thought provoking. He cackles, tossing back his head contemptuously.

'You've got no more idea than the last lot! You're wasting your time. Come and speak to me when you've got something sensible to ask!'

And at this he rises from his seat and walks away without another word, limping slightly, but otherwise continuing purposefully between two checkouts and out of sight along an aisle marked 'Foreign Food'. The detectives watch him in silence. With good reason DS Leyton appears exasperated that his boss's ham-fisted question has just kyboshed his interview – but in formulating a complaint he notices Skelgill's expression of satisfaction, and adjusts his words to be more charitable.

'That was interesting, Guv.'

Skelgill is nodding. But now his gaze switches from the disappeared man to the display boards up behind the fast food service counter, advertising the fare that is the source of the fried aroma that ebbs and flows like a perpetual tide.

'I was out of milk this morning. You can only swallow so much sawdust.'

DS Leyton sees where this new conversation is headed. 'We've got plenty of time, Guv.' There is perhaps a slightly sarcastic note in his voice – that their interview has ended prematurely.

'I never come to these places, Leyton. What's the score?'

DS Leyton inhales resignedly.

'Our nippers always have the nuggets. The missus likes the grilled chicken wrap. I usually plump for whatever special burger they've got on.' He indicates with an outstretched arm. 'See – *Montana Bison Double Cheeseburger with Hungry Horse Relish* – just the ticket.'

Skelgill is squinting – he looks frustrated. He is trying to conflate the Photoshopped images with what he might feel like eating at ten in the morning.

'What's that – chicken leg end – I'll try that.'

DS Leyton splutters and cannot wholly suppress a spontaneous laugh, and he hauls himself to his feet and lumbers away towards the counter to conceal his mirth.

'It's *legend*, Guv. Hah! It comes in a bun. Large fries and tea, yeah?'

When his sergeant returns after what seems like an inordinate wait (so much for 'fast food') Skelgill eyes suspiciously what appears to be a plain-looking chicken burger bulked out by lettuce and mayonnaise. But upon tucking in he falls silent, and DS Leyton watches him with amusement as he alternately eats and gulps down the prohibitively scalding tea; it might almost have been prepared to order. While his superior is thus engaged, he reprises his prepared notes pertaining to Aidan Wilson. After a minute he picks up on Skelgill's conversation stopper.

'The geezer had a fairly sound alibi, Guv.' He glances inquiringly at Skelgill who signals with his eyebrows for him to continue. 'He was a sales rep for a food wholesaler in Carlisle. His patch was more or less the whole of the county. He used to call on the independent grocery stores. His journey plan that day had him starting over in Whitehaven in the morning, then he worked his way back across country via Mockerin, Lower Lorton and the Honister Pass, arriving home at about 5pm.'

Skelgill interrupts his eating to speak.

'One of the lads in the rescue, he used to be a rep – retired now – he was a law unto himself. When you're out on the road there's no one looking over your shoulder. How did they know Wilson was telling the truth?'

DS Leyton refers again to his notes.

'It seems to me, Guv, at one stage they had Aidan Wilson under the microscope. I mean – they had no suspects, so they probably thought he was the most likely bet. But it wasn't until a couple of weeks later that they checked his movements in detail. The decision report states that if he'd wanted to cover up a gap in his timetable, he probably could have done it. He collated all his orders for the week and took them into the wholesaler's on a Friday. There was nothing to prove he completed his journey plan in the order he was supposed to. Officers questioned all the shopkeepers – but there was no way they could remember whether he'd called exactly when he said he did. They got a dozen or more reps some days.'

Skelgill is frowning.

'He'd have been taking the risk of his car being recognised. There's only one road through Borrowdale proper.'

'Then again, at the time it might not have stood out, Guv. A familiar car doesn't attract attention. And most of the locals would have been occupied at the shepherds' meet.'

Skelgill nods, but continues to play devil's advocate.

'Strikes me that the last thing Aidan Wilson would have done is arranged to meet his wife for a cosy dog walk in the middle of the day. But if he did it on spec, how would he have known where and when she'd go? Like you say, folk were busy – if you'd been running a stall and wanted a break you'd likely have played it by ear.'

DS Leyton's eyes widen a little.

'But maybe that's it, Guv? The fact that she went at one o'clock – the sort of time you'd arrange to meet with someone. What if she had a date and Aidan Wilson had got wind of it? He could have seen them together – and then confronted her afterwards.'

Skelgill does not reply. He has finished his burger and is preoccupied with prising the last of his fries from their unsuitably narrow packet. With a groan of frustration he tilts his head and knocks back the remnants like the dregs of a drink.

'Was there one scrap of actual evidence that pointed to Aidan Wilson?'

DS Leyton stares rather forlornly at his notebook – but he seems already to know the answer.

'Unless DS Jones has found something that she didn't highlight – not really, Guv.' But then he perks up. 'What about like we discussed – him leaving the kid and moving out – possibly for a woman? None of that makes him look too clever.'

Skelgill's countenance is clouded by pessimism.

'Folk'd probably say I've done plenty of things that don't make me look too clever, Leyton – but that doesn't mean I've murdered someone.'

For a second DS Leyton appears inclined to ask Skelgill what he has in mind – but he thinks the better of it. While he is pondering his response, Skelgill raises a question.

'What did *he* say about his movements?'

DS Leyton flicks to and fro through several pages.

'That he left Slatterthwaite at his usual time of 8am – drove over to the coast – followed his journey plan as I've mentioned – arrived back home just after five. That was confirmed by his mother-in-law. The first thing they knew was the local farmer Pearson called in shortly afterwards to say Mary Wilson hadn't reappeared to close up her stall at the shepherds' meet. They didn't have a phone at the house, so Aidan Wilson drove over to the pub at Balderthwaite – of course she wasn't there. That was when he rang the police at Keswick.'

'Who gave our lot the idea to look at the Bowder Stone?'

DS Leyton's dark brows contract.

'I don't reckon that's documented. I suppose between them and the locals they'd have put two and two together. She'd been seen leaving with the dog at lunchtime. The dog had come home alone. Her car wasn't back at the pub. They'd have discussed the likely places she might have gone.'

'It was our patrol that found the car, aye?'

'Yeah – it was, Guv.'

'And there was nowt queer about it?'

DS Leyton shakes his head.

'Don't reckon so, Guv. Apart from it was locked and the keys were never recovered.' He stares pensively at his notes. 'That was about it – plus now we reckon the pink headscarf she was wearing is unaccounted for. Strange that they found the little key fob but not something that was much bigger and brightly coloured. Maybe someone came across it and took a liking to it – then they were too frightened to come forward.'

There is a silence. Skelgill is contemplating that, the keys aside, the two items that have become salient were both knitted by Mary Wilson, personal to her. He pulls out his mobile phone and types an abrupt five-word message and sends it to DS Jones. Then he glances up at his colleague.

'Next?'

'Interview, Guv?' He correctly divines his superior's meaning, for Skelgill nods. 'It's the woman, Megan Nicolson – formerly Atkinson. She was at school with Mary Wilson and worked with her as a barmaid. She's one of the four that witnessed her leaving. She still works in that same pub.' He consults his wristwatch. 'We ain't due with her for three-quarters of an hour.'

Skelgill shrugs and rises as if this is unimportant. He strides away but checks himself to glance at the display boards, as if seeing the menu in a new light. DS Leyton catches up and now grins.

'That trumps my Bowder Scone – Chicken Leg End. *Hah!* Nice one, Guv.'

Skelgill is about to reply when his phone rings – it is a familiar jingle: DS Jones. They scuttle through the sliding doors of the store and Skelgill answers as they reach the car and begin to clamber inside.

'Hold fire, Jones – we're just about to head up into Borrowdale.'

Skelgill manoeuvres in suitably cavalier fashion to exit the supermarket lot and then turns more sedately onto the road towards the lake. Grey bellied, straggling herds of stratocumulus radiate from the Scafell pikes, shepherded by a brisk southerly, skimming the high tops and streaking the fellsides with creeping shadows. Squinting, Skelgill squirts his washers, but the reservoir is dry and insect debris becomes smeared across the screen. Meanwhile he engages the speaker setting on his handset and places it on the console.

'Leyton can hear you now.'

'Hi – how's it going?'

'Alright, girl. You sound like you're in the ladies' room.'

'I am.' She chuckles. It seems she means it. 'It's the best signal I can find. Apparently this place was built in 1868 – they say the walls are so thick that they don't need jammers to stop the inmates using smuggled mobiles.'

DS Leyton turns inquiringly to his superior, who responds with a rather pained look. This is not about her anecdote – but that they both realise she must be calling them without the knowledge of DI Smart, who no doubt would not approve of such contact. DS Leyton leans towards the handset.

'Well – we're sitting comfortably, if you are.'

'*Ha-hah!* I'd better be quick. The cleaners are working their way along the corridor.'

Accordingly, Skelgill interjects.

'What's the verdict?'

'*I* don't think it's him, Guv.'

Again Skelgill and DS Leyton exchange glances. DS Jones has placed the stress on the first personal pronoun.

'What does Smart reckon?'

DS Jones takes a moment to settle upon a suitable form of words.

'I'd say he's a little intoxicated by the prospect of success.'

Skelgill nods grimly. He knows she understands that DI Smart will be desperate to trump him, to steal in like a goal poacher when Skelgill's shot was about to cross the line.

'Are we talking gut feel – or actual facts?'

There is the impression that DS Jones is nodding as she replies.

'Actually both, Guv, now that you mention it. But the facts raise question marks. I spent last night going through his records. The pattern of his M.O. doesn't fit certain aspects of our case. There was a string of attacks – initially five sexual assaults – culminating in two murders. They were always in an urban environment, never beyond Greater Manchester. In each case he'd stalked the victim beforehand. It's true he picked on women that worked in pubs – he'd drink in the bar and follow them as they walked home after their shift – always at night and knowing at which point there was a suitable alley or patch of darkened waste ground where he could pounce and drag them away. And it's true he choked his victims. His crimes were committed over a nine-month period; the first one was more than a year after Mary Wilson went missing.'

'What's his story about being in the Lakes?'

'Unconvincing, Guv. He claims he visited alone for a few days – stayed in Keswick at a B&B that he can't remember. He demonstrates no real knowledge of the geography. He says he was walking in woodland – came across a woman – she began behaving provocatively towards him – but somehow it ended up in a tussle and he accidentally strangled her – he panicked and concealed the body beneath stones in a cave.' DS Jones hesitates, as though she thinks she may about to be disturbed. But she continues without recourse to such an explanation. 'This level of detail has just been broadcast – never mind that he would have had access to contemporary news reports. I questioned him about the cave and he wasn't able to describe the

103

fact that the rocks came from several distinct sources on the scree slope. He was slippery, but I'm pretty sure I caught him out on that one. Besides, compare that to his other assaults – he left his victims for dead on the spot and made no attempt to conceal them.'

'What did Smart reckon – about the rocks?'

'Er – I didn't discuss it with him, Guv. I don't think he realised what I was getting at. I thought I'd bounce it off you.' DS Jones sounds sheepish, though Skelgill makes a growl of satisfaction – but before he can respond she has more to say. She speaks with added urgency. 'You texted me about trophies, Guv? There's absolutely nothing in the records – no items belonging to his victims were found in his possession or at his lodgings. He didn't even rob them of their purses or jewellery.'

Skelgill stares pensively at the road ahead. DS Leyton takes the opportunity to pose a question.

'Emma – did he admit to the other crimes?'

'No. He declined to give evidence.'

'So why now for this one?'

She inhales with a deliberate hiss, as if to warn that she is about to be indiscreet.

'I don't know what his mental state was twenty-odd years ago – but I'd say he's unbalanced. I think it's opportunistic attention seeking. Possibly for notoriety – possibly for variety.'

Now Skelgill comes back in.

'Have you discussed that with Smart?'

'No, Guv. Like I say – you know when someone's on a mission. It's easy only to see the similarities. That she worked in a bar. That he could have been watching her. That he may have followed her unseen. The same cause of death. I've just tried to ask the right questions and keep my head down.'

Skelgill is scowling.

'Don't be too cooperative, lass.'

DS Jones chuckles apprehensively.

'He's planning to conduct a further interview this afternoon. Is there anything you want me to cover?'

Skelgill does not answer, and there is such a long pause that DS Jones must wonder if the signal has been lost, for she says "Guv?" with sudden vigour. Skelgill starts, and then replies somewhat absently.

'See if there's anything that connects him to anyone in the Borrowdale area.'

'Sure, Guv.'

Again there is a silence before Skelgill speaks.

'When are you coming back?'

DS Jones is hesitant.

'I'm not certain – what DI Smart's plan is, Guv.' She pauses, and then her voice drops to a whisper. 'Oh-oh – that's someone come in. Can I call you later?'

Skelgill has little option but to agree.

'Aye.'

'Nice job, Emma!' DS Leyton cries out – but she has ended the call.

9. MEGAN NICOLSON

Wednesday 11.30am, Balderthwaite

Megan Nicolson, fifty-two, conjures for Skelgill the image of the saucy seaside postcard stereotype; though it is not so much the full figure in a barmaid's outfit a size too small, or the manufactured blonde shock that is a little larger than life, but the cherubic countenance with its rosy cheeks, button nose, bright blue eyes and preposterously ingenuous smile. Once more he finds himself reflecting upon the number of people on his local patch whom he has never really come across.

The *Twa Tups* is not due to open for another half an hour – although in asking them if they wanted a drink she seemed to suggest that alcohol were an option, and Skelgill had admired the cask ales on offer as she leant invitingly between the handpumps. They have settled on coffees with cream, to his immediate regret (tepid and cloying; tea is just so reliable). They have a table in the empty snug bar at the front of the establishment. The floor is of hefty slate slabs, the distempered ceiling low and black-beamed, the walls crowded with local scenes corrupted by age and nicotine. The interior is gloomy; Skelgill, seated upon a settle that was once a church pew, has his back to a small sash window; accordingly he can only be a silhouette to the woman who faces him. DS Leyton has taken up a more neutral position; at the end of the table his sturdy form is accommodated by a solid sack-back Windsor chair.

While Megan Nicolson has been identified from the historical files as a person of interest to the police, and has been contacted by a junior officer in their team, she acts rather as if she does not quite know what is going on, and gives a coo of astonishment when Skelgill introduces the subject.

'I never thought it would come to this – Mary Tyson found murdered after all these years.'

Skelgill notes that she uses Mary Wilson's maiden name. He glances at DS Leyton, who has en route assured his superior that he is well prepared to conduct the interview (as he was for Aidan Wilson, until Skelgill's intervention brought matters to an abrupt conclusion). Skelgill sees his sergeant open his notebook, preparatory to speaking. However, despite their official line – that they seek from the public fresh insights in the context of the discovery of Mary Wilson's remains – Skelgill privately has a tactic that is diametrically opposed. He is more interested in enduring memories, those that have percolated like the rain that began as a veil of fog upon the high fells, filtered by the rocks and time, to emerge clear and sharp, a zesty spring down in the dale; impressions that are untainted by the desperate promptings of a detective. He speaks before his colleague can catch his breath.

'Tell us something about Mary.'

'As a bairn, like?'

'You were at school together, aye?' He waves a casual hand and sinks back against his seat; he seems in no rush.

'She used to play alone in the woods – believed in fairies and whatnot. She'd go off into her own little world. When we were in primary, I mean. But she still went for walks when she was older. And later she had the dog.'

She seems to think that Skelgill is asking about Mary being in Cummacatta and is answering this point directly. But he wants to know what Mary was like – and she inadvertently tells him something of that. To spend time in one's own little world does not feel so alien.

'Was she popular?'

'So-so.'

It takes Megan Nicolson a moment to conjure such an economical reply, and Skelgill is drawn to read more into her ambivalence – that Mary was a little smug, that she thought she was special; but there was no cause to dislike her.

'You know her remains were found in the Kissing Cave?'

When sinister would be justifiable, Skelgill's tone is conversational. It is of the order of one local to another, with no special emphasis upon the location and its possible connotations.

Nevertheless, she seems to bite fleetingly at her cheek.

'Aye – I heard that. But they called it something else on the radio – the archaeologists' name.'

Skelgill continues offhandedly.

'Mary would have known it well enough?'

Her mascaraed lashes flutter with a hint of diffidence – or it might be coyness.

'Most of our generation would know it. You went up there as teenagers.'

Skelgill grins amiably.

'Like they say – a rite of passage, aye?'

The woman simpers.

'But it weren't a grown-up thing.'

'She never mentioned it?'

She shakes her head, the semblance of a puzzled frown creasing her brow, that he might be suggesting an adult tryst in such an unfavourable location.

'Did Mary have many boyfriends?'

He asks in a way that allows for promiscuity to be the answer, or more a bland interpretation, but Megan Nicolson is clear in her response.

'Aidan were her only proper boyfriend that I knew of. They were going together from when she were still at school.'

'She didn't go out with any of the other village lads?'

'Nothing serious – like I say, she weren't old enough.'

Skelgill makes a gesture of instability, moving his hands simultaneously from side to side.

'Her and Aidan Wilson – they never broke up for a period – nothing like that?'

'Aidan never gave her chance. He were all over her like a rash.'

Skelgill does not immediately react to this rather more prickly statement, despite that it contradicts the impressions he has formed of the Wilsons' relationship.

'I got the feeling they were independent of one another.'

She offers a clarification.

'You're asking me about when they first started.' (Skelgill may not be, but he does not interrupt.) 'Aidan was a good bit older – he'd got a car. He'd take her out of the village a lot of the time. So they didn't knock about with the rest of us so much. They used to drive back for last orders – maybe a lock-in. But he were always glued to her side.'

'I thought he was the one considered to be a bit of a catch.'

Megan Nicolson begins to scoff at this suggestion, but then qualifies her response.

'Some might say that. Happen it was more him that'd got his claws into her. But she didn't seem to mind.'

Skelgill nods phlegmatically; it is an action barely affected, for he absorbs the information with no attempt to be analytical.

'What about around the time Mary disappeared?'

It is something of an open question – he could mean had it been a good summer, or who was Prime Minister. He waits to see what she will say. Her reply suggests she has remained on message.

'They'd been a couple for a long time by then – maybe fifteen years.'

She seems to feel it unnecessary to expound upon her rationale.

'You worked here together – on the same shifts sometimes?'

'Aye – Friday and Saturday nights – and Bank Holidays.'

Skelgill looks at her appraisingly.

'I've seen the pictures in the files of Mary. The pair of you behind the bar must have turned a few heads.'

Though her crossing of her legs might imply a certain guardedness, a slow alternate movement of her shoulders suggests she is not immune to the compliment.

'That's just par for the course. It doesn't mean anything. Well –'

But Skelgill knows she doesn't want it to mean nothing – that men still find her attractive. And why wouldn't that be okay for her ego. But she adds a rider.

'It's part of your job to flirt a bit.'

Skelgill combs the fingers of one hand through his hair in a seemingly hopeless gesture.

109

'I can tell you – it would be easy enough for some dimwit like me to get the wrong idea.'

She grins sympathetically.

'You get to know how to handle it.'

Skelgill scowls, an attempt at self-reproach.

'Could she have got herself into a situation where she felt obliged in some way?'

Megan Nicolson's smile turns down disapprovingly.

'They'd not long had their bairn. He weren't above a year.'

She says no more. Skelgill allows a respectable pause before he continues.

'Besides – you would have noticed if there were something more to it.'

His intonation is definitive rather than questioning. But in response she shifts forward, placing her plump barmaid's hands on the table, with their tight rings and prominent veins and recently lacquered nails.

'I remember – they looked into all that – the police. There weren't anything came of it – and that were when things were fresh in folk's minds. Twenty-plus years – it's a long time to go back.'

She glances at DS Leyton, as if for corroboration of her logic, and then looks again at Skelgill. He nods; he appears convinced. But it is the second time today he has received an oblique answer to an enquiry of this nature. He casts about the snug, surveying superficially.

'There's not a lot changed in here, though, I reckon.'

'It's been like this for centuries, they say.'

Skelgill gestures over his shoulder.

'You saw Mary on the day she disappeared.'

He does not elaborate but she knows what he means.

'Aye – I were behind the bar – facing the window.' She tilts her head towards him to illustrate her statement. 'I were serving Pick Pearson and old Walter Dickson. I said – there's Mary – and they turned round and saw her. Thankfully it weren't just me. I shouldn't have liked to be the last one – alone, like.'

'It was definitely her?'

'Aye – she stopped to look through.'

'As if she was trying to make out who was inside?'

'I suppose so. Pick Pearson thought she were looking for him – he said something about judging her stall. But then she never came in. But it were definitely her – we couldn't have all been mistaken.'

Skelgill nods pensively. He points past Megan Nicolson to the small counter with space for just two stools where Walter Dickson and Patrick Pearson had been stationed. Set into the wall behind is a framed serving hatch – it is convenient for handing through drinks or bottles only available on one side; the lounge bar in particular stocks a more exotic range of spirits and liqueurs, advocaat for snowballs, and tomato juice and Worcester sauce for bloody Marys.

'Could she have gone into the lounge without you knowing?'

Megan Nicolson seems unconvinced by this suggestion, that it would be improbable.

'I would have heard her come down the passage. Happen she'd have had a word – stuck her head round the door.'

'Were there folk in the lounge?'

Now the woman looks decidedly unsettled, as though she feels this is an unreasonable question, and that he puts her in peril of giving inadvertently a false answer.

'There were a bell on the counter – there still is – if anyone needs served. But most folk were over the road. On the day of the meet the pub's quiet first thing – until the fell runners are back and the first round of judging's announced.'

Skelgill is looking rather like he is not that bothered; indeed that he has some other more important job to do and is largely going through the motions. He sighs before he speaks, his tone one of resignation.

'The thing is, Mrs Nicolson,' (she looks uncomfortable at his formal address) 'if Mary were meeting someone, or had had the notion to look for someone – well, that could go a long way to explaining what happened.'

The woman nods willingly, her expression puppy-like. But she can offer nothing more, and they sit for a few moments in a kind of limbo. Eventually Skelgill breaks the silence.

'Your husband, it's *Sean* – aye?' She nods, looking apprehensive. In their introduction they have mentioned that they are seeing him later this afternoon – although of course she had been made aware of their intentions. 'He knew Mary quite well?'

There is a faint but discernable tensing of the muscles of her face.

'We were all in the same class at school.'

Skelgill, however, is nodding agreeably. He glances at DS Leyton in the way of getting advance confirmation from one who knows of something he is about to say.

'He supplied Mary with wool for her knitting business?'

The woman nods, more curtly than before, a sharp movement that dislodges a strand of hair and causes her to brush it from her rouged cheek with a nervous jerk.

'It weren't a commercial arrangement – nowt like that – it were just waste. You can't hardly get 50p for a Herdwick fleece even now.'

Skelgill banks the information, though it is not the aspect that interests him.

'I were more thinking along the lines of what he reckoned to her disappearing.'

Megan Nicolson inhales slowly; she seems discomfited.

'He were shocked – like we all were. But he were mainly took bad about our Alison – she were just a young lass – all that scaremongering about a murderer loose in the dale. Us folk that had bairns couldn't sleep nights.'

Skelgill nods, his expression understanding, in blank kind of way.

'She'll be grown up now.'

'Aye – she's thirty-three. She's married and lives in Leicestershire. She's got two of her own.'

There is something in her intonation, perhaps the faintest hint of an inquiry, that wrong-foots Skelgill, and for a moment he finds himself thinking that Megan Nicolson must have borne her child at a relatively tender age. He wonders if he should say she doesn't look old enough to be a grandmother, but having already risked one such compliment he feels he has probably used up his professional quota. Perhaps rather abruptly he moves the conversation on.

'It must have come as a relief when the DNA tests gave the all-clear.'

She seems to take a small involuntary gasp; her breathing has become more noticeable, and there is a trace of a flush on her chest around her exposed collarbones and creased cleavage.

'Truth be told – it were more that time went by and nothing else happened. Eventually folk began to feel safer. I don't know if anyone properly understood that DNA business – and it all seemed to come to nowt. Course – there were talk that Mary had just run away of her own accord – such that there never had been anything to worry about.'

'You sound like you never thought that.'

She shakes her head; there is a look of defiance in her eyes that is a little at odds with their sparkling blue.

'She might have had her differences with Aidan – who knows what goes on in a marriage – but what mother would abandon her bairn? Especially after all that time.'

Skelgill makes an apologetic face on behalf of humanity.

'We come across it.' He looks at DS Leyton who nods willingly. 'There's nowt stranger than folk.'

She makes as if to speak but then checks herself. It appears she was about to contest the morality of his claim, if not its veracity. Then she does utter a rejoinder.

'Now we know she didn't.'

It interests Skelgill that she has in a fashion put the ball back in their court, employing the sort of phrase he might have chosen himself. In turn, he picks up the thread of her logic.

'Young Nick – we saw him yesterday.' His inflection invites her acknowledgement, and she nods to indicate there is no need to specify to whom he refers. Anything else would be unlikely in a community where they have both lived continuously. Skelgill gestures towards the bar. 'Is he a regular?'

She hurriedly shakes her head.

'I don't reckon he drinks.'

Skelgill looks a little disappointed.

'Sounds like he's handy on the guitar – this would be just the thing – live music on a Sunday night. As I recall, it's a standing attraction – turn up and jam?'

Skelgill is being somewhat disingenuous, for in days gone by in planning to meet a mountain rescue pal for a Sunday night pint and in suggesting possible pubs with decent ale and a warming hearth they had eliminated the *Twa Tups* for the very reason that conversation would be drowned out by those who liked to blow their own trumpets. But Megan Nicolson quickly puts him right.

'Must be above ten years since we've had that. The *Tups* changed hands – the new owners wanted to make it less cliquey – more for visitors. That were when they started doing B&B and bar meals.'

Skelgill inhales with apparent dismay.

'Time flies. I didn't realise it were that long ago. He'd have been too young – but didn't his dad play, going back?'

The woman seems perplexed by his question.

'You mean Aidan? Aidan Wilson? Not as I recall.'

Skelgill shrugs as though this were unimportant in any event.

'Did he drink here?'

She makes a gesture of appeal, holding out her hands palms upward.

'As youngsters – though he were older – most of us used to drink here. Friday nights, maybe Saturdays. It were a crowd from the village and the surrounding district. But he stopped coming in. After his Ma died and they took over the cottage – Mary used to say they were hard up – though the rent couldn't have been that bad, and he had a decent job, according to Mary.' Now she lowers her voice a little, almost conspiratorially. 'Mary didn't like to admit it – but I'd say he were tight – didn't approve of either of them spending money. Going right back I've seen them have a row over a round of drinks – when it were their turn and he wanted to leave. At least Mary weren't like that.'

Skelgill absently scratches the top of his head.

'Is it possible there were money troubles at the time she disappeared?'

Megan Nicolson appears doubtful.

'Happen they were stretched – they'd just had the bairn and Aidan had changed his job. But they were living with Jean Tyson, so they could share the same overheads. I don't reckon they were any more hard up than most folk.'

Skelgill nods.

'Would you say you were close to Mary?'

'I knew her well enough.'

'But if there'd been something going on – say she owned money – or say she were borrowing from someone – would she have confided in you?'

But the woman is beginning to shake her head.

'I shouldn't say I were *that* close. I were willing, like – but Mary were more the sort to keep her troubles to herself. And I wouldn't say she were under the thumb – but you could tell she were always worrying what would Aidan think about something or other – that he might not approve.'

Skelgill nods again, though he must appear a little disinterested – for she regards him interrogatively, as though she is dissatisfied with his reaction. But he is indeed distracted; at least three attempts to make specific headway have been rebuffed, and it feels like the conversation is drifting somewhat aimlessly. He knows that if DS Jones were sitting beside him she would be itching to haul the interview back onto a more even keel, a course plotted, a destination in mind. DS Leyton seems to have been lulled into easy-listening mode, leaning back holding his cup and saucer and sipping occasionally. Skelgill suddenly rises to his feet.

'I must pay a visit to the little boys' room.' He affects a bow to the surprised woman. 'Thanks for your time, Mrs Nicolson. Sergeant Leyton has a couple of quick questions to finish off.' He looks directly at his colleague. 'I'll meet you at the car.'

DS Leyton appears momentarily panicked – but he nods obediently and puts down his coffee and takes up his notebook from the table. As Skelgill exits the snug he pauses to take from the bar a leaflet advertising the forthcoming Balderthwaite shepherds' meet; as he folds and pockets the item he hears his deputy ask permission to update the woman's personal details.

A stone-flagged corridor leads to the main entrance, which is at the side of the old building, and there are doors on the left, as he looks, successively signposted to the ladies' and gents'. But Skelgill takes a door on the right, marked 'Lounge Bar'. It is a substantially larger room than the snug, and brighter, having both of these qualities by virtue of a flat-roofed extension that has been added to the rear of the inn. It is still a few minutes shy of opening time, and the lounge is empty. It has that strange pub-non-pub atmosphere that Skelgill first noticed after the smoking ban, when combusted tobacco could no longer mask the smell of fermented beer in the carpet.

He approaches the extension, which stretches left and right along the back of the building, halfway to being a conservatory. The long windows give on to the beer garden – merely a collection of picnic benches set on gravel that merges with that of the car park; his own car is there beside a couple of others filmed with condensation that look like they have been left overnight. He walks to the extreme left and takes a seat in a slipper chair. Now he looks over his shoulder. He cannot be seen from the bar counter or the serving hatch; on the other hand he has a clear view of the exterior, the beer garden and car park.

*

'Why are we stopping, Guv?'
They have travelled barely two minutes and Skelgill has slewed his car into a recessed gateway between dry stone walls. He replies as he springs from the vehicle.
'Call of nature.'
'I thought you just went?'

Skelgill is standing with his back to the open door, facing the wall.

'I got sidetracked.'

DS Leyton waits to see if his superior will elaborate, but Skelgill seems either unwilling, or sufficiently preoccupied with his pressing needs to deem that a reply is low on his list of priorities. After some time – when he continues to stand and stare over the wall into the paddock – he returns to the driver's seat.

'Herdwicks gathered for the Balderthwaite meet.'

'Herdwick's what, Guv?'

Skelgill looks impatiently at his subordinate, as if he ought to know what he is talking about. But, of course, a more natural assumption would be the creatures' human namesake, in the shape of the long-serving police pathologist. Skelgill casts a hand towards the gate that impedes their view. As he does so a thick-coated sheep ambles into sight.

'The yowes in that field – happen they've brought them down off the fell for shearing.'

DS Leyton raises a finger to signal his recall.

'Oh, yeah – it did say that, Guv – on that poster we were looking at?'

Skelgill nods.

'Aye – hand clipping. The way it were done before the electric came.'

'That's gotta be a dying art, Guv. Must be some old boy they've dragged out of retirement.'

Skelgill glances sharply at his colleague.

'It's her husband, Leyton.'

'What's that, Guv?'

'Megan Nicolson – it's Sean Nicolson that does the hand clipping demonstration.'

'Oh – right, Guv. You've got local knowledge on me.'

Skelgill grimaces.

'His name was on the notice, Leyton.'

Now the penny drops.

'Ah – so he were doing that at the shepherds' meet when Mary Wilson disappeared?'

'I reckon that's the story.' But now Skelgill folds his arms – for he is not entirely sure of this. 'He might have entered some sheep – most of the shepherds hereabouts would do – they have upward of forty classes.'

'I suppose we'll get it from the horse's mouth soon enough, Guv.'

Skelgill does not immediately reply. The engine is idling but he is showing no inclination to drive off. Though it is not entirely overcast and there are scrappy patches of blue, rain is in the air and large drops are streaking the screen. He flicks the wipers onto the intermittent setting, taking the opportunity to erase some of the insect smears.

'What did you make of his missus?'

'You what, Guv? Megan Nicolson?' But Skelgill does not answer.

After some apparent racking of his brains, DS Leyton reaches a conclusion that he tentatively puts forward.

'I don't reckon she told us much new, Guv. Leastways, not about Mary Wilson – nor what happened back then. I'd say if anything she seems to have a downer on Aidan Wilson. Not overboard – but she had a few little digs at him.'

Skelgill broods for a while. The rhythm of the wipers is soporific, their regular movement verging on the hypnotic. He stares beyond the bars of the gate, his gaze unaffected by sheep that cross his field of vision.

'How about what she didn't tell us, Leyton.'

'How do you mean, Guv?'

Skelgill's face becomes painfully distorted, as if he cannot stomach the effort of voicing his thoughts.

'She grew up with Mary Tyson – Wilson. They were at school together, knocked about together in the same clique, worked together. She didn't have a bad word to say about her – but not a good word either.'

DS Leyton is a little perplexed. On occasion his boss will be deliberately cryptic – out of frustration, or devilment – and then there can be a more profound aspect that is not always apparent at the time. In this case he seems to be highlighting the contradiction. DS Leyton experiences a small spark of inspiration.

'You mean, like – she's keeping mum, Guv?'

Skelgill nods pensively.

'Aye. Sommat like that.'

But Skelgill is no more forthcoming – whether out of unwillingness or simply that he is unable to provide a clear explanation of his thoughts. However, DS Leyton produces his notebook and begins to thumb methodically through its pages. He makes a small grunt of triumph.

'Yeah – now you mention it, Guv.' He turns to Skelgill. 'If anything, she's changed her tune. Remember DS Jones saying there was a suggestion of Mary Wilson having an affair? I've made a note here from the files – that came from Megan Nicolson. When originally interviewed about it she said, "Mary's a dark horse, I wouldn't be surprised if there's been something going on". There was nothing specific and no names put forward, but the officer made a note to the effect that he believed it was a definite hint. But then of course that aspect was investigated and there was no indication of any relationship.'

'As the pair of them reminded us, Leyton – her and Aidan Wilson.'

DS Leyton looks keenly at his superior, as if in Skelgill's tone of voice he detects a deeper meaning beneath its cynicism. But Skelgill without warning rams the car into reverse gear and, taking a chance on there being no oncoming traffic – human, ovine or otherwise – swings blind onto the lane, brakes with a harsh jolt and surges forward.

'Pearson, aye?'

DS Leyton is desperately lurching from one brace position to another. But he manages to blurt out a response.

'That's it, Guv – Patrick Pearson – farm beyond Slatterthwaite, if I got the map reading correct.'

10. PATRICK PEARSON

Wednesday 12.50pm, Slatterdale Rigg

'Struth, Guv – this is hillbilly country if I ever saw it.'

Skelgill, concentrating hard on navigating the rutted track, which is unsuitable for much less than a *Defender* and comfortable only for a tractor, smirks without looking aside. It might be his sergeant's turn of phrase, or perhaps his tone of consternation that amuses him. His colleague, of course, is a stranger to such environs. A Londoner, with a young family and metropolitan instincts for multiplexes and malls, he has little inclination to explore the fells, so bereft are they of chicken nuggets. But he is probably inured to urban badlands that might cause Skelgill equally to baulk.

To his more complacent eye their surroundings hold no fears; it is simply wild country of the sort that makes up much of the Lakeland landscape. A rising U-shaped valley with its foaming beck and fellsides that steepen as grass becomes bracken, becomes heather, becomes scree; the bleat of sheep, the mew of a buzzard, the stone-tapping *chack* of a wheatear on a stretched telephone wire, tilting into the wind; against an exposed crag a solitary browning rowan; blooming late in the verges canary-yellow tormentil and flimsy powder-blue harebells.

He knows of dozens of such places, where metalled roads end and rough tracks continue to isolated farmsteads. Not so long ago – as vouchsafed by his treasured Victorian map – even some of today's essential routes, taken for granted, were similarly hostile to motor vehicles; not least the nearby Honister Pass – there was no shortcut from Buttermere to Balderthwaite in those days!

Still, it strikes him that it is several years since he last came this way, and he likely paid scant attention, being on a mission to complete some substantial circuit, or was running, or was toting heavy rescue gear – he can't quite remember which. Perhaps he ought to heed those features that are the cause of his sergeant's wonderment. For on reflection he might agree that, yes, perhaps Slatterdale, as this upper limb of Borrowdale is sometimes called, does possess a more sinister quality than other uplands. The atmospheric conditions are playing their part – what was patchy cloud when they left Keswick has merged and descended to cloak the fell tops, a dark lowering ceiling from which wraiths stretch ghostly fingers that seem to warn or even threaten to assail them. And the rain that had begun to patter during Skelgill's pit stop has become a steady drum, requiring the wipers on maximum and obscuring sight between sweeps of the blades. The interior is steaming up, amplifying the claustrophobia, the sense of being walled in by the ever-encroaching mountains and oppressive sky; if this were a horror movie they would ultimately be crushed.

But it is not the landscape alone that has triggered his partner's response; there is the human-inflicted blemish upon it, a lack of care. It had begun with the first gate (to open which his long-suffering sergeant was despatched into the rain). Rickety, collapsing, it was tethered by a loop of frayed blue baler twine. Skelgill's shouted reminder for it to be shouldered, scraping the rocky ground, back into place had seen it almost disintegrate. Thence, onward and upward, they have passed tumbling walls; paddocks overgrown with inedible rush and poisonous ragwort; precious few sheep, looking unhealthy and unresponsive; randomly abandoned machinery, corroded and overrun by nettles, a harrow, a baler, a rusted manger, a muck-spreader with a sapling growing out of it. Then a small breaker's yard populated by the rotting carcasses of obsolete cars, variously cannibalised, lacking wheels and doors, piles of rotting tyres, bumpers and miscellaneous fragments of vehicle scrap. And the farmstead itself, which they now approach, a straggle of buildings clinging to the fellside, irregular sheds and byres with their roofs holed and sagging – and finally the narrow farmhouse, smothered by an invasive thicket of elder and blackthorn within an area walled off to keep out sheep, once upon a time a kitchen garden, but now unguarded by a rotting gate lying off its hinges. So overgrown is it that a virtual tunnel leads to the lean-to porch, and only part of the upper floor is visible; render flakes from the stone beneath, the paintwork of the first-floor windows is long beyond redemption, roof tiles are missing, and cast-iron guttering leaks profusely.

Skelgill halts the car and lowers the window by a couple of inches. He stares, unblinking. The chimney lacks a pot – from here a miserly stream of smoke is pressed flat in the wind, spun like a strand of grey wool; incongruously, amidst the dilapidation and decay a new-looking satellite dish juts from the southern side of the stack.

'Come on, Leyton.'

The second Skelgill steps out dogs set up barking manically. DS Leyton hesitates – he stands close to the vehicle in case he should retreat for his own safety. But there is no onslaught – the animals must be penned at the rear of the property. The sergeant grins nervously.

'I pity the postie, Guv.'

Skelgill shrugs indifferently.

'There were a box by the first gate, Leyton – old Pat, she doesn't have to come up here.' He evidently knows the lady in question.

Skelgill slams his door – unusually for him; typically he presses it shut – but it seems he wishes to announce their arrival, as if the dogs' clamour were not enough, or perhaps not sufficiently specific. He leads the way, ducking twigs and tendrils, moving purposefully through the downpour. Beneath the porch the inadequate front door is ajar and Skelgill pushes it wider. He can hear a radio or television; the sound muted by a closed door somewhere ahead. He steps over the threshold into dank air heavy with spores. He calls out into the gloom of the passage.

'Mr Pearson? It's the police.'

There comes a shout – unintelligible – but he takes it to mean they are to proceed – although equally it may be a command to the dogs; on cue, they fall silent. The hallway zigzags past a dingy kitchen on their right – a glimpse of a single tap dripping into a stained Belfast sink – and then on their left a cramped staircase. A little further is the plain door of the living room. Skelgill knocks and in the same movement pushes it open.

The inharmoniousness of the exterior is carried through to this interior chamber. In a bare room ineffectually darkened by frayed and shrunken curtains, upon exposed floorboards beside a small tiled hearth where meagre embers glow in the grate stands a state-of-the-art widescreen TV set. On the other side of the hearth the sole piece of furniture, a shabby wingback chair, faces the television and – at a diagonal – the detectives. They are consumed by the second incongruity: the giant of a man slumped in the armchair.

Jean Tyson, Nick Wilson, Aidan Wilson and Megan Nicolson – despite their local origins, these were all effectively strangers to Skelgill. But this time he recognises their interviewee. Even now, reclining and in his seventies, he seems enlarged in all proportions, feet, hands, limbs, torso – it seems a wonder he finds clothes to fit; he wears an old-fashioned collarless shirt, much stained, and equally disreputable trousers fastened by a belt of twine; the elongated feet are stockinged, hob-nailed boots cast aside; perhaps the explanation for the biting rancidity that permeates the air. But it is not only the man's size that makes him distinctive. His long cadaverous head has a great square forehead above a massive ridged monobrow, beneath which his heavily lidded eyes are cloaked in shadow. He makes no word of greeting, nor any effort to rise.

DS Leyton seems dumbstruck by the man's appearance. Skelgill, too, is staring hard – although no longer at the person – but at a shotgun that is propped within his reach beside the fireplace. Skelgill clears his throat. He realises he is going to have to speak over the television.

'Mr Pearson. It's DI Skelgill and DS Leyton. You received a call from one of our colleagues.'

Patrick Pearson seems to be regaling them – he in particular – with what Skelgill sees as a look of contempt, and he wonders if the mention of his own surname has given the man cause for disdain; some ancestral family reason of which he is unaware (but

123

would not be surprised about). Or it could simply be that he is a policeman, not a universally popular profession.

With great gnarled hands that seem crippled by arthritis Patrick Pearson fumbles for a remote control and contrives with knotted fingers to lower the volume to about half of its original level.

'Tha's early.'

Skelgill has acquired the distinct impression that the man would complain whether they were early, late or even on schedule – but DS Leyton takes him at his word, and addresses him in a friendly tone of voice, taking half a step forward and gesturing to the television.

'I believe you can pause the programme with that model of equipment, sir.'

Patrick Pearson responds with some phrase that is indecipherable even to Skelgill's native ear, but shows no inclination to adopt the suggestion. Skelgill thinks he has mentioned the word *yowes* – so he takes it that there is some imminent task, and no time to spare. He opts to press on.

'Mr Pearson, the case of Mary Wilson is now a murder investigation. Naturally we're talking to those folk who last saw her.'

He curtails any further words of introduction. The man's gaze seems to have drifted back to the popular local bucolic soap opera that is playing out its repeat upon the screen. For his part, Skelgill remains silent. He senses that DS Leyton is becoming agitated at his side. But, finally, his patience draws a response.

'Thou won't be talking to arl Walter.'

Skelgill glances at his colleague.

'No, sir. That makes you an even more important witness.'

Patrick Pearson produces a phlegmy growl; he sounds like he suspects he is being buttered up. But just when it seems nothing more will be forthcoming, he responds.

'We were in t' *Twa Tups* – me an' Walt conferring. Lass deeked in t' window. That were it. That's the story.'

Skelgill responds somewhat offhandedly.

'There was a suggestion that she was looking for you – something to do with judging her stall.'

The man's massive brow seems to gather, if it were possible to appear more ominous.

'If she were, she changed her mind.'

'She didn't come in?'

There is a grunt and a lateral movement of the huge head that Skelgill takes as a negative.

'What about after that, sir?'

The man seems disinclined to answer – as if the question is too vague, and does not sufficiently compete with the on-screen drama. Skelgill tries again, more incisively.

'What did you and Mr Dickson do after you left the *Twa Tups?*'

'Went back t' meet. There were judging to be finished.'

By coincidence a change of scene in the soap opera sees a Border Collie gathering a flock of Swaledales. Skelgill finds his gaze drawn to the television. While the dog looks like it knows what it is doing, the actor playing the shepherd is unconvincing. He is clean-shaven, his complexion too even when it might be ruddy, no hair out of place; and Skelgill is thinking that a real shepherd would use not voice commands but whistles over that distance. Meanwhile the background birdsong is wrong for the time of year. Patrick Pearson, however, does not seem to share his scepticism, and is watching intently. Skelgill resumes his questioning.

'I understand you raised the alarm, sir? You alerted Mary Wilson's husband – at her mother's cottage – Jean Tyson's place.'

It is only the final mention of Jean Tyson that prompts the man to look sharply at Skelgill. His expression is one of annoyance, as though there might be some hint of an insinuation to which he objects.

'I were driving right past her front door.' Again he makes the disagreeable sound in his throat. 'For all I knew, Mary were there. Gone back for t' bairn or sommat. That's what folk thought.'

He says it scathingly, as though Skelgill must be stupid for asking such an obviously pointless question. Skelgill, however, is unperturbed.

'But her car wasn't there.'

The man does not answer, but continues to look at Skelgill.

'What was Aidan Wilson's reaction?'

Now Patrick Pearson looks away. But though he fastens his eyes upon the television a movement of his jaw muscles suggests he is contemplating more than the inadequacies of the shepherd. And perhaps – although Skelgill considers it an optimistic notion – there is the realisation that he is being asked to be the eyes and ears of the detectives – and that what he says might be regarded as significant.

'He didn't seem fussed. Except he were complaining about her stock being left.'

Skelgill shows some interest in this statement.

'I thought he went straightaway to look for her?'

'Aye – after Jean mithered him. It were her that were spooked. Cur dog had garn yam itsen.'

Skelgill snatches a glance at DS Leyton, and winks to advise him he has understood the dialect. The man merely means the dog found its own way home.

'What did you do, Mr Pearson?'

'Might have stayed for a mash.' His tone sounds resentful of Skelgill's question. 'Went on us way after a bit. There were no reason to think owt of it.'

Skelgill, who has been standing perfectly still, shifts from one foot to the other and presses the knuckles of both hands into the small of his back. It seems to mark a hiatus, as though he has dealt with whatever significant questions there were to be asked.

'Have you always been on your own up here, sir?'

But his more casual manner seems to cut little ice with Patrick Pearson. And though his reclusiveness is local knowledge that Skelgill might reasonably possess his reply comes grudgingly.

'Since t' arl folks passed away. Above thirty year.'

It is evident that he refers to his immediate forebears, though it seems odd that he uses the descriptor when he himself is in his seventies. Skelgill raises his head in comprehension, and then he produces from his jacket the Balderthwaite shepherds' meet brochure he took from the *Twa Tups*. In keeping with its traditional layout it is mainly occupied with the forthcoming programme of events; on its back cover, however, is a list of all the previous year's winners. He displays the reverse to show to what he refers.

'You must know some number of folk hereabouts.'

'I keep to mesen – can't show favouritism.'

Skelgill peruses the densely typed page of classes, with the names of those triumphant, runners-up, and highly commended. While there are the likes of the Johnsons and the Thompsons, he sees no representative of the Pearson clan. But are there any other Pearsons in the dale? It would appear this man has no issue, no sons or daughters to take up the farm in his lieu. Perhaps what he says has something in it – there is no temptation to show prejudice. But then the familial name does catch his eye, at the foot of the sheet: *"Judges. Senior – P. Pearson, Understudy – S. Nicolson."* He raises the leaflet.

'I see you're head judge these days.'

'Since arl Walt died.'

'And that's *Sean* Nicolson?'

'Aye, he's understudy now.'

Skelgill nods. The man is being rather more forthcoming.

'How does that work?'

Patrick Pearson casts his eyes briefly back at the television, as if he cannot be bothered with this explanation. But then he yields.

'Sheep classes – you judge separately. Then confer. Senior judge holds sway. Exhibitors and ancillary classes – understudy judges them.'

Skelgill makes as if to speak, but then checks himself. The action seems to be exaggerated, as if to suggest he is thinking on his feet, as though ideas are occurring to him.

'Mr Pearson – going back to the meet – the year Mary Wilson disappeared – you were judging the stalls, aye?'

'What if I were?'

Despite Skelgill's best efforts the hostility is never far below the surface; he is obliged to row back.

'It's just that you probably looked at her stall more closely than anyone else. Say there'd been a note pinned – about when she was due back. Especially if she knew she was being judged for best exhibitor.'

'How would I remember that? There weren't nowt.'

That he adds the rider seems to Skelgill to gainsay his proposition. But rather than highlight the contradiction he simply continues.

'Had she made an effort? I mean – was she trying to win?'

Skelgill glances at DS Leyton, whom he can sense is wondering where the conversation is headed. But when he looks back he finds Patrick Pearson staring at him, properly for the first time during their visit; the eyes are dark and brooding.

'She *did* win.' His voice is thick with acrimony. Skelgill blankly returns his gaze; it seems to have the desired effect. 'I fixed the winner's rosette to her stall. *It was us that noticed she'd gone.*'

He places an unusual degree of emphasis upon his final sentence – it is hard to say why – perhaps he resents that there is some credit overdue for this, recognition that he never received. Though it seems a small and rather dubious accolade. In what Skelgill considers is inconsistent with the pitiless nature of this man, he wonders if the disappearance of Mary Wilson might have affected him more than anyone would guess; after all, Mary was a close neighbour's child, of parity in age had he fathered offspring of his own. Skelgill is prompted to play a little trump card, that of his own provenance.

'I were just a strip of a lad. I were at school with Jud Hope. I went with Arthur Hope's search party. Between Seathwaite and Seatoller.'

Skelgill's gamble elicits a reaction from the big man, who shifts awkwardly in his seat, although from his bleak expression there would be no cause to anticipate a positive rejoinder.

'He's alreet, Art.'

'He's retired now – just fixes up his bikes. Jud's got the farm.'

Patrick Pearson scoffs.

'There's no such thing as a farmer retiring.'

Skelgill chuckles amenably.

'Aye – happen that's what Jud probably thinks half the time.'

It is possible that the man forces an ironic grin. Skelgill senses a small breakthrough.

'The Tysons – you'd know the family well.'

'Like I say – I keep to mesen.'

To Skelgill's mind this is not a practicable standpoint. The man might live a mile up a dead-end track – but every time he needs to visit the local shop or post office in Balderthwaite he must pass through the tiny hamlet of Slatterthwaite. Never mind that in these isolated upland communities there can be no such thing as anonymity – how many times would he have directly passed Jean Tyson's cottage? *Thousands?* Hadn't he run over one of her dogs, for Pete's sake!

But Patrick Pearson has folded his arms and his gaze has reverted firmly to the television. The bogus shepherd is now kissing an improbably beautiful milkmaid in a romantically darkened barn. Skelgill feels their welcome (if that could ever be the word for it) has expired – and, besides, there is an accumulating sense of going through the motions in these visits to the historical eyewitnesses. But the legwork has to be done, and at least he can console himself with the phenomenon that, even if little is gleaned – in a way, a lot is absorbed. He long ago realised that he does not have to catch a fish to learn most of what there is to know about an unfamiliar water; the actual experience of having been there frames future speculation in a real context. He catches DS Leyton's eye and signals with a short jerk of his head that they should retreat. DS Leyton does not look disappointed, much as though he has a list of prepared questions in his notebook. They can always come back. For his part, Skelgill feels no need to beat about the bush. Fell folk appreciate straight talking. He gestures casually towards the television.

'We'll leave you to it, sir. Thanks for your time.'

A grunt is all they receive in return. Skelgill glances at the shotgun and inhales and then sighs as if he were about to comment but has thought the better of it. As they depart they hear the volume return to its former level. Outside, they duck into the rain – but instead of diving for his car Skelgill leads his colleague a short distance past the farmhouse where a long, low windowless stone barn stands as the last edifice before the bare fells extend into the cloud. It seems more ancient than the other buildings, roofed with massive roughly trimmed slates. Its muddy yard is heavily rutted; there are no cattle prints; just rain falling in puddles and running in channels. The heavy planked doors are padlocked with a rusty chain. Skelgill begins to approach, but the dogs start up and he turns away.

'Come on Leyton.'

'What were we looking for, Guv?'

'If I knew, Leyton, I wouldn't be getting soaked.'

Back at the wheel, Skelgill executes a three-point turn. His expression is surly as he bends to snatch a parting glance at the farmhouse. Above the undergrowth he sees a curtain of an upper window twitch back into position. He does not mention this to his colleague, but DS Leyton has his own reflections at the ready.

'Crikey, Guv – that was like meeting Frankenstein's monster – I shouldn't like to run into him on a dark night.'

Skelgill nods grimly. Similar thoughts have visited him over the years that he has caught glimpses of the man out on the fells.

They pass the car graveyard again.

'I didn't see a motor, Guv.'

Skelgill understands he means a functioning model.

'There were quad tracks outside that barn. Plus I reckon he's got an old tractor – the sort with no cab. *Massey Ferguson 35*. Nowt else would fit.'

DS Leyton seems unconvinced.

'He weren't exactly dishing out the hospitality, Guv. And I got the feeling he'd burnt all the furniture. I reckon the floorboards are next.'

'You probably think folk are tight in Yorkshire, Leyton.' Skelgill's tone is scornful. 'You've not seen owt. He's probably got thousands stashed under those boards. Besides – what about that TV? It must have cost a pretty penny.'

DS Leyton shakes his jowls phlegmatically.

'Right enough, Guv – and his satellite subscription. That don't come cheap, neither.'

Skelgill nods, but the demands of the track, increasingly treacherous as the ruts fill with run-off from the fellside, begin to occupy his attention. And he is content to be distracted, to defer the post mortem of their encounter. No fish were caught; in time he might understand what exactly he has absorbed of the ostensibly unproductive water.

11. SEAN NICOLSON

Wednesday 3pm, Jopplety How Farm

'It's chalk and cheese, Guv. It makes that geezer Pearson's place look like nuclear winter.'

'The sunshine helps, Leyton.'

While Skelgill is correct to point out that the weather front has hustled through to put a bright face on affairs, his sergeant is equally perspicacious in seeing that Jopplety How Farm is an altogether different prospect from the primordial squalor of Slatterdale Rigg, despite the challenging second-gear climb up the flank of Grange Fell. Having taken a signposted right turn barely a minute out of Balderthwaite, they have found themselves navigating a metalled lane that is both pothole free and bordered by immaculately maintained walls. It is a standard of husbandry contiguous as they reach the farmstead, a square cluster of clean-washed grey stone buildings set around a freshly hosed working yard. *Spick and span* is the cliché that comes to Skelgill's mind; this is the workplace of a conscientious artisan.

Their welcome is of another order, too. Sean Nicolson, a tallish slightly bowed man in his early fifties, stands hospitably on the threshold of the main house. He wears a smart blue boiler suit, that would suggest to Skelgill he has changed for their visit – for not even the most fastidious sheep farmer can still be clean by mid afternoon. And instead of manic barking, a slick young Border Collie slips past the shepherd's legs and, ignoring her master's call of "Lady", prostrates herself at Skelgill's feet; imploring that he should stoop and tickle. It is an irresistible entreaty.

The man wryly laments his misfortune.

'She's daft as a brush. Happen she's going to take a bit of work.'

His voice is gentle, his local accent distinctive (he says "tek" for "take") without being coarse. He turns, leaving the door wide open for the detectives to follow into what is a spacious kitchen, its walls of natural stone and its ceiling beams exposed.

'Make yourselves comfortable, lads.' While he says "mek" for "make" his brogue does not descend to "theesens".

The centrepiece of the kitchen is a broad oak table – they ensconce themselves while he pours tea into patterned mugs from a matching pot that has been readied and left upon a coal-fired *Aga*. On the table itself are milk and sugar and side plates, the latter with reference to a pyramid of familiar bakery produce. While the man's back is still turned, an animated DS Leyton points and mouths "Bowder Scones".

He seems to sense their interest (or perhaps his hearing is especially sharp), for as he approaches with two mugs in one fist and a third in the other he speaks.

'Meg brings them up from the village. Young lass that's got the farm café does the baking. Tuck in if you fancy one.'

Given that the detectives have stopped off at the said establishment, for once Skelgill looks like he is not hungry, and he preoccupies himself with shovelling sugar into his tea. In fact his concentration is engineered, for in Sean Nicolson's manner he finds some recognition – it is hard to place – but he determines not to stare and draw attention to his disquiet. Somewhat ostentatiously he casts about the kitchen as though admiring its features. But in this deliberate act there is a second realisation that perplexes him. While the exterior of the farm is immaculate in its orderly asceticism, the kitchen – though clean and tidy – is extraordinarily fussy. The table sports a colourful embroidered cloth and a bristling centrepiece of dried flowers, and all around are superfluous ornamental items (such as pincushion hearts, corn dollies, and candles) hanging from cupboards and set in niches in the walls; there are wafts of bergamot, cloves and sandalwood, such that the impression is of a rustic gift shop. This stark exterior-versus-interior disparity throws into sharp focus the concomitant contrast between the farmer and his wife.

They say opposites attract – but in Skelgill's personal experience the maxim does not adequately deal with its corollary:

for opposing poles that converge impetuously, a cataclysmic collision is inevitable. Indeed, in most long-standing marriages that he can call to mind, surely *compatibility* is the watchword? Yet never, in some game of 'match the couples' would Skelgill have successfully paired the coquettish barmaid they met at midday with this softly spoken, unassuming shepherd.

He brings his gaze back around to the man. He must have seen him about the dale over the years, which would account for the sense of déjà vu that now visits him. Sean Nicolson is of an age – as Mary Wilson would be – that puts him between generations for Skelgill; he does not fit into the pattern of people with whom he might have mingled. Unlike Patrick Pearson his appearance is not especially distinctive – short-cropped greying hair that might once have been fair, a broad head with regular features. Only in his pale eyes is there a doggedness, an inner determination to fulfil his calling to a small patch in the great rural tapestry. Skelgill becomes conscious of his thoughts beginning to meander, and he makes an effort to tune in to DS Leyton. He is expounding upon their meeting with Mrs Nicolson, and of their understanding that she will be occupied until the evening in her role behind the bar.

'And is that you done for the day, sir?'

It seems his sergeant has dispensed with their standard introduction. Perhaps he assumes the man's wife will have relayed such information. Sean Nicolson's reaction is to avert his eyes – but it might just be a kind of modesty, a self-effacing nature common to many of his ilk. And this is an unaccustomed situation – not least being interviewed by a detective with an accent straight from *The Sweeney*, which has Skelgill wondering if he should have done the talking. However, Sean Nicolson answers evenly.

'There's a couple of other flocks that I mind. I need to go over by Watendlath. But it'll be light while six.'

DS Leyton tilts his head in a birdlike fashion.

'Do they need a lot of looking after, sir? I thought the whole idea with sheep was they took care of themselves.'

Sean Nicolson glances at Skelgill – but he is no wiser than the shepherd as to why his colleague might have chosen this line of questioning. He raises an eyebrow in a way that suggests they are in no hurry and that the man should answer.

'The Herdwicks – they're more self-sufficient. They're what we call *heafed*. It means they roam free – they learn to hold to their own patch – that's the *heaf*. But you still need to make sure they're healthy, or they've not got themselves tangled in twine or wire or sommat like that. The other breeds – there's yowes and their lambs still in-bye – again you need to watch them – and there's always fences and walls to fix, maybe extra feed to put down, and the drinking troughs to be flushed out.'

It is a patient explanation, and DS Leyton seems genuinely interested, and compliments the man on his expertise. Skelgill is beginning to wonder if there is any merit in this soft-soaping, indeed any need for it. He exhibits none of the contempt they have encountered in their interrogation of either Aidan Wilson or Patrick Pearson, nor the outright shell shock of young Nick Wilson. Sean Nicolson's demeanour is more akin to that of a captured airman who, shot down over enemy territory, suspects that despite their pleasantries a worse fate awaits him, but accepts it stoically.

'It's what I've done all my life.'

Now DS Leyton glances at Skelgill, an expression of satisfaction about his features.

'Mr Nicolson, we noticed that you perform a shearing demonstration at the shepherds' meet. Is that what you were doing – going back to the time when Mary Wilson disappeared?'

The man shows no outward sign of diminished composure.

'Aye – I've exhibited since I were a teenager. I were taught by my granddad.'

DS Leyton nods in a businesslike manner.

'And you knew Mrs Wilson well?'

If anything there is perhaps just a hint of surprise in the man's eyes that the detective need ask him this question. DS Leyton qualifies his enquiry.

'What I mean, sir – there's no doubt it was her that you saw leave – at lunchtime, from the shepherds' meet?'

'I were at school with her. We'd known each other since we were bairns.'

DS Leyton inhales between gritted teeth, as though it is the precursor to a more difficult question.

'I appreciate it's going back a long time, sir – and that you probably weren't thinking about it – but was there anything out of the ordinary, like Mrs Wilson leaving when she did? Would that have been a regular thing to do?'

While these queries were raised – probably *ad nauseam* – at the time of the original investigation, and have been met with impatience, obstruction and obfuscation in the last few days, there is no such reaction from Sean Nicolson. His pale blue eyes watch DS Leyton carefully. He bides his time – he does not rush to jump in, nor shake his head nor nod prematurely. Skelgill observes him with interest, wondering what memories, in his case, have percolated through the rocks of ages.

'I were shearing. I looked up. She were just passing. She had the dog on a lead. She were wearing jeans and a white top and a pink headscarf.'

It is a precise answer, delivered in the economical way of fell folk; when there is nothing to say, they will say nothing; when there is something, they will use just the requisite words. But Skelgill detects a misting of the pale eyes. It is fleeting, superficial, but it reveals an undercurrent of what must surely be regret. It is understandable; a girl with whom he grew up; and now the definitive news that she was struck down in her prime. And in that very moment he has just described, the realisation that she was heading to her death. Skelgill thinks he perceives more care, more concern, and more quiet vengeance in this man, than he did in the woman's husband. And yet this too makes sense to him; here is a shepherd, a fellow outdoorsman – after all, he was present, too – and some marauding wolf took one of their flock. Does the man carry a burden of responsibility? Is he thinking, what if he had called out – inquired about her sales success – detained her in some way? Who knows what small intervention might have precipitated a different outcome. But, then again, she may have been determined in her mission. It is along such lines that DS Leyton picks up.

'Mr Nicolson – how would you describe her behaviour?'

'In what way?'

DS Leyton rephrases his question.

'What we're getting at – in light of what we now know – could she have been trying to avoid being noticed?'

'I don't see how you'd do that – in public view. Besides, she looked in at the *Twa Tups*, didn't she?'

It seems the point he makes is that, if anything, Mary Wilson advertised her departure.

'That's correct, sir – her leaving was confirmed by other witnesses – including your wife.'

'Aye.'

DS Leyton screws up his features, as though he is trying to decipher something from his notebook.

'And what did you do, sir – I mean just after that?'

Again there is perhaps the hint of curiosity in the man's eyes, that the detective would be asking him about something he would surely know – yet at the same time he is unperturbed that he does so. And once more his reply comes in measured tones.

'I were called to an emergency. A prize tup had bloated.' Now he glances at Skelgill, who nods to demonstrate his understanding. 'You see, the grass in the holding pen, it's often lush and thick with clover. One of the other shepherds had noticed the tup had cowped, but the owner weren't there. Because I stay for the full day I always keep some *Bloat Guard*. I managed to get the tup to take some – I put a tube down its throat – but it were a bad case. I stayed with it until the vet came – he had to perform a rumenotomy. It weren't a pretty sight.'

DS Leyton is now the one that is looking alarmed. While he does not understand the precise details, there being a mixture of dialect and veterinary science terms, he gets the gist, stomach contents, and all that. He moves quickly on.

'What about afterwards, sir?'

137

'There weren't a lot of time. I start the demonstrations again at two o'clock. There were bait laid on at the *Tups*. I managed to grab a quick bite.'

'And you didn't notice Mary Wilson? Either there at the pub – or in the vicinity?'

Sean Nicolson is shaking his head pensively. But he has no answer.

'Sir, I realise you would have been asked this – but what do you think now, of the suggestion that she was meeting somebody – a person she didn't want others to know about?'

There is a pause before the man replies.

'It's possible, int' it?'

'Was it likely?'

Now he looks intensely at DS Leyton.

'Why would I know Mary's mind?'

His intonation is rather strangely profound, and causes Skelgill to look up (he has been stroking the dog at his feet, which settled upon him as the softest touch immediately they sat down). DS Leyton expounds upon his logic.

'I suppose if she'd said something to you – or someone – that you overheard.'

'Like I've said, I were busy shearing. I happened to glance up – caught a glimpse of her. She didn't look like she were doing owt unusual. It were common knowledge that she took walks with her dog.'

'And the woods were her favourite place?'

Sean Nicolson does not appear convinced by this suggestion.

'I reckon she mainly walked it between her Ma's and the village.'

'Between Slatterthwaite and Balderthwaite?'

'Aye – along the beck. It's a good place to take a dog – the footpath's walled off from the in-bye land.'

Skelgill is nodding to this – as an owner himself, he is acutely aware of the issue of dogs and sheep, that they do not mix; and the risk to the dog if they should. He pictures Patrick Pearson's shotgun – no doubt he would loose off both barrels first and ask questions later. But even this mild mannered shepherd would probably put his flock before a family pet, if push came to shove. DS Leyton continues.

'It makes you wonder why she didn't do that. It would have been her chance to see the nipper.'

He says this rather musingly, as though realising it would be a natural state of affairs. Meanwhile a small furrow seems to have formed on the brow of Sean Nicolson.

'Happen she thought there weren't time for that. She took her car, didn't she?'

DS Leyton shrugs.

'But if she were tight on time, why not just walk round the village?'

'If she wanted to let t' dog off lead. It'd been tied up at her stall all morning.'

There is a pause while DS Leyton glances at his notes. Now he seems to take his cue from the man's last comment.

'What was the arrangement you had with Mrs Wilson regarding the supply of wool, sir?'

Rather as his wife had done, he exhibits a hint of alarm, as though he thinks they believe there was something untoward about this.

'I wouldn't call it an arrangement. I gave it her free. As much as anything she took it off my hands.'

DS Leyton motions as if he is turning imaginary dials.

'What I mean, sir, is what was the practical arrangement. How did she get the wool?'

Sean Nicolson jerks a thumb to indicate out of doors. He has the stout fingers of a farmer.

'I kept some fleeces baled in the barn. She could come for it when she needed it. It were no use to me. It's coarse – and it's deceptively light. A Herdwick's fleece weighs half of most breeds' – that's another reason it don't fetch a lot. Wool's bought by weight. But Mary made a feature of it being traditional local knitwear.'

DS Leyton is nodding.

'So – when would have been the last time she collected some wool, sir?'

Sean Nicolson makes a face of slight bewilderment, as though this is a near impossible question. But after a moment's consideration he replies.

'Mostly the shearing's in August. So it were maybe a month before the meet that she last took some. I reckon she'd have been running low – and she'd have wanted to make plenty of stock for her stall.'

DS Leyton turns his head from side to side, as though his shirt collar is becoming uncomfortable.

'Would that have been the last time you spoke with her, sir?'

Sean Nicolson shakes his head.

'I'd have talked to her at the meet. When we were all setting up, early on – there were the usual crack about the weather – it being good for a change – that there ought to be a decent turnout.'

'Would you say you were on friendly terms?'

Now the man frowns more distinctly – and it might occur to the observer rather odd that he would need to recall this; perhaps the thought simply pains him.

'I knew her well enough. Like I say, we were at school, together – grew up in the dale. And of late she'd been working behind the bar at the *Twa Tups*. I might see her if I went in to pick up Meg on rainy night. Mary had her own car, mind.'

Skelgill, from his more detached viewpoint registers both the addition of the rider and the avoidance of an entirely straight answer. DS Leyton, however, is nodding readily and continues.

'You knew a bit about her business – were you aware of any problems – financial, I'm thinking of? Could she have got into trouble, borrowing money, owing money?'

'Folk could always do with more money – but I doubt if it were that, with Mary.'

There seems to be a flush of colour upon the man's cheeks. Skelgill wonders if this is simply an ingrained principle coming to the fore, neither a lender nor a borrower be, one that is all pervasive in these parts. But this time DS Leyton is quick to pick up on the possible ambiguity in his words.

'What could it have been?'

Now Sean Nicolson reaches for his tea. He drinks as though his mouth has suddenly become dry. When he puts down his mug he stares into it, avoiding eye contact. Then the reason underlying his reticence becomes clear. He speaks with some difficulty.

'Aren't most women murdered – by sex attackers?'

DS Leyton glances at Skelgill, but his superior remains implacable.

'Actually, sir, not statistically. But most female victims *are* murdered by someone known to them.'

Sean Nicolson looks up, his eyes distinctly troubled. He gazes for a moment at Skelgill, and then back at DS Leyton.

'Is that what you think?'

DS Leyton gives a slow shrug of his broad shoulders, like a giant tortoise momentarily retreating into its shell.

'We have to keep an open mind, sir. Reviving an investigation that was closed over twenty years ago – at this stage we're just playing catch-up.'

Sean Nicolson shakes his head slowly.

'I'm not much help. I wish I could be.'

*

'What is it, Leyton?'

Skelgill's sergeant appears to be brooding over a text message he has discovered on his phone.

'Ooh – it's the – er – missus, Guv. Seems like she's in a bit of a pickle. She's got an appointment – one of these ladies' things, you know – regular check? But the littlun's playing up.'

'You talking Keswick?'

'Yeah – the health centre. At four-thirty. The other nippers have got after-school clubs until five-fifteen, so they're under lock and key.'

Skelgill glances at the clock on his dashboard.

'I'll drop you off – we'll be there in ten minutes.'

DS Leyton casts a suspicious glance at his boss.

'What about writing up these interviews, Guv?'

'Leyton – it's kept twenty-odd years – I think the case can wait until tomorrow. Besides –' (and now Skelgill makes an agonised face) 'if Smart gets his way we'll just be going through the motions.'

DS Leyton looks torn. It is obviously a tempting offer, but he suspects he ought to reject it.

'What about my motor, Guv – it's back at Penrith?'

'Get the bus, Leyton – else someone's going to be driving across in the morning. Failing that, I'll come and pick you up.'

DS Leyton is now really wide-eyed. It is a rare double dose of altruism from his boss.

'I'm sure I can manage the bus, Guv – thanks all the same.' He looks rather forsakenly at his handset. 'But that'd be great if I could get the missus out of jail. I can work on the report tonight.'

Skelgill does not answer – but he begins to drive in a more rapid, yet carefree fashion, and might almost be humming a tune under his breath. In fact, it is a reaction to a day in which he feels his head has been stuffed full of everything and nothing, such that these ineffable properties have cancelled one another out. The flickering sun, slanting between the ancient oaks of Borrowdale seems to have a mellowing effect upon his craggy features.

'There they are, Guv!'

DS Leyton's exclamation comprises the first words spoken since their discussion. Skelgill swings the car into an entrance marked "Emergency Vehicles Only" and stops on double-yellow lines where Mrs Leyton waits under the entrance canopy. She is leaning over a pushchair; she looks up despairingly and then with relief at their arrival. They are dead on time. Skelgill's sergeant bales out like a paratrooper warned of an imminent crash landing, in his desperation inadvertently displaying an expanse of unseemly flesh.

Skelgill ducks to catch a glimpse across the car of his sergeant's troubled spouse, who forces a thankful smile and exchanges a quick word with her husband before she dashes into the building. The buggy has its rain cover fitted and most of what is visible within, from Skelgill's angle can be summed up in the word tonsils, from which cavity emanates a prodigious yowl. Here is a predicament outwith his comfort zone, and he is compelled to observe how his colleague will deal with it. DS Leyton looks momentarily at sea – but then he produces from his jacket a bunch of keys, with its Millwall-supporter's plastic lion key fob. He dangles the little creature and the child's two small hands reach out, snatch the bunch and feed the toy directly into its mouth. Silence! DS Leyton glances across at Skelgill, and grins, and gives him the thumbs up.

But Skelgill does not respond. He stares at his sergeant, or the infant, or both – almost unseeing – and then, without a wave of farewell, crunches the car into gear and speeds off. Almost immediately he fishes for his mobile phone, sets it ringing in speaker mode, and traps it in the sun visor above his head. After quite a long delay, a tentative DS Jones answers.

'Oh – hi.'

He knows immediately she is with DI Smart – and is he irked that out of some misplaced good manners she has not called him "Guv". It sounds like they too are travelling. He guesses that she will not have him on speaker – but he cannot take it for granted there will be no eavesdropping. Moreover, it is generally possible to decipher a one-sided conversation. His voice is low, his words curt.

'If asked I'm phoning about when you're coming back.' He does not wait for her assent. 'Did they test Nick Wilson's DNA?'

There is a significant pause; she is clearly thinking about how to couch her answer.

'Almost certainly not.'

'Right – I'm getting it organised. I'm fetching one of Herdwick's crew now. Can you chase it up once it's in the system?'

Skelgill is referring to the test result, since it is she that has been liaising with the various forensic departments in this regard.

'I should be able to let you know tomorrow.'

'Call me when you get a chance – on your own.'

DS Jones does not answer – and it becomes evident why. A male voice, a Mancunian drawl comes over the airwaves. There is glee in the tone.

'Is that you, Skel? We've got the slimy pervert bang to rights, cock! I expect the Chief's already told you to drop everything your end.'

DI Smart must have grabbed his colleague's handset. Skelgill pulls his mobile phone from the sun visor and tosses it over his shoulder into the flatbed of his car, where accumulated fishing paraphernalia cushions its fall. He jams his right foot on the accelerator and overtakes the vehicle in front of him, a brewery company's dray with an advertisement featuring boozing England rugby union players and the slogan *'Swig Low'* painted on its side. A driver coming the other way flashes him, but he merely grimaces; he is too preoccupied to think either about beer or road rage. As per his instructions, DS Jones's answers were shrewdly couched. It would have sounded to DI Smart like he wanted to know when she might return to Cumbria. But that is evidently not going to be tonight.

12. MEMORY LANE

Thursday, early morning

There are only three ways by car to reach Buttermere village – three ways 'home' – up Lorton Vale from the Cockermouth direction, skirting Crummock Water and sometimes the last resort in winter; or via one of the high passes from Derwentwater, either the Honister or the Newlands. Skelgill has opted for the latter. The approach is from the western side of the lake, traversing the gravity-defying screes of Causey Pike. It is a route he considers both more direct and a refreshing change of scene; it avoids Balderthwaite, for the time being. But there is another reason that he won't quite admit to himself: had he taken the Honister Pass he almost certainly would have met his mother coming the other way on her boneshaker of a bicycle. Complications would ensue. He would offer a lift; she would give him short shrift. She would want to know his business; he would be taciturn. And so on – an uncooperative exchange sidetracking them both from their ends. That said, he experiences a small nagging regret – because no doubt she could more than usefully answer some of the questions bobbing about in the slack water of his subconscious.

And he can hardly claim to be in a hurry. He has halted at Newlands Hause; his soot-stained Kelly kettle is on a rumbling boil and streaky bacon spits in a dented aluminium pan on his meths stove. Better here than in his kitchen, with Cleopatra (now in the custody of his daily dog-sitting neighbour) drooling down his trousers. Besides, there is the scenery to savour. The autumn rains have saturated Buttermere Moss, and the tumbling waters of Moss Force are foaming white in the low early morning light. Beneath a clear sky the air is still – though likely as not this will change as the day wears on – but in the meantime an exaltation of meadow pipits celebrates the benign conditions, swirling and chasing about the deserted parking area; a sure sign of winter to come, that they have abandoned their territories and are readying to head for the salt marshes of the Solway.

Skelgill's volcano kettle begins to erupt, and he turns his attention to fixing up his tea and bacon roll. He clears a space on the flatbed of his shooting brake and sits facing due west. Way down below there is just a glimpse of one of the Holme Islands, like a raft becalmed in the southern reaches of Crummock Water; beyond, the fells rise to the distant rounded summit of Great Borne, part of the great rollercoaster ridge that divides Lorton Vale from its neighbouring valley, the real-life Ennerdale. Skelgill's thoughts drift accordingly – after all, this morning he is on a trip down memory lane. And he cannot banish the earworm, the theme tune of the soap opera that Patrick Pearson was watching yesterday. Just as he and DS Leyton were leaving, a cliffhanger ending had seen the lustful milkmaid's axe-wielding fiancé about to enter the barn to replace his tool; a sure fire case of *in flagrante delicto*. The credits had rolled and the band had struck up. To Skelgill's mind it is a mournful dirge – but, his mother being an aficionado, it has long been embedded in his psyche, a Pavlovian stimulus that conjures feelings of a compulsory early bedtime with only school to look forward to (thirty years ago *Ennerdale* was screened on Monday and Wednesday nights, and no repeats). Skelgill chews contemplatively. He supposes there is some compensation in being an adult. That said, the day's duties remain to be done, with the additional obligation to change the world.

Morning twilight slips down the dale like an ebbing tide, and strands of sunlight are just illuminating the grey slate rooftops of Buttermere village when Skelgill rounds the end of his mother's terraced cottage and enters via the unlocked back door. The small kitchen looks much as it has always done; it will have been cleaned and swept this morning, like every morning; a stockpot of soup simmers on the range, the familiar aroma of lamb, potatoes and onions; his habit would be to sample it – but he has had his fill, and besides has other things in mind. He passes into the narrow hall and enters the tiny parlour at the front of the house, by custom a room rarely used, where his great-grandparents' oak casement clock has ticked away the generations in splendid isolation, sometimes its only human contact the weekly wind. Against the opposite wall stands a traditional walnut sideboard, and from its middle drawer Skelgill extracts a large, well-thumbed scrapbook – the family album, no less, though infrequently used these days he guesses; at clan gatherings even the old folks cluster round their mobile phones to exchange videos of the exploits of their progeny.

He shifts a vase of artificial hydrangeas and lays the album on a cross-stitch cloth that covers a mahogany drop-leaf table. The thick pages lie like layers of geological sediment; he makes a stab at the desired epoch, and is not far out. He half squints at the contents; there are reminders he would rather not receive; strange how arguably the most profound entries – births, marriages, deaths – are the minutest clippings of all. A lifetime, ten million moments, encapsulated in the space of three postage stamps. And then, to his relief, he finds what he is looking for: an A5-sized leaflet, black print on yellowing white stock, so like the one he has in his pocket that it is quite remarkable; here is something that hasn't changed: the design of the Balderthwaite shepherds' meet brochure. The archive copy, pressed for posterity by his mother, dates from the year after Mary Wilson disappeared; by custom it lists the winners at the preceding meet.

The cellophane pages covering the contents of the album have become brittle and have lost their adhesive properties. As he raises the board leaf to extract the pamphlet a press cutting escapes from the reverse side and flutters to the floor; he ignores it for the time being. He turns the leaflet over; sure enough the results are displayed on the back page. There are so many classes for sheep – the likes of Best Mouth Female, Best Gimmer Lamb, Best Horned Tup, and so on and so forth. He scans the dense type, squinting now for good reason; rivers of white seem to criss-cross a black hinterland. But his persistence pays off, for there it is – near the foot of the page: "Best Exhibitor – Mrs M. Wilson, *Shear Bliss Knitwear* – 1st Prize." So Patrick Pearson was right.

And she never got to wear her rosette.

Skelgill is staring at the clock when it begins to strike. Eight. He doesn't count – but he has heard eight so many more times than any other number that he doesn't need to; he knows eight is coming, and he knows what eight feels like when it is just an echo. Eight am – time to leave for school, or be late and get a clout round the lug. Eight pm – when the last haunting strains of *Ennerdale* have died away and the adverts are coming on – time for bed, or get a clout round the lug.

On the last stroke he snaps out of his reverie. The pale newspaper cutting on the burgundy mat is obtrusive in his peripheral vision; salient in the speck-free parlour, like the first leaf of autumn to fall upon a freshly mown sward. He stoops and swoops it up – and the headline catches his eye.

"Buttermere Lad Shatters Dickson's Record!"

He stares at the piece. There is a photograph, black and white, grainy – hardly distinguishable, really. Except of course the callow youth breaking the tape (and not knowing how to celebrate) is he. No other runners are in sight. He remembers the content of the article, despite that he has not set eyes on it for a good decade and a half. Jake Dickson – the invincible Jake Dickson from Balderthwaite – twice his age back in those days, a man to his boy, the record holder and unbeaten for years on end. And yet he had beaten both him and the record.

He scrutinises the shepherds' meet brochure once more. Sure enough – there is his event: Scawdale Fell Fell Race (by belligerent tradition a double 'fell'); and his category: Senior Male: 1st D Skelgill (Buttermere, 39:59), 2nd B Underscar (Keswick, 42:43), 3rd J Ingshead (Grange, 43:18). He stares at the page – fighting hard it seems to contain his bewilderment. He might be thinking that he won by almost three minutes – an unprecedented margin of victory in the entire history of the race – and no wonder there was no one else in the photograph! But, actually, he is contemplating something else altogether. *Where was Jake Dickson?*

*

'You'll be getting sick of the sight of me, lad.'

Guided by a loud clanging Skelgill has arrived at a dank corner of Walter Dickson & Co's premises to find mechanic Nick Wilson employing a lump hammer to shift the recalcitrant brake disc of a dung-spattered farm pick-up. It conjures a reference on his previous visit to his own primitive manual of motor maintenance. Indeed the young man starts as though caught red-handed using such an illicit method – but his fears prove to be grounded elsewhere. He remains on bended knee beside the vehicle, his eyes averted and his head bowed as though for an executioner.

'Is it me – am I the suspect?'

Skelgill is both perplexed and disarmed by the meek rejoinder.

'What are you talking about?'

'I heard it on the radio – it said the police have interviewed a suspect.'

Now it is Skelgill that looks dumbfounded. For a moment he flounders to find a response.

'Nick, lad – how could you be a suspect?'

It takes the young man a few seconds to answer.

'But you took me DNA last night. Then it was on the news this morning.'

Skelgill has to stem a torrent of questions that threatens to swamp his composure. The radio? The police? A suspect? He digs his hands into his trouser pockets and turns a circle on the spot.

'Aye – and I explained that was nowt to do with you personally.'

He realises it would be accurate to say he did not go into convincing detail when he and Dr Herdwick's assistant visited the caravan to take the cheek swab. However, the boy now nods dejectedly. Skelgill, meanwhile, cannot restrain his curiosity any longer.

'So, what did you hear on the radio?'

The fresh-faced mechanic looks up, surprised that either the detective doesn't know or – surely more likely – he is testing him out in some way.

'It just said the police have found a suspect and the investigation is continuing.'

Skelgill now drops any pretence of omniscience.

'Did it say where, or who – or what did it say?'

Nick Wilson shakes his head.

'I reckon that was all.'

Skelgill looks dissatisfied, though he turns away to suggest his annoyance is directed elsewhere and not at the sensitive young man.

'Was it on local radio – or national?'

'Local. That's what I listen to, any road.'

Skelgill nods, and again perambulates in a circle, wider this time, requiring him to step over discarded tools and car parts. How has the information got out? Has DI Smart held a press briefing? Has the Chief approved a media release? Or has there been a leak of some sort? Only a handful of people know about the Manchester suspect. A leak is a matter for concern – but nothing compared to a release authorised by the Chief, for she would not have done so unless she gives credence to Smart's end of the investigation. But why has he not been informed? And why has DS Jones not contacted him?

But he must park these anxieties. There is little he can achieve without making inquiries, and he cannot do that here. Besides, there is his own lead to follow up, despite the body blow of this new development.

'I'm here to see your gaffer.' He sees the boy flinch. He reaches and pats him firmly on the shoulder. 'And you're in the clear, right?'

Nick Wilson forces a reluctant grin.

'He went to Keswick to pick up some brake pads and stuff. He said he'd be back by nine. We've promised the job done by ten.'

Skelgill checks his watch. It is a few minutes to nine.

'I'll wait in my car – that way I can see him coming.' He turns away, and mutters under his breath. 'And I can listen to the radio and find out how the police are getting on.'

*

'Morning, sir – have you got a minute?'

Though taken unawares – carrying a stack of boxes and not seeing that Skelgill is actually seated in his car with the window wound down – Jake Dickson reacts coolly to Skelgill's presence.

'Alreet, laddo?'

Skelgill indicates with a jerk of his thumb the passenger side.

'Do you want to jump in, sir?'

The man, both arms laden, gives a bow of the head.

'Let me just give these pads and discs to the lad.'

Skelgill watches as Jake Dickson disappears into the gloom and emerges half a minute later; little time to have conferred, albeit Skelgill had relayed nothing of note to Nick Wilson. It is the first proper look he has had of him; previously he was in overalls, up to his chest in the inspection pit, shrouded in darkness. He has longish black hair, strong features and an almost unnaturally tanned complexion. He wears a leather bomber jacket over a t-shirt and tight-fitting *Levi's,* and Chelsea boots. It is an ensemble that, to Skelgill's eye, smacks of the faded rock star, a man who still fancies himself, blind to the crow's feet and pot belly that betray the self-image. He swings himself casually into the passenger seat and eyeballs Skelgill.

'What's all this "sir"? You're one of us, laddo. What's wrong with good old Jake?'

Skelgill determines that he will not yield to this subtle coercion, despite that he suffers small pangs of guilt; there is respect for an elder, and a once formidable reputation.

'How about we compromise on Mr Dickson for the time being.'

Skelgill frames his reply as a statement that is not up for negotiation.

Jake Dickson slaps his hands on his thighs and then upon the console in front of him.

'You don't see many of these around.'

'You mean I'm easily recognised.'

'You are plain-clothes, after all.'

Skelgill raises an eyebrow.

'I shouldn't like to creep about incognito. I'm here to help, not spy.'

The man makes a hissing sound, and looks sideways at Skelgill, a confident smirk across his full-lipped mouth.

'And I'd help you – if only I could.'

His retort seems to preclude an involvement that has not yet been requested; it seems he still vies to control the situation.

'Mr Dickson.' It must be clear that he is not going to escape whatever Skelgill wants; and in his dark eyes there is a flicker of alarm as Skelgill produces the leaflet borrowed from his mother's scrapbook. He hands it over. 'I wanted to ask you about this.'

Jake Dickson again makes the hissing expiration; he is like a smoker shorn of his cigarette.

'Ee, lad – this is going back some.'

'The results are for the year Mary Wilson disappeared.'

Jake Dickson flips over the pamphlet as though he is familiar with its layout. He permits himself an ironic chuckle.

'Have you come to rub it in at long last?'

Skelgill inwardly bridles at this remark – as if this were the most significant event in his later-to-be-curtailed fell running career; it might have been a milestone, but in hindsight parochial in the scale of things. But that is an argument for another day, if ever. Instead he speaks generously.

'You were the next best in the field by a country mile.'

Jake Dickson moves as if to respond positively – but then he checks himself as though there is something double-edged about Skelgill's praise. He stares almost fearfully at the leaflet. Then he remarks, somewhat half-heartedly.

'Brian Underscar were a decent runner.'

'Two minutes behind your record. He wouldn't live with you.'

Jake Dickson's face has become taut, he is tight-lipped; the bravado has seeped away. He nods slowly; he appears to know what is coming. Skelgill intones calmly.

'Mr Dickson, you didn't run.'

Now the man reacts, unexpectedly as far as Skelgill is concerned, his features morphing into a mixture of the slightly obsequious and the slightly patronising. He rubs his oil-stained hands together as he must have done a thousand times with *Swarfega* at the end of a job. He dips his head and looks at Skelgill through narrowed eyes.

'Truth be told, lad – your reputation preceded you. I decided I weren't going to be shown up by a bairn.'

Skelgill looks away. He stares directly ahead into the cavernous mouth of the garage, his gaze unseeing, his mind's eye recalling the day. It was hot for late September. The runners, so often gloved and hopping up and down on the start line of a Lakeland fell race, were subdued, taking on drinks, several even crowding in the shade of the great oak on one side of the field. He knew nothing about sports science or dehydration; he'd grown up thinking headaches were just something that happened when the sun was cracking the cobbles and you were outdoors too long, too much radiation on your head. And when the gun had fired, he'd sprinted for the gate. He was first there and never once looked over his shoulder. Had he wanted an easier race he could have relented and jogged with the chasing pack. As in life, he ploughed his own furrow. In consequence he saw little of the grown men who were his fellow competitors.

'Mr Dickson, what did you do?'

The man regards him, slyly it seems – but he does not withhold an explanation.

'I allus ran from the back.' His inflection elicits a nod from Skelgill. 'Starting gun went off – I nipped round the side of the *Twa Tups*.'

Skelgill is trying not to react – albeit he feels like he is experiencing the unravelling of one of several promising threads that dangle from the confused web in his mind.

'Then what?'

'Sneaked into t' lounge. Had a couple of pints while t' race were on.'

Skelgill senses he must be looking unnaturally unresponsive. He makes an effort to seem more casual.

153

'Aye? Who served you?'

Jake Dickson strangles an exclamation, as if to say how would he be expected to remember something like that? But then he answers.

'It would have been arl Jim, as used to keep the place. Retired to Whitehaven. They say he's dead now.'

Skelgill nods, but he does not allow his thoughts to drift to the coastal town and the purportedly deceased witness.

'How long did you stay there?'

'Until after I reckoned the last runners were down.'

Skelgill is perplexed. Jake Dickson was generally expected to win; there would surely have been an inquest.

'Didn't they want to know where you were?'

The man shrugs.

'Can't say as folk were that bothered. I'd put my tracksuit on – I limped around a bit. I might have said to one or two that I'd pulled a hamstring. Once the fuss were over folk were paying attention to other things – announcement of t' sheep classes – and all that. Soon enough they were getting kaylied int' pub – it were all forgotten.'

Skelgill is pensive. He does not want his next question to sound portentous.

'In the time you were in the *Twa Tups*, did you see Mary Wilson?'

'I never saw her.'

There is something about his answer, not least that it comes almost imperceptibly too quickly, that sets a little alarm bell ringing for Skelgill. But to probe any further just now would show more of his hand than he is ready to reveal. He nods, in the manner of expressing disappointment.

'What did you say at the time – about not running?'

'Whatever I were asked, I answered. I can't recall.'

Skelgill means what was the man asked by the police – and, interestingly, Jake Dickson seems to interpret the question as such. Though he is not sufficiently au fait with the files, Skelgill imagines that the fell runners would have been considered unlikely suspects. There is a vague memory of his own sentiments – knowing that suspicion hung like an autumn mist over Borrowdale, over everyone, including himself – but that it could not really be attributed to him because he was running when Mary Wilson left the meet and drove to a spot on the opposite side of the valley. The race went off at 12.30pm; the stragglers were back within the hour. But not so Jake Dickson. He never left the village. And yet, it seems, this fact was overlooked in the original investigation.

Skelgill also wonders why it had never registered with him that the multiple-times previous winner, record holder and pre-race favourite wasn't in the frame – indeed hadn't figured in the race. But then, not only had he been front-runner, having broken the tape he was chaperoned away by his supporters. Swamped by a concoction of exhaustion and euphoria, and bearing a youthful ignorance of the protocols of congratulating fellow competitors, he hadn't paid much attention. And, at fifteen, none of his relatives would have had the notion of marching him over to the *Twa Tups* for a celebratory pint (despite that he and Jud Hope had been managing to buy halves of mild from the landlord in Buttermere for the best part of a year).

Skelgill is nodding somewhat blandly in response to Jake Dickson's last answer. Beneath the surface, his instincts are telling him to get out of here – not so easy, since they are in his car. But he needs some time and space to digest what he has absorbed. He finds himself asking what must sound like an ill-informed question.

'You knew Mary Wilson, aye?'

The man regards him a little warily.

'Course I knew her – we were all in the same crowd growing up.'

At this juncture Skelgill might pose one of several highly pertinent questions – concerning Mary Wilson's boyfriends, affairs, relationships – but he has a strong sense that Jake Dickson has not provided the whole truth thus far, and he does not want his impressions clouded by further evasion and fabrication. And why spook him any more than is necessary? In this respect, his next question perhaps wrong-foots the man.

'How come her lad works for you?'

Jake Dickson leans back in the passenger seat and folds his arms. He makes a face that is rather condescending, perhaps as he thinks befits his position in charge.

'He used to hang around – come down on his bike from his nan's place – Slatterthwaite.' Skelgill nods to show he understands the social geography. 'He never said much, but I could tell he liked to watch. I started giving him little jobs – like washing cars, sweeping up. Then one day I got called away in the middle of replacing the headlamp bulbs on a *Defender*. When I got back he'd done it.' Jake Dickson shrugs, as if to rest his case. 'I started him with a Saturday job – then when he left school I took him on full time.' He grins sardonically. 'He's not one for looking at the *Haynes* manual, but he's got a good knack. Works things out for himself.'

Skelgill is listening reflectively. A 'kinaesthetic learner' – a rare plus point that he scored in an aptitude test; some police training course, back in the mists of time. When he does not respond, or ask something else, Jake Dickson takes it upon himself to make the running.

'He reckons you gave him a DNA test last night – what's that all about?'

Skelgill sets aside his reminiscences; his demeanour stiffens.

'There's a few gaps in the original investigation – we're just trying to fill them in.' He screws up his face, momentarily revealing his front teeth. 'Something and nothing.'

He notices Jake Dickson is now, if not *wringing* his hands, then again going through the motions of applying the invisible cleaning gel.

'Nick reckons he's heard on the radio you've got a suspect. He can't be a local man – that were ruled out at the time.'

This statement is clearly couched to winkle some answer from Skelgill.

'That'd be about right, Mr Dickson.'

The man makes a humming sound, which might be a sign of satisfaction, possibly even relief, though it is quickly truncated, and now he begins to shift rather impatiently in his seat. Skelgill obliges him.

'Mr Dickson – I'd better not keep you from your work – I believe you've got a rush job on.'

'Aye.' The man reaches for the catch and begins to open the door. 'Should be done in time.'

Skelgill's tone becomes more conversational.

'How long have you been proprietor here?'

Jake Dickson seems happy to answer.

'Me uncle Walter died five years back – but it's been above ten since I've been running it myself. He were crippled with rheumatism. That were another reason young Nick came in handy.'

Skelgill is looking at the sign above the lintel. It strikes him that it states 'Walter Dickson & Co' rather than the more usual '& Son'.

'Are you married?'

The man grins, and his boyish good looks momentarily flicker beneath the seasoned veneer.

'Not me – footloose and fancy free, as they say.'

He clicks his tongue and slides out of the car, closing the door perhaps more firmly than is necessary. Skelgill watches, he has a jaunty walk, and he sweeps his hair back over his ears with both hands as he disappears into the workshop.

Skelgill engages the ignition, reverses and turns the vehicle, and accelerates past the sign for Balderthwaite farm café. His stomach protests, but his mind is preoccupied. Jake Dickson seems satisfied with his morning's work. Yet it is a curious statement, his failure to run – an admission of cowardice, of a sort – and surely quite out of character. Therefore is this the lesser of two evils?

13. HELIX UNWINDS

Thursday midday, Penrith

'The Chief's been on the warpath all morning, Guv.'

'Tell me something new, Leyton.'

'She even came down in person – in case you were ignoring your phone.'

Skelgill glances at the handset that now lies upon his desk; there are numerous missed calls and messages.

'What's all the fuss?'

DS Leyton does a double take, as if he knows his boss is being disingenuous – but when he sees only belligerence in his superior's expression he quickly readjusts.

'Oh, well, Guv – I suppose you've been busy. I didn't hear it myself – but there was an unauthorised report on the local radio – that we're interviewing a suspect in the Mary Wilson case.'

Skelgill stares implacably at his subordinate.

'That'll be Smart, then. Piling pressure on the Chief.'

But DS Leyton shakes his head.

'George on the front desk says it was claimed as "a source close to the police" – besides, DI Smart's been screaming blue murder. Seems he was planning a press conference this afternoon down in Manchester – and was going to make a big fanfare of it. Now we're being inundated with requests from the media to name the suspect.'

Skelgill seems relatively indifferent to the predicament.

'I'm surprised she's been taken in. That confession's got more holes in it than my old hiking socks.'

DS Leyton shrugs resignedly.

'Maybe it's the chance to crack such a high-profile case – the limelight can be dazzling. Except now it's rained on their parade and the Chief wants to know who was responsible.'

Skelgill shifts in his seat and draws his mug towards him, but it contains only tepid dregs from yesterday and he is plainly irked by this state of affairs. He speaks tersely.

'What's to stop the con telling someone he's put his hand up for it?'

'I believe they've had him in solitary since he started to sing, Guv.' DS Leyton frowns introspectively. When he continues his voice is more tentative. 'Reading between the lines, I wondered if the Chief suspected DS Jones.'

'What!'

Skelgill looks like he would summarily shoot the messenger. DS Leyton holds up his hands in surrender.

'Just the impression I got, Guv.'

'Leyton, there's not a cat in hell's chance that Jones would leak something.'

DS Leyton is a little relieved that Skelgill has not asked him directly what the Chief said to prompt him to form this hypothesis.

'Thing is, Guv – DS Jones is quite pally –' (he sees further disapproval, a blanching of Skelgill's grey-green eyes) 'well, not exactly pally – but she knows that Kendall Minto geezer. I'm sure she once said they were at school together. And George reckons he saw him trying his chat on her when he was here for the press briefing on Tuesday.'

Skelgill is now sufficiently annoyed as to have risen and crossed to his window. The weather is transitioning yet again, in keeping with the unpredictable pattern that is typical of an English autumn, and wood pigeons and jackdaws are being swept across a chequered sky like windblown leaves. A scudding cloud obscures the sun and the browning landscape seems to darken beneath his scowl.

'If it were Minto why was it on the radio? Why not in his newspaper – or on their website?'

'I was thinking about that, Guv – but say he wanted to cover his tracks? They're in cahoots anyway, that media lot. He gives them a little tip off, next time it's the other way around.'

Skelgill does not reply. He stalks over to the map on the wall behind his desk. He stares, unmoving; it is not apparent that he is seeking some detail. DS Leyton twiddles his thumbs as if to distract himself from his boss's displeasure. Yet when Skelgill speaks it is as though he has banished their conversation from his mind.

'What Jones said – about treating the witnesses as suspects – remember?'

DS Leyton nods obediently, glad for the change of subject. He senses his superior wants to make some announcement, but that it is against his nature to do so.

'Are you onto something, Guv?'

'Might be something and nothing.' Skelgill realises it is the second time today he has employed the platitude.

DS Leyton continues brightly.

'You always say, Guv – you never know when the truth might be staring you in the face – or the lies – *hah!*'

Skelgill appears only to be half listening. Perhaps he is picturing the events up in the oak woods of Borrowdale. He intones slowly, still addressing the map.

'At the time Mary Wilson disappeared there were half a dozen possible explanations, and nobody seemed to be panicking. If our lot had known what we do – Jones is right – they would have come down on the dale like a ton of bricks.'

DS Leyton is nodding, but also beginning to look doubtful.

'At the end of the day, though, Guv – they did implement the mass DNA testing. That was unprecedented. And it put the locals in the clear.'

Skelgill turns on his heel – and is about to gainsay this point – that only a positive result would have been meaningful; a negative proved very little. But there is now another twist in the tale – in the microscopic double helix that is deoxyribonucleic acid – news of which he awaits from DS Jones. He relents, and instead decides to relate what he has discovered this morning.

'Hark, Leyton – here's just one example. Nick Wilson's gaffer – Jake Dickson – he were supposed to be in the fell race. That went off at 12.30pm and would have kept him busy for three-quarters of an hour. Except he never ran. He made himself scarce – he went into the back room of the *Twa Tups*. From there he could have seen Mary Wilson going to her car.'

DS Leyton is literally wide eyed.

'What – are you thinking he followed her, Guv?'
But Skelgill shakes his head, and his expression is sour.
'Leyton – he could have hitched a lift with her for all I know – but the point is, was he even interviewed?'
DS Leyton glances up a little sheepishly at the stack of files that he has deposited on Skelgill's tall grey metal cabinet.
'I dunno, Guv. Mind you – if he were – it would be interesting to know what he said.'
Skelgill remains far from enthused. Perhaps surprisingly he is more concerned about the general point than the specific.
'If this had happened yesterday we'd want to know what folk did between 1pm and 2pm – chapter and verse, backed up by witnesses. While it was fresh in their minds we'd speak to every man Jack who knew her, and plenty that didn't who turned up at the meet.' He slumps heavily into his chair, his head flung back like a patient preparing for his dentist. 'Twenty-odd years later – it's the perfect excuse to be unreliable.'
DS Leyton rests his stout forearms on his compatibly broad thighs and exhales deeply.
'Except that geezer Dickson has remembered, Guv.'
Skelgill allows the chair to spring forward. He grimaces pensively – his vague notion of the confession being a lesser evil passes fleetingly across his thoughts once more. He does not reply.
His sergeant remains upbeat. He jerks a thumb above his shoulder.
'I can start working through the files, Guv – see what we've got.'
But Skelgill does not share his colleague's enthusiasm.
'I reckon I know the answer, Leyton – like Jones said, folk were asked what they saw, not what they were doing.'
'But – Jake Dickson, Guv. I mean – if it's at odds with what he's just told you?'
Skelgill nods reluctantly at his colleague. He suspects that, if Jake Dickson were even formally interviewed, he sheltered behind the assumption that he ran the fell race, and therefore was considered of little significance as a witness. That would

161

have suited him; plainly he did not intend to advertise the fact that he chickened out of the event.

After a few moments' silence, DS Leyton launches himself to his feet with an accompanying groan.

'I'll go for some cha, eh, Guv?'

Skelgill does not object. He continues to sit broodingly, until after a few minutes his mobile phone bursts into life. The ringtone tells him it is DS Jones. Slowly, he reaches to tap the speaker button; and his greeting is monosyllabic.

'Jones.'

DS Jones hesitates – her intake of breath is audible – as though in his single word there are kaleidoscopic nuances to be decoded before she can appropriately respond. In the event she decides to skip formalities.

'You're not going to believe this, Guv.'

At this moment DS Leyton reappears in the doorway bearing two mugs – he catches her words and hesitates, wondering if he should make a diplomatic retreat. But Skelgill beckons him impatiently.

'Jones – hold your horses – here's Leyton just come in. Start from the beginning.'

DS Leyton reaches to pass Skelgill his tea, and leaning over the handset he greets his colleague.

'Morning, Emma – or, afternoon, I should say. How's rainy Manchester?'

'Hi –' She is about to extend the exchange – but then must think the better of it. 'We have the DNA test results back on Nick Wilson.'

DS Leyton gazes inquiringly at Skelgill.

'What's this, Guv?'

Skelgill scowls, but – having taken a palliative sup of his steaming tea – he softens.

'Leyton – last night – when I saw your bairn chomping on your lion mascot key fob. I thought, what if the DNA we've been chasing after belonged to Mary Wilson's bairn?'

Now DS Leyton is flabbergasted.

'But – why didn't they think of checking that?'

Skelgill shrugs contrarily, but when he does not answer DS Jones offers some mitigation.

'I guess they were set on a particular frame of reference. They were trying to match an adult male – not to eliminate unlikely or impossible suspects. They had limited resources and they were swamped. The processing of samples took days and even weeks – not hours like it does now. The comparison procedure was manual not computerised. In any case, it's not Nick Wilson's DNA.'

'*Not?*'

Now Skelgill jerks indignantly into life. He stands up and rests his hands on his hips, like a traffic policeman preparing to halt the flow but unsure of which direction to select. He had assumed she was about to tell him that his hunch has proved correct. Instead, she has casually tossed a spanner into the works.

DS Leyton, meanwhile, has gathered his wits.

'Whose DNA is it?'

'It remains unidentified – there's no match on the system – except –'

For some reason DS Jones falters – and it takes a prompt from her fellow sergeant.

'Go on, girl.'

'Well, the lab didn't just compare Nick Wilson's sample with the key fob profile – they automatically cross-referenced it with the entire database collected for Operation Double Helix.' Now she clears her throat. It is perhaps just a nervous affectation, but nonetheless it creates a small moment of suspense around what she is about to say. 'The thing is – Nick Wilson's biological father is not Aidan Wilson. It's Sean Nicolson.'

*

Skelgill finds himself trying to remember exactly *when* do the leaves fall off the trees? Sure, there are leaves down, and some yellowing or browning, but the great bulk of deciduous matter has yet to be shed. He supposes it is the second half of October when 'fall' as the Americans call it actually gets into full swing. Right now, with sunlight filtering through a largely green canopy, he could be excused for believing it is still late summer. A little earlier the erratic weather produced a spike in the mercury that touched seventy, though it is cooling now as the sun slides from its modest zenith. But Mother Nature shows few signs of pulling in her horns. Striding from the Bowder Stone he has already heard a chiffchaff – too late to be a breeding bird, instead a swansong of sorts, before it sets off for its sub-Saharan wintering grounds; warm pockets of air buzz with insects – there is plenty for a hungry warbler to eat, to fatten up for his journey. And though the path-side vegetation is in retreat, resilient herbs are flowering: stinging nettles, red campion and wood woundwort. More autumnal, true, are the airborne seeds of rosebay willowherb that drift on the breeze; they possess the magical property of being able to pass through the dense forest unhindered, they are fairies, of course, and impossible to grab, and Skelgill has made half a dozen unsuccessful attempts.

Such esoteric musings are pricked as he reaches the offshoot of the path that DS Leyton had noticed on their last visit. The gate is unlatched and half open and Skelgill frowns with concern. Just beyond is the worn platform of bare rock from which climbers practise their abseiling technique, Devil's Lowp, they call it – though he has no idea if this is just a modern appellation, it being a colloquial rather than an historic name. Someone had joked about witches being made to jump, to 'lowp', to prove their innocence. He leans over carefully; the smooth slab is slick with lingering dew, and it might only be a hundred feet to the bottom, but that is more than enough to kill. As he stares down upon the tumble of fractured boulders beneath the sheer cliff, he feels the little pang of fear and excitement that an abseil entails – the moment of truth, the half-second between having one's feet firmly rooted and the point of no return, the rush of adrenaline and relief that the equipment has taken the strain, that the rope, sheriff and harness are working in harmony. Free fall is averted; the climber is in control.

Control seems a far cry from his present situation. And yet the disruption of control is something he specialises in – certainly the powers that be would paint him in such a light. He detected in his meeting with the Chief before setting out a palpable displeasure. While a neat pattern has presented itself in the Manchester confession, he insists on worrying at the edges to no obvious purpose. And yet – to give her her due – she had reversed (or, at least, postponed) any decision about curtailing the Cumbrian side of the investigation. Thus, while he was unable to present any concrete reason why this should be the case, he evidently succeeded in swaying her with his loose ends.

It was strange that the subject of the leak did not come up. Yet he had felt unnerved by her demeanour of incisive perspicacity. It was like a forbearing schoolteacher giving an ink-stained pupil the benefit of the doubt in a case of an ink-pellet war perpetrated behind her back. Did she think it was he? That would be ridiculous.

He backs away from the precipice and fastidiously closes the gate. It would take very little for a child or animal or even a careless adult to make a fatal mistake of navigation, even in broad daylight. His own path now takes him through the second gate, close to which twenty-two years ago Mary Wilson's infamous knitted key fob was found. He emerges into the more sparsely wooded heathland of Cummacatta and picks up the all-but-indeterminate zigzags, which he introduced to his sergeants as the 'obvious' route to the Kissing Cave. Its vicinity is deserted now – all forensic examinations complete, tents dismantled, police tapes untied and rolled up – and he realises that it probably falls to him to tell the archaeologists they may return. He makes a mental note to contact Professor Jim Hartley. However, given their gruesome find, maybe they will not hurry back.

But Skelgill's final destination is neither Friggeshol nor its spousal Odinsgill, with its babbling beck. He scrambles across the rocky gully, and follows a faint but – to his outdoorsman's eye – definite path, onwards and upwards through the woodland until he reaches a boundary wall. There is no stile, which makes him think the path is beaten by wild animals alone, and the sporadic stink of fox along the way would bear this out; likewise Mr Tod would have no difficulty in scaling the wall. For his part Skelgill finds toeholds that serve his purpose. He thumps down into marshy ground, sphagnum moss populated by bog asphodel and bell heather. Beyond, the open fellside rises towards the indistinct summit of Grange Fell – "an up-and-down tangled plateau" is how Wainwright saw it, of bracken, grass and heather, scattered rocky outcrops, and the occasional rowan bereft of leaves but hung with crimson berries.

He gets his bearings and sets a course that will take him to Watendlath, site of an isolated farmstead that he could actually have driven to. But he has his own reasons for coming this way – he has no plans to reach the hamlet itself; instead he is absorbing the lie of the land. Besides, his primary goal is a moving target, and one that he is not guaranteed to find.

As it turns out, only a few minutes have elapsed before these roles are reversed: he becomes the target, and a guided missile – black-and-white, like a miniature orca cutting through the undulating waves of vegetation – streaks towards him with uncanny precision. Lady! The little collie has picked up his scent and has remembered this is the kind human that does a good line in stroking behind the ears (and, truth be told, to a dog's keen nose he has more than a whiff of canine about him; a double endorsement). Having subdued the unbridled greeting, Skelgill rises to see the silhouette of her master appear over the horizon of Jopplety How Moss. And Skelgill metaphorically kicks himself.

How he could not have seen the resemblance between Sean Nicolson and Nick Wilson, at this moment seems extraordinary. In their meeting, while his faculties were diverted by the man's answers, his subconscious was screaming at him to recognise the subtle signs, to join the dots. There was same tall, gaunt frame; the same unassuming mannerisms; the same broad fair head and pale, sad eyes.

And now they close on one another. A different man, Skelgill thinks, and this could be like a conflagration of gunslingers – and certainly he would be on his guard for some dastardly move. But though he carries a working stick, Sean Nicolson's demeanour reads like a book – and what Skelgill sees is resigned acquiescence, verging on relief. A lamb to the slaughter? Yet he surely cannot know why Skelgill has come looking for him.

Perhaps for this reason, Skelgill finds himself procrastinating.

'She might be daft as a brush, but she's got some turn of speed on her.'

'Aye – the raw potential's too good to ignore.'

Skelgill nods in agreement.

'She covers the ground more like a lurcher.'

The man regards Skelgill thoughtfully.

'Thee'd know a bit about that – the fastest in the dale.'

Now Skelgill makes a self-deprecating exclamation.

'That crown slipped long ago – I'm not even the fastest in my family.'

Now the man grins ruefully.

'We all have to slow down sometime.'

'Aye – step aside for the next generation.'

Skelgill is speaking from direct experience, but perhaps there is something in his choice of words that resonates with Sean Nicolson. The man looks at him mournfully, and to his surprise he lowers himself to sit on a low ridge of exposed rock, squinting into the afternoon sun. Skelgill accepts the unspoken invitation, and he too sits, leaving a yard between them. As one taciturn northerner to another, he decides he must cut to the chase.

'I know about Nick.'

From Sean Nicolson there is only silence. He is unmoving, merely blinking.

'We had a DNA test done – for another reason. In case the DNA on Mary Wilson's key fob were from her baby. That it were a wild-goose chase all these years. We got the result this morning. The computer made the match with your original sample.' Skelgill is taking pains to let the man know he was not trying to trick him in their meeting yesterday.

'So that's it.'

Skelgill is unsure of the man's meaning.

'Did you know?'

Another pause ensues.

'Happen that's what she were going to tell me.'

Skelgill feels a surge in his pulse rate, when his heartbeat has only just recovered from his ascent.

'On the day she disappeared?'

Sean Nicolson looks at him; there is barely concealed anguish etched across his broad countenance.

'She had on her bright pink scarf. That's what she used to wear. It were our sign.'

Skelgill is about to pounce on the admission – when inexplicably he apprehends something of the time warp.

'You mean it was a sign to *meet?*'

Now the man stares broodingly in the direction from which Skelgill has ascended.

'It were one afternoon.' He glances at Skelgill, suddenly wild eyed. 'It were – like – Christmas Day. Not that I could forget. About this hour – it were just getting dark.'

'Aye. It would be, that time of year.' Skelgill waits patiently for him to continue.

'I were here. Inspecting the flock.' He indicates loosely around them. 'I heard her calling – I suppose I didn't know it were her. From Cummacatta. Just sounded like it were a lass in trouble. I ran down and climbed over, into the wood. As I got closer I realised she were calling her dog. It had run a fox to earth – in the –' (he pauses and looks again at Skelgill) ' – in the Kissing Cave.'

Skelgill finds bizarre images forming in his head concerning the cave, as though he has floated above the fellside, and can see it far below, and the story unfolding in a vivid hallucination. His hands at his sides, he grips stalks of heather, like an airline passenger hanging onto his seat knowing a bumpy landing is imminent. But still he holds his tongue.

'I'd shouted as I approached – so she must have known it were me. I got the dog out, checked it were alright.' Now he begins to struggle to put into words what he wants to say. His mouth is dry and his speech becomes more disjointed. 'There were something about her – I mean, not bad, like?' He refers to Skelgill, as if seeking his approbation. 'She said I want to thank you. I said what do you mean? She said – it *is* the Kissing Cave. A Christmas kiss.' He breaks off again. He shakes his head, now staring at the ground between his feet. 'It were like a dam breaking.'

Still hunched he turns his head and gazes appealingly at Skelgill.

'Me and Mary – we didn't know what we were doing. Aye, it were wrong – but we couldn't stop. You see – it should have been us together – she kept saying that. She'd always loved me. And I were the same. But – the time with Megan – we were just eighteen – we weren't even courting. I had to stand by her.'

Skelgill is reminded that he has divined something of this very misalliance.

'You knew Mary at school, growing up, teenagers, then as young adults, the pub, the wool. You were close.'

The man seems a little shocked by Skelgill's apparent empathy.

'Happen she wanted a baby.'

Now Skelgill gives a slow exaggerated shrug, as if to say isn't this the way of things.

'Were it just the one time?'

Sean Nicolson shakes his head forlornly.

'Like I say – she had on the pink headscarf. She said she'd wear it again. Come up with dog to the edge of the wood – it would be a sign she were free, alone. Afternoons between her shifts – and when I were over here. I always come in the afternoons.'

Skelgill is frowning perplexedly; yet he speaks in a conversational manner.

'And on the day of the shepherds' meet, when she disappeared – were you still seeing each other then?'

The man looks alarmed – that Skelgill, who seems to understand so much, is so wide of the mark with this question. He shakes his head, his expression pained.

169

'She suddenly stopped coming. In the spring, it were.' He glances sharply at Skelgill. 'Later I worked it out. Megan told me she was pregnant – she came home from work all excited – Mary and Aidan were having a bairn after all that time.' The man's features are tortured. 'She were even laughing – because of what had happened to us. Took them twelve years of trying, she said. Took us twelve minutes by accident.'

Despite his outward calm, diverse thoughts and questions are jostling for prominence in Skelgill's mind. But particularly salient is the man's last remark, and his observations of the ostensibly barren Mary; fecundity was not an issue, after all – for either of them. Such reasoning prompts him to make what he knows to be a rather banal observation.

'You and Megan – you had no more bairns.'

Sean Nicolson shakes his head philosophically.

'She had a difficulty with the birth of our Alison. She took a fit – it were bad. She didn't feel she could go through it again.'

A silence ensues; it seems to Skelgill that he must revisit the central issue.

'Just to be clear – you didn't know about Nick?'

Again the man cranes to stare at him.

'How could I know?'

Skelgill feels entitled to inflect a hint of scepticism into his rejoinder.

'You didn't have a conversation about it? About her being pregnant?'

But Sean Nicolson resolutely shakes his head.

'Like I say – she stopped coming. I didn't know what to think. If it were Aidan's – that she were too embarrassed to face me. Or if it were mine – too late, she'd already made her bed – patched up whatever problems there were. Or she might not have known herself – and she were mortified. I were mortified. Megan and me – our lass were eleven – what could I do? In the end I had to settle that the bairn must have been Aidan's. She withdrew for a while and then gradually I'd see her at the pub, she were distant – then it were nodding terms. When she came up for wool, she always picked a time when Megan were there. Like she knew that's how it had to be from now on.'

In the silence that ensues Skelgill ponders what he would have done. Grasped the nettle, surely? But perhaps it is something easier said by an outsider than done by a participant.

'She must have known. She must have been in turmoil.'

Sean Nicolson flashes an agonised glance in response to Skelgill's analysis.

'If only I'd followed her.'

Skelgill realises he means on the day of the meet.

'Would she have gone to the Kissing Cave?'

The man seems too troubled to answer directly.

'I could have protected her. She wanted me to come.'

Skelgill finds himself playing devil's advocate.

'You don't know that. You're going by the headscarf. She had a stall full of them for sale. Happen she just picked one without thinking owt about it.'

But Sean Nicolson is shaking his head.

'She waited.'

'What do you mean?'

'When she was leaving – with the dog. She stopped – until I looked up from shearing. She was looking right at me. I knew it from her eyes.'

It does not escape Skelgill that yesterday the man had denied he could know her mind. But was that no more than a self-referencing denial – a wish that he could not have known that Mary Wilson had something of great portent to impart? But Skelgill persists with his appeasement.

'You think it now – you're putting two and two together. You couldn't have known it then. You can't blame yourself.'

Sean Nicolson regards Skelgill with a sudden urgency, though in his pale eyes confusion reigns.

'Meg – she doesn't need to know about this? It were all int' past. The lad – he doesn't need to know?'

Skelgill stares back, alarm gripping his own features. The man hunches over once again, catching his head in his hands and tearing agitatedly at his scalp. Skelgill feels a strange sense of awe

171

– the shepherd is fifteen years his senior – in the man and the fells around him he sees his long life of labour, loyalty, and love. But what he speaks of is police knowledge – effectively public knowledge. The authorities cannot choose which stones to turn, or turn a blind eye to what they discover. The new DNA evidence is a fact that could have a bearing on a murder investigation. It is not as simple as sweeping it under the carpet.

But he notes the man has made no overtures regarding his innocence, or any attempt to reiterate an alibi. Has he not considered why the detective might be sympathetic to his predicament? Does he not see that the very fact of what he believes Mary Wilson was about to reveal could underlie the motive for her murder? Skelgill has to plumb the depths of his emotions in order to fashion a response to the man's entreaty – but eventually the right words come to him.

'Do you want your Mary's killer brought to justice?'

Sean Nicolson seems to take an age to answer.

'Aye. More than owt I can think of.'

14. ALL SAINTS

Monday morning, Balderthwaite

'I mean, Guv – it all adds up. If he got wind that she was going to spill the beans – or even if she told him outright – that'd be the motive he'd need to do away with her. Just look at him. Crocodile tears.'

'Leyton – *shush!* Leave it till after.'

Skelgill hisses through gritted teeth, a reprimand he supplements with an elbow into the ribs of his colleague. Thus reproached, DS Leyton makes a face of insubordination, unseen by his taller superior at his shoulder. He licks a drip that has trickled from his nose onto his upper lip, and resets himself to stand to attention.

For his part, Skelgill is glad about the rain. From a self-conscious perspective the charcoal trenchcoat he has excavated from a rarely visited cupboard masks the inadequacies of his one and only 'funeral suit' – which, on reflection, is pretty much his only presentable formal outfit these days. Though he is no follower of fashion, even he can discern that those cheap polyester suits he purchased for his probation as a detective are a good fifteen years out of date – and, truth be told, snapped up in a clearance sale from a traditional tailor in Penrith were probably already well behind the mores of the time. So he is relieved that the preening DI Smart, in his immaculate designer wear, cannot make some direct comparison, to steal a devious edge in their exchanges, or less subtly humiliate him in the eyes of DS Jones.

But there is another reason, far more profound, that he welcomes the downpour. Had it been a spring day resonant with birdsong, of floating butterflies and gently swaying golden daffodils, of electric blue sky and fair-weather cumuli – perhaps the kind of day Mary Wilson herself would have chosen – that would have seemed to Skelgill to cheat her of the solemnity that is due to her memory. It would be an acceptance that, at last, everything is fine; the birds a-singing, the bees a-buzzing; and

Mary Wilson is at peace and light prevails over darkness. Not so. All things are not bright and beautiful. Far better that cloud cloaks proceedings. That the heavens have opened up to lament her short life; that the fells that ring the dale in which she grew up, that she would have known so well, are shrouded from sight and run with invisible tears; that the scene is reduced to a small pocket of dank claustrophobia into which the funeral-goers have been pressed. Opaque is the low stone church of All Saints, the most ancient building in the dale, of stone and slate and moss and dripping gutters; the walled churchyard, its turf muddied underfoot; on one side the gate into the village school, where Mary and her classmates learned and laiked; and came through sometimes – perhaps for religious services, perhaps just for mischief. Perhaps Mary, who liked her own company, would lie amongst the silent gravestones, their weathered entreaties straining skywards, to gaze in wonderment at the cerulean heavens.

Now her coffin is poised to be lowered into the cloying earth. From a respectable distance the detectives watch on. To Skelgill's eye the scene is reminiscent of a Remembrance Sunday, a gathering around the village war memorial. Men and women in knee-length overcoats, tilted figures, their heads bowed, their ranks diffuse in the mist, such that those they mourn might mingle like ghosts in their midst; long lost kin, local lads that fell in France and Flanders and futility, their shattered bones forsaken. Except this morning there is only one spirit that wanders lonely among the crowd, touching their hearts, their souls, their consciences; seeking to reassure, or to reproach; or perhaps seeking the bright pink headscarf that was never found.

Despite the inclement weather there is a creditable turnout. But Skelgill wonders how many (or, rather, how few) are actually closely associated with Mary Wilson. Her only near relatives of whom he is aware are her mother and her son. There must be cousins of sorts, but he is not familiar with them; in twenty-two years some of her relatives will have died, or moved away. Perhaps less so for her contemporaries, who now are in their fifties. Coming late into the church the police contingent had found a pew near the rear. It had taken Skelgill's eyes a while to become accustomed to the gloom. In time there materialised identifiable silhouettes. At the very front, closest to the coffin on its bier, Jean Tyson, Nick Wilson – and Aidan Wilson. Should he be surprised that Aidan Wilson occupied the same row? There were others from the dale. Sean and Megan Nicolson (she beneath a hat that was surely more suited to ladies' day at the races). Jake Dickson, his black hair slicked back, seemingly rocking agitatedly. Also unmistakeable from the rear, the towering hunched form of Patrick Pearson, just behind the family. And others that Skelgill could recognise, such as the present tenants of the *Twa Tups* (their minds perhaps half on the wake); and – to his annoyance – the flamboyant quiff that can only belong to the reporter, Kendall Minto – and Skelgill wonders how many others among the congregation are of his ilk, incognito, sniffing for a story. He hopes at least any photographers – or, heaven forbid, a camera crew – will have the decency to stay away.

As it is, that the police are there mob-handed is far from ideal. Skelgill alone, he could have blended in, sufficient of a native to merit his attendance; perhaps even he and DS Jones, judged solely on this criterion, might have passed as genuine mourners. But DI Smart's insistence on coming – inexplicable, in Skelgill's view, given his slant on this investigation, his dismissal of the local angle – has destroyed any such illusion. No doubt he wants to parade himself as the white knight who has ridden to the rescue of the ailing case; yet he shows scant interest in those present; instead aloof, self-important, he seems more absorbed in DS Jones – he has contrived that she shares the shelter of his ostentatiously branded *Boss* umbrella, albeit she has positioned herself tactfully between her two superior officers.

Skelgill tries not to think about this. On his other side stands DS Leyton, the pair of them exposed to the elements. Despite having quashed his sergeant's whispered outburst concerning crocodile tears, the point has sharpened his wits. The reference was made to Aidan Wilson. In fact, Skelgill would beg to differ; he sees no such thing, only the same stony contempt they had encountered during their abortive interview at his place of work. Skelgill has observed no engagement between the man and any other – certainly not with Jean Tyson (there is the impression of mutual disdain) – and not even with his son. His *son!*

Therein lies another kettle of fish. If anyone strikes Skelgill as unnerved by these proceedings it is Sean Nicolson. His natural demeanour, of apprehension, of anxiety, seems amplified – as if at any moment the Sword of Damocles will drop to shatter his fragile secret. And it is a dilemma that is double-edged: there is the painful insight that he revealed during their fellside exchange, the loss of his beloved Mary. During the singing of Psalm 23, *The Lord is My Shepherd*, a movement of his hand attracted Skelgill's eye – it was surely the involuntary act of wiping away a tear? There had been a sudden glance of alarm from Megan Nicolson – and her spouse's reaction was to exaggerate the motion as if subduing an itch, and to ignore her attention, since to do otherwise would acknowledge the basis of her concern.

Skelgill had wondered who might carry the coffin, and what this may reveal. But, in the event, the undertakers' men had acted as pallbearers. Watching pensively he had contemplated whether they are recruited for their uniform height – and therefore if once a team is assembled, there is discrimination whenever a vacancy crops up: only candidates of five-foot nine need apply. Six burly men seems extravagant to haul such scant remains; but then his own memory is of just how heavy a coffin is; how first taking the weight almost causes the knees to buckle; how it digs into the unaccustomed shoulder; how hard it is to walk through a veil of tears.

And so the congregation had followed the casket from the church into the churchyard. The gravel path that has led them to the prepared plot curves between waterlogged turf, and its narrowness has restricted the cortege to processing two-by-two. Jean Tyson together with Nick Wilson had been first in the line, Mary Wilson's mother and son respectively. Then, a little to Skelgill's surprise, Aidan Wilson with the Frankenstein creation that is Patrick Pearson. He is no relative as far as Skelgill is aware – but the others seem accepting of his presence; he is of course a near neighbour of lifelong tenure; moreover he owns some standing in the community in his capacity as senior judge at the annual meet. Perhaps he has been closer to the Tyson family than Skelgill has appreciated; after all, his hostility at being questioned, and his proclaimed self-exclusion from the folk of the dale was contrived for the benefit of the prying detectives; there is nothing to say such an extreme state of affairs pertains in reality.

Frankly, if Skelgill has formed an impression of the graveside gathering it is something of a paradox. At family funerals – especially those of his own maternal clan, the prolific and widespread Grahams – his experience has been of a palpable oneness, all present with arms linked or around shoulders, a collective expression of distress and support. Here today the watchword is not collective but *collection* – an assembly of individuals, each insulated from their peers, standing silently apart, isolated by their thoughts and memories – and maybe, he wonders, by their suspicions. Though there is little in the way of probing eye contact, of surreptitious glances to gauge the guilt of others; gazes are universally cast down to the ground, to the grave, to the casket as it descends and Mary Wilson is laid to rest. And now Skelgill senses at last some unanimity, relief that the mourners may retreat and traipse through the steadily falling rain the short distance to the *Twa Tups*, to shed their damp outerwear and partake of sandwiches and sherry.

While DS Leyton pays an overdue visit to the gents', Skelgill stations himself beside a tea urn in the conservatory section of the lounge. Waiting here he experiences his own moment of remoteness, despite that he knows several of the folk – not least having interviewed them in the past days, and others by sight and even one or two better than that – the Hopes are here, for instance, his old schoolmate Jud with his parents Arthur and Gladis; and Debs from the farm shop and café, with her other half, Rebekah; the pastor, still gowned; and the local postie, Patricia Stampson. But as the alcohol begins to flow, and reticence melts, it is a phenomenon that takes place around him; he stands marooned on his own little islet. DS Jones has departed, with DI Smart – they left from directly outside the church to return to Manchester – the latter's words ringing in his ears, a snide cackle and a disparaging "Good luck in your sleepy Borrowdale – we'll bring home the bacon by the end of the week – don't you worry, cock." DS Jones had flashed him an apologetic glance, the best she could offer as DI Smart kept her under close surveillance. His cunning use of the umbrella had assisted in this regard – and Skelgill could hardly object, for her stylish outfit looked far too good to be allowed to become sodden; indeed he had noticed members of the congregation stealing glances at her and DI Smart – perhaps wondering that so trendily dressed and well groomed a pair could be from the police; perhaps they were at the wrong funeral, or were en route to some society event. Skelgill grinds his teeth – but now his uncomfortable thoughts are interrupted by the arrival of the somewhat less urbane DS Leyton.

'Lor' luv a duck, Guvnor – standing room only.'

'There's some of them won't be standing for long, the way they're sticking it away.'

DS Leyton nods sagely; sure enough trays of sherry borne by a couple of young village girls pressed into waitress service are being emptied as fast as they appear, and behind the bar the landlord and his wife are already working themselves up into a frenzy of flailing arms as pumps are pulled and optics pressed and swilling glasses distributed above shoulder height. Skelgill postulates that at this rate it won't be long before Megan Nicolson will have to swap sides and put in a shift. He absently serves himself a top up of tea from the urn; then he seems to realise his colleague has none and moves aside for him. DS Leyton's dark mane plastered down by rain makes his fleshy face appear unnaturally large, but then Skelgill runs the fingers of one hand through his own hair and realises he must look like a species of vagrant. He affects a shiver and resorts to a series of thirsty gulps from his piping hot beverage. DS Leyton can only inhale across the surface of his own drink; he casts about the crowded lounge; he seems to share something of Skelgill's frustration.

'I know there's a saying about being a spare part at a wedding. What's the equivalent for a funeral, Guv?'

Skelgill makes an ironic scoffing sound. He does not have a ready quip, other than 'detective' seems apposite. His sergeant is right in that no matter what the state of the case (even completely solved to the satisfaction of the bereaved) – to attend a funeral in an official capacity puts the policeman in an invidious position. He is either suspected of going through the motions, of paying lip service when he cannot be emotionally invested, or (as is likely to be the perception in this instance) is open to the accusation of spying. Such concerns have left Skelgill feeling in a state of limbo. But he notes the reporter, Kendall Minto, experiences no such weight of conscience; already assiduously circulating, dispensing commiserations, he is no doubt gleaning titbits of information. DS Leyton is alert to his superior's scrutiny.

'I'm surprised that cove's not been bending your ear about the leak, Guv.'

Skelgill seems irked.

'What are you talking about, *my* ear? What's wrong with yours?'

DS Leyton back-pedals.

'Well – what I mean is, Guv – you being the senior officer. He's more likely to ask you for confirmation.'

'He knows he'll get short shrift from me, Leyton.'

DS Leyton looks doubtful. It strikes him that if Kendall Minto were ignorant of the leaked information then surely he would be crawling all over them, playing catch up? That he does not do this might suggest he is indeed already in the know.

But at this juncture Kendall Minto receives short shrift of another kind. Above the hubbub there is the sudden raising of a male voice, angry, threatening – and without further warning the distinctive thwack of a fist upon human flesh and bone; instantly the outraged cries of other men, the shrieking of several women, and the crash of furniture and glass. Automatically Skelgill and DS Leyton abandon their teas and begin to wade through the crowd. It is only a matter of yards but nonetheless not

179

immediately apparent exactly what is afoot. As Skelgill squeezes past the portly form of postie Pat Stampson she enlightens him, evidently having had a better view.

'Old Jake's kaylied – he's gone an' twatted yon reporter.'

Breaking into the nucleus of the conflict Skelgill is confronted by a scene that neatly illustrates this succinct description. A dazed-looking Kendall Minto is sprawled back in a slipper chair, which appears to have cushioned his fall, blood streaming from his nose upon the front of his white shirt; Jake Dickson, nostrils flaring like a rearing stallion, is being held back at the shoulders by a tag team of Nick Wilson and Sean Nicolson; side by side, they are men of startling congruity; they grapple to get him into a more effective arm lock. Skelgill also takes in that the bowed giant Patrick Pearson seems to have assumed a protective stance in relation to Jean Tyson, their height disparity giving the impression of the manner in which a parent would begin to chaperone a child away from a threatening dog.

Skelgill can see that the danger has passed – Jake Dickson is firmly pinioned and Kendall Minto looks in no condition to retaliate. He steps between them and jerks his thumb at the prone journalist.

'Leyton – take him to the washroom.' Then he addresses a shocked-looking Megan Nicolson. 'Have you got a first-aid kit behind the bar?'

The woman nods obediently and reaches to touch DS Leyton on the back, as he bends to take hold of Kendall Minto.

'I'll fetch it to the toilets.'

DS Leyton responds with a grunt as, employing a firefighter's lift, he hauls the stupefied young man to his feet and steers him through a passage that opens up in the crowd. Skelgill turns to the remaining protagonist, who has been vainly struggling and loudly protesting, though not particularly coherently. Skelgill speaks quietly but with considerable authority in his voice.

'Mr Dickson, I suggest you shut it – else I'll have no alternative but to arrest you.'

There is plainly a rebellious streak in Jake Dickson – never mind whatever it is that has caused him to fly off the handle –

and never mind that it would appear he was well tanked up before the church ceremony had even begun – and he makes a desperate if futile lurch in the direction of the departing Kendall Minto.

'Keep thy bloody nose out of what's none of thy business!'

That his oath is literally accurate takes only a slight edge off its offensiveness. Then, still struggling, he catches the eye of Aidan Wilson, watching on, a disparaging sneer fixed upon his pinched countenance – and Jake Dickson vents more fury upon him.

'And thou can hop it, an' all – if it weren't for thee none of us would be here now – and Mary'd be behind t' bar!'

Aidan Wilson glares with disdain, though he may well be relieved that Jake Dickson is restrained. Meanwhile, Skelgill is infuriated that the latter has failed to obey his order. He steps menacingly closer, and perhaps the man detects that he is a millisecond from receiving a sharp silencing jab to his solar plexus – it must be evident in Skelgill's eyes (although there is an irony here, for in the back of his mind a little voice tells him to let Jake Dickson spout forth); but in any event it would not look good for a policeman to punch a defenceless prisoner, and he is uncertain of quite where the crowd's loyalty lies. However, conveniently for all, the man falls grudgingly mute. Skelgill addresses Sean Nicolson.

'Take him through to the bar will you? Get some black coffee down him.'

Sean Nicolson nods and glances at Nick Wilson, so that they may set off in tandem with their charge, overwhelming his inertia. But perhaps that Skelgill has not carried through his threat of incarceration has a palliative effect, and Jake Dickson visibly sags and seems ready to acquiesce. Accordingly, Sean Nicolson speaks in his gentle voice.

'Come on, marra – let's be garn.'

And they duly go. The crowd sways apart once more and then reconstitutes itself. It seems in only a few seconds that normal service is resumed, as if the incident were only to be expected. Skelgill casts a look at Jean Tyson; once more, unsuitably, she seems to be being comforted by Patrick Pearson – at least he reaches for a sherry and passes it down to her from his great height – she has occupied the seat vacated by Kendall Minto. She appears unperturbed by the fracas, though Skelgill is reminded of the natural severity of her demeanour; perhaps today her emotional defences have been doubly deployed. A succession of folk find their way across to her, and bend to express their sympathy – commiserations that she accepts with due dignity, her station almost regal, with the towering, glowering form of Patrick Pearson standing like an imperial sentry a pace behind and to one side. It seems he has stepped in where her grandson might be expected to oversee her welfare.

Above the crowd Skelgill notices DS Leyton appear in the doorway. He raises a palm, indicating his sergeant should wait, and he makes his way over to him, apologising as he pushes through the now more animated throng.

'Where's Minto?'

'He's scarpered, Guv.' DS Leyton sees his superior's look of alarm. 'He's fine – it were just a nose bleed – no permanent damage to his pretty-boy looks.'

Skelgill appears unimpressed; he is tempted to remark that more is the pity, but refrains.

'What did he say?'

DS Leyton suppresses a chuckle.

'Don't bring any charges – it'll damage his reputation – his ability to get information.'

Skelgill makes a scathing exclamation. But then he offers a more reasoned observation.

'I'm surprised he didn't want to stick around – tongues are loosening.'

DS Leyton nods.

'I heard Jake Dickson start mouthing off. Who was that aimed at, Guv?'

'Take your pick – I reckon it would have been anyone in his line of sight.' Skelgill seems reluctant to name an individual, but then he yields. 'Aidan Wilson – in the first instance.'

DS Leyton listens reflectively – then another thought comes to him.

'Minto got some text message. He tried to make it seem like nothing – I reckon that's what's dragged him away. But I don't reckon he's abandoned his crusade just yet.'

'What do you mean by that?'

'Just as he left, Guv. He said, "Good news about the Manchester suspect" – but then he winked like I was supposed to know something.'

Skelgill's features become unyielding; it is a look that is intended to suggest indifference, but it tells those familiar with him exactly the opposite. After a moment he speaks.

'Smart was bragging he'd have it all wrapped up by the end of the week.'

But DS Leyton seems unwilling to accept this proposition.

'I don't reckon he's any closer, Guv – surely that's one thing DS Jones would tip us off about, save our shoe leather?'

'Happen she might.'

But Skelgill does not sound convinced. It falls to DS Leyton to make the running,

'I've finished going through the files, Guv – if you want to hear that – when we get back?'

That DS Leyton has emailed a report the previous evening, and received no recognition from his boss has come as no surprise.

'Have you got it on you?'

'Er, yeah – I can get the file on my phone, Guv.'

Skelgill nods, more decisively now. He steps past his colleague and makes towards the exit door.

'Let's head over to the café – stick around in case we want to speak to someone later.'

DS Leyton shuffles hurriedly after his superior.

'Reckon it'll be open, Guv?'

'Aye, I spoke to Debs. She's got a couple of lasses up from Keswick. They're still getting tourists this time of year.'

'Right you are, Guv. The Bowder Scones are on me.'

183

15. CAFÉ CONVERSATION

Monday midday, Balderthwaite

'I, er – I noticed Minto was trying to get a word with DS Jones as she was leaving, Guv.' Skelgill glowers over his sausage sandwich but does not attempt to interrupt his sergeant. 'I don't think he'd expected her to shoot off directly from the church – he kind of shadowed them when he realised they were heading for the car – then DI Smart headed him off, sent him packing. I wonder what that was all about, Guv?'

'Leyton, we've got enough mysteries without inventing new ones.' But despite these words it is plain that Skelgill is discontented. 'Like you said, if there's something to know, Jones'll tip us the wink soon enough.'

DS Leyton has little alternative but to accept this reminder of his own analysis.

'I suppose so, Guv.'

Skelgill glances over his shoulder, as if to check their privacy. The garden, his preference for seclusion, was not an available option; the downpour shows no sign of relenting, and was beginning to slant in on a freshening breeze as they made a dash for the café. By comparison the interior is warm if foggy. A boisterous gaggle of middle-aged ramblers have entered just behind them, well soaked and full of their morning's achievements and calamities. It seems they belong to a club based in Lancaster, and are walking the Cumbria Way, a seventy-mile hike from Ulverston in the south to Carlisle in the north; tonight's stopover is in Keswick, roughly seven miles hence by way of the western shore of Derwentwater. Skelgill, eavesdropping whilst waiting for DS Leyton to place and return with their order, found himself tempted to butt in; they were arguing over whether their route would take them past the legendary Bowder Stone (which it does not, save for wading the River Derwent at its nearest point – foolhardy at the best of times, and suicidal in today's spate conditions). Skelgill, of course, knows of a simple detour – but he found himself abruptly biting his tongue when there came the sudden mention of Mary Wilson.

"That's where that Wilson woman was murdered – I heard it ont' radio again this morning."

"They never solved that, did they? The police were baffled."

"And they DNA-tested all the men around."

"They never tested me!"

(This quip raised a round of laughter.)

"But, Eric – you didn't live up here."

"Aye – but I've done walks in the area. Seathwaite's only a couple of miles down t' road – and that's the most popular start point for Great Gable and Scafell Pike. There must be loads of folk like me – just come in for the day. Three Peakers and whatnot."

This had prompted a round of pensive silence before there was another contribution.

"The police must have been sure it were a local man – else they wouldn't have gone to all that trouble. It's usually the husband or lover, so they say."

"I must get one for my missus!"

After the mirth had died down the original speaker had chimed back in.

"They've got someone for it – that's what the radio said. A prime suspect – believed to be a prisoner."

"Aye?"

"Aye. I reckon it's that nutter they called the 'Solway Strangler' – remember him – used to choke women with their own clothing?"

"Aye, that's reet. So he did."

This had shaken Skelgill – for it seemed more information has been released – there was no mention of the man's status in last week's leaked news. What had not unnerved him, however, was the wilder speculation, for the infamous 'Solway Strangler' had been eliminated on the grounds that he was incarcerated at the time of Mary Wilson's disappearance. However, the ramblers' pragmatic opinions had reminded Skelgill of the

185

challenge he faced, his indistinct trajectory beneath the dark clouds and mist-shrouded fells of Borrowdale, versus the sunlit tree-lined avenue down which DI Smart appears to have enticed the Chief, with its promise of laurels for the taking. He was brooding over this dichotomy when DS Leyton's words had pricked his reverie.

"There you go, Guv – sausage sarnie. Times two."

Food had taken precedence over conversation for a few minutes, until DS Leyton's opening gambit concerning Kendall Minto trying to speak to DS Jones. Now, having evidently given up on this theme, he delves into the inside pocket of his jacket, and produces a sheaf of lined A4 paper, folded into thirds. He flattens it out on the surface of the table. The page is covered by his scrupulous manuscript, which always strikes Skelgill as incompatible with a fellow he regards as not entirely meticulous in his habits.

'Can't get a flippin' signal on the mobile in here, Guv. I've been trying while I was waiting at the counter. These are the crib sheets I made before I typed the report. They're a bit out of order – if you see what I mean – but I'll make do, shall I?'

'Aye.'

DS Leyton raps with his knuckles upon the document. 'Thing is – I started with Jake Dickson, being as he'd set the alarm bells ringing – though what with the developments we've had since it's hard to know where the priority lies.' He glances up at his superior for guidance.

But Skelgill shrugs somewhat laconically, and slumps back, lifting his tea plate against his breastbone.

'Whatever, Leyton – we've got till Friday.'

It seems he refers to the timetable indicated by DI Smart – and for all DS Leyton knows the Chief has formally issued such a diktat. But they are sitting comfortably, have food and drinks, and shelter from the elements – and, he supposes, a few hours to kill. He traces a course with a stout index finger until he arrives at an underlined heading.

'If you recall, there were eleven statements provided by the known eyewitnesses and family, and then about a hundred people who were identified as being in the vicinity before and roughly up to the time Mary Wilson disappeared. So Jake Dickson fell into that category. The investigating team divided them up into batches and did short interviews. There are notes against each person's name, but no verbatim quotes or statements that could be brought in as evidence against someone. On top of that there's the database of males who were DNA-tested over the next few weeks – that's north of five hundred. But the testing centres were just that – show your ID, give a blood sample, have a cuppa; Bob's your uncle. There was a duty PC, but no interviewing – the staff were nurses drafted in from Workington hospital. Oh – and there were thirty-seven fell runners – that was a separate list based on those who'd registered to compete.'

At this juncture DS Leyton stops; plainly Skelgill's name was on that list. He resumes rather tentatively.

'Did you know, Guv – you were the youngest by five years? You must have been a flippin' child prodigy, racing against all those full-grown geezers.'

Skelgill affects a degree of nonchalance.

'Leyton, when you've got big brothers like mine, you soon learn how to make yourself scarce. Out the back door and straight up the fell was the safest bet. Billy Whizz, me Ma used to call me.'

DS Leyton chuckles, amused at the image conjured by his superior's anecdote: a scrawny kid hot-footing it with a swiped Cumberland sausage gripped in his fist. But he sticks to the business in hand.

'Anyway, Guv – you were excluded because of your age. The rest, they were all spoken to. Of course – that includes Jake Dickson. Despite – as he now admits – that he never ran.'

Skelgill looks like he is impatient for a punch line, and DS Leyton gets to it.

'He was interviewed the following day. All it says, Guv – I'll tell you exactly: "Jake Dickson. Age thirty-two (as he was then). Runner. Had known Mary Wilson since primary school. Clearly recognised her photograph. Had noticed her presence in the morning at her stall. Had not spoken with her. Did not see her at the shepherds' meet after the time of the race. Was aware of the publicised details of her disappearance – such as the location of her car – unable to shed any further light on these." That's the lot, Guv.'

It is almost exactly as Skelgill has anticipated. The investigating team had established that Mary Wilson had left at shortly before 1pm and had driven to park in the vicinity of the Bowder Stone. She had not returned either to the shepherds' meet at Balderthwaite or her mother's cottage at Slatterthwaite, and when her car was found it was logical, therefore, to assume that her disappearance (or 'abduction') had occurred in the woods soon after her arrival – given that she ought to have returned to her stall by around 2pm. Questions were couched to the many possible witnesses accordingly. Skelgill does not speak as he mulls over these details.

'So, it's just a matter of whether he's telling the truth about going to the pub – and what he saw, or didn't see.' DS Leyton hesitates. Then he leans forward, his expression hopeful. 'Your gut feel's usually pretty reliable on these things, Guv.'

Skelgill remains pensive. His sergeant is putting the ball in his court. What does he really think about Jake Dickson? More to the point, what does he *feel?* The man was uneasy when confronted with the fact of his absence from the fell race – a partial guess on Skelgill's behalf, for had he been placed fourth or below, he would not have figured in the published frame. But with little prevarication he had provided an explanation, ostensibly honest in its candid admission of cowardice. It also juxtaposed him to the known movements of Mary Wilson – surely if he had wanted to distance himself from her, he would have made up a story that placed him elsewhere? There again, that may not be wise if he knew there was a risk of his presence in the *Twa Tups* being independently confirmed. After all, Megan Nicolson was working on the other side of the serving hatch. Skelgill exhales heavily, as though releasing with the breath his building frustration; he responds grudgingly.

'He was picking my brains about the Manchester suspect.'

'Plus he lost the rag with Minto, Guv – made it quite clear he didn't approve.'

Skelgill nods but follows up with a shrug as if to cancel out the positivity before they get carried away. If the ramblers know about the latest 'news' then no doubt so do the locals. And Jake Dickson's tirade (well, a little more than that) probably reflected the communal sentiment – they didn't appreciate Kendall Minto's inquisition, it struck the wrong note for the occasion. He somehow doubts that Jake Dickson would comprehend the clandestine nature of Kendall Minto's mission. Besides, perhaps he simply exhibited an understandable protective instinct – that Mary Wilson was at least a schoolmate, and for the thick end of a decade her son has worked under his wing. Skelgill bites irritably into his second sandwich, and makes a face that conveys to his sergeant he should move on.

DS Leyton turns over a page of his notes.

'Well – obviously, Guv – the big bombshell is Nick Wilson – and Sean Nicolson being his old man, biologically speaking.' He glances up to check that Skelgill concurs with his assessment, and seems to read agreement. 'Just because that never came out at the time don't mean there weren't those who knew about it. Like I was saying in the churchyard – Aidan Wilson wouldn't be the first geezer to do in his missus on account of her playing away.'

Skelgill swallows in order to respond.

'Delicately put, Leyton.'

DS Leyton is unsure if Skelgill is humouring him – or whether indeed he should have employed a less coarse expression. But he can see that Skelgill does not dispute the putative motive.

'On paper he's got a strong alibi, Guv – all those repping calls – yeah. But like we discussed – no concrete proof of where he was just after 1pm on the actual day. It's a perfect alibi in a way – sounds convincing but impossible to confirm – they couldn't even pick holes in it back then. Most of those little shops have probably closed down. We'd have no chance now – and he must know it.'

DS Leyton's inflection invites a response, but Skelgill is eating again. The sergeant seems to understand he should thus play his own devil's advocate.

'Sure – how would he know she was there in the woods? But he might have guessed she'd been planning to meet Sean Nicolson. Or she might have told him she was going to come clean about the baby – perhaps they'd had it out the night before. All he'd have to do was wait nearby in his car and follow her. He might not have intended to kill her – just to intercept her and stop her from letting the cat out of the bag.'

Now Skelgill is free to speak once more.

'What was in it for him? Not long after, he left the family home – and the bairn. He could have done all that without putting a noose round his own neck. There was no joint inheritance and he obviously wasn't interested in getting custody.'

DS Leyton frowns.

'Well, there's revenge, I suppose, Guv. Being cuckolded – that's it, ain't it?'

But Skelgill is glaring belligerently.

'Why not kill Sean Nicolson instead?'

DS Leyton can see that this would have been a more pernicious form of retribution. But he has a counterpoint.

'If Mary Wilson was going to blab, Guv – then she surely would have done if Sean Nicolson were murdered. And Aidan Wilson would have been the obvious suspect.'

Skelgill makes an indeterminate growl, another expulsion of air in frustration. They are beginning to drift into the realms of the red herring and the wild goose. He brings the debate abruptly back to basics.

'Leyton, we've got nowt on him. No witnesses, no circumstantial evidence, no forensics.'

They fall silent, each half-heartedly racking their brains. Eating takes over to fill the hiatus. It strikes Skelgill that the only weapon they have in relation to Aidan Wilson is surprise. They know about Nick Wilson. The question is, when to deploy that weapon – there will be only one chance to register a reaction.

And there is a potential fly in the ointment. That is their obligation to Nick Wilson – to tell him what they know, the unforeseen by-product of his voluntary DNA test. At this juncture Skelgill is not even sure of the protocol – indeed of the ranking of competing rights of those persons concerned. Does the human right to know trump the human right of confidentiality? Nick Wilson surely has a right to know. But does Aidan Wilson have a right to suppress such information? Does Jean Tyson? And what about Mary Wilson – does she have a right from beyond the grave to protect her son – or to protect her reputation? And then Sean Nicolson – what are his rights?

In raising the new lead with the Chief, she had treated it as an issue on which he ought to be informed, and for fear of showing his ignorance he had shied away from further discussion. He could buy time by ordering a back-up DNA test, on the grounds that the result was inconclusive, or of such potential significance that it required the validation of a second laboratory. But the clock is ticking – he has revealed the information: he used the 'weapon' on Sean Nicolson – and it flushed out the story of his affair with Mary Wilson. Okay, the man's initial reaction was that he does not want the news to go any further. But that may change. As it sinks in, the truth he has long suspected may prove too great a burden to bear alone. And there is the small matter of a belated relationship with his estranged son.

Finally, DS Leyton speaks and hauls Skelgill's thoughts back to their conversation.

'Like I said, he got guilty written all over his boat if you ask me, Guv.'

'Who? What?' Skelgill's tone is antagonistic – he automatically assumes that his sergeant refers to the man he is thinking about, Sean Nicolson. And perhaps he is momentarily blind-sided by his colleague's Cockney slang.

'Aidan Wilson, Guv. I mean – what about his behaviour when we interviewed him? And this morning, what Jake Dickson said – blaming him that Mary Wilson was gone? I still reckon it's most likely that he knew, Guv – about her affair, and the baby – and he went and done her in and flew the coop soon enough.'

But Skelgill is reminding himself of the caveats he drew at the time to which DS Leyton refers. Of the 'suspects' they have encountered, there is nothing he would like more than to pin the guilt on the obnoxious specimen that is Aidan Wilson. But he knows that to tilt at such an apparently obvious windmill is exactly the way to disappear over the horizon and off an unseen precipice, a point of no return. Unhindered, DI Smart will be free to frame some halfwit of a convicted lifer who seeks bizarre notoriety. He regards his colleague censoriously.

'What else have we got in the statements?'

DS Leyton appears to want to advance the subject of Aidan Wilson, but for the moment he retreats. He pores over his notes, and turns the pages back and forth a couple of times.

'Naturally, Guv – I had another look at Sean Nicolson.' He taps the sheet as though he is squashing a bug; it is a reminder of something of significance. He looks up with a searching expression. 'In Sean Nicolson's statement there's no mention of what he told us – that malarkey with the champion sheep and its guts exploding. All it says is that Mary Wilson passed his stand with her dog as he was doing his shearing demonstration, and that was the last he saw of her.'

There is a silence as Skelgill digests this information. In time, DS Leyton adds a rider.

'Course that don't mean he didn't do what he said. But if we're treating it as an alibi to be confirmed, we'd need to find the other shepherd, and the vet – something like that.'

Skelgill's features are creased with doubt.

'I can tell you now, Leyton – the vet's long dead. That was Winston Skipton-James. It's his lass Harriet that's taken over the practice – she does all the farm work in Borrowdale.'

'Think they'd have records, Guv?'

Skelgill shakes his head.

'You'd be whistling in the wind, Leyton. Winston was old school. Cash on the nail.'

'Maybe we can track down the other shepherd, Guv?'

But Skelgill looks like he thinks that is no more likely.

'If you recall what Sean Nicolson said, Leyton – someone brought the sick tup to his attention – the owner was away.'

Skelgill's contrariness is realistic. However, he is about to surprise his colleague.

'Leyton, if you think Aidan Wilson had a strong motive – then why is it any different for Sean Nicolson?' He pauses as if to invite a response, but DS Leyton just regards him in an open-mouthed fashion. 'What if he did go to the woods with her, like he says she wanted? Say she told him about the bairn being his. He had plenty to lose – a wife and an eleven-year-old lass. Simple explanation.'

DS Leyton puffs out his cheeks.

'When you put it like that, Guv.'

But as is Skelgill's wont, his hypothesis has a sting in its tail.

'You know what, Leyton – I don't believe it was him.'

DS Leyton avoids eye contact. It is a rare event for Skelgill to declare anything of this nature; and perplexing given that he has just laid out the facts that would support the opposite view. After a moment's hesitation, however, he turns his superior's capriciousness to his advantage.

'In that case, can I come back to Aidan Wilson?' Now he looks up more purposefully. 'He's the one person that the others have consistently bad-mouthed. We've heard he was controlling, tight with cash, he didn't pull his weight – and he was indifferent when Mary Wilson disappeared.'

Skelgill looks unmoved, and this seems to take some of the wind out of his subordinate's sails. A prompt becomes necessary.

'So what, Leyton?'

'Well, Guv – I was working on this last night – I had the files spread out over the dinner table while the missus was fighting the Battle of Bedtime. Afterwards she came and asked me what it was all about. So I told her the story, top line. First thing she said – straight out – was, "Did Aidan Wilson have a fancy woman?" – and you know, there was that broad he supposedly shacked up with after he slung his hook from Jean Tyson's place.'

Skelgill's creased brow suggests his sergeant's train of thought threatens to derail the established order of things in his mind. But he does not interrupt, and DS Leyton continues.

'That aspect was never investigated. Immediately after the disappearance, there was no indication that Aidan Wilson might have been having an affair. He continued to live at his mother-in-law's with her and the baby. In due course Operation Double Helix gave the all-clear – and the investigation began to be wound down. Aidan Wilson left home well after the dust had settled. By that stage no one was keeping tabs on him – or anyone else, come to that. And there's nothing in the files to indicate that someone came along and said this looks a bit fishy – Jean Tyson being the most likely to do so. Course – she mentioned it to us the other day – but that came across as resentment built up over the years, because he's had sweet Fanny Adams to do with her grandson.'

Skelgill has temporarily abandoned the last of his sandwich; still he does not speak.

'Anyway, what if we can find this woman, Guv?'

Skelgill breaks his silence.

'More to the point, Leyton, what if we can't?'

DS Leyton knows Skelgill well enough to understand his meaning. The remark is made in an offhand manner – but is nonetheless provocative; his boss has postulated that she, too, could be a missing person.

'*Hah* – that's just what the missus said, Guv. I mean – I told her she's been watching too much of that *Ennerdale* – she's a sucker for the soaps.' He makes a dismissive gesture with one hand. 'But I have to admit, she got me thinking.'

Skelgill's demeanour remains sceptical, despite his controversial interjection.

'As I recall, Jean Tyson said it didn't last for long.'

DS Leyton has evidently transferred his earlier notes from his pocket book to his handwritten summary. He refers to a paragraph at the end of the document.

'Here we are, Guv. She said he moved to a B&B at Grange between six and nine months after Mary Wilson disappeared.' He glances up briefly, and then continues. 'She implied it became a relationship – but that he moved out to Keswick within the year.'

It is a week since the three detectives interviewed Jean Tyson at her Slatterthwaite cottage. Skelgill is wondering why this is something they have not yet followed up. Surely DS Jones will have put someone onto tracing the woman? She is not the type that has to be asked twice to do something – generally not even once – such that he is not in the habit of registering this kind of action point. If the woman is still alive – and, frankly, there is no reason to think she would not be – then she may indeed be able to enlighten them as regards Aidan Wilson.

'Check with Jones – she must have one of her team onto it – and they've drawn a blank, is my guess.'

DS Leyton nods and makes a little mark with a biro in the margin of his page. Then he frowns; it is the precursor to a suggestion that he suspects will prove unpopular with his boss.

'We could always go back over to the pub, Guv – once it's quietened down a bit. If Aidan Wilson's still there – we could ask him about this – and there's the business of the DNA – hadn't we better knock that one the head?'

That his sergeant has obviously been mulling over the same issue as he, comes as a small surprise to Skelgill – irrationally so, it being such a salient aspect of the investigation – but now he reiterates his own conclusion in this respect.

'Leyton, when you want to knock a limpet off the rocks you need to hit it hard and fast. Give it a gentle prod and you can forget about it.'

There is a silence while DS Leyton gazes uncomprehendingly, until the significance of this metaphor sinks in. He makes a sucking noise, perhaps subconsciously induced, and nods resignedly.

'And I don't suppose we could really speak to Jean Tyson today, Guv.'

195

Skelgill nods grimly. While she may be able to shed further light on the Grange B&B episode, to interview her on the day she has buried her daughter feels, out of common decency, to be a matter for a rain check.

DS Leyton opts to move on. He reverts to his draught report.

'Megan Nicolson, Guv.'

Skelgill is quick to pick up this new thread.

'Why didn't she notice Jake Dickson were in the lounge bar on the day Mary Wilson disappeared. Or if she did, why didn't she say.'

He intones these words as statements of fact, as though they are long-recognised tenets of the investigation. Nonetheless, it is a response that engages his sergeant.

'Exactly, Guv! Remember after we'd interviewed her – I said she'd changed her tune? In the first place she had Mary Wilson as a candidate for an affair – and then last Wednesday she was putting a dampener on it. Against that, in her original statement she made no mention of Aidan Wilson – yet the other day she had plenty to say about him, none of it flattering. And now it looks like she might have covered up for Jake Dickson having been in the pub.'

Skelgill scowls somewhat disapprovingly.

'Happen she had a fancy for him, Leyton.'

DS Leyton looks a little alarmed.

'What do you mean by that, Guv?'

'I reckon he was a bit of a Jack the Lad – he thinks he still is.'

'Are you suggesting she thought he had something to do with Mary Wilson, Guv?'

'*Whoa* – hold your horses, Leyton.' Skelgill raises a restraining palm. 'All I'm saying is you can't assume everything was simple. We've already found out that Mary Wilson had an affair with Sean Nicolson. It's not hard to imagine other permutations – before, at the time, or since.'

DS Leyton absently pulls up a clump of still damp hair, in the fashion of Stan Laurel.

'I suppose so, Guv.'

Skelgill regards his sergeant earnestly.

'Megan Nicolson likes to come across as artless – but she's wily, if you ask me. Don't you reckon if her husband were carrying on with her workmate – her old schoolmate – she'd have got wind of it? There's Sean Nicolson saying he and Mary were childhood sweethearts. Megan would have been right on her guard. On top of that, she's not shy of a bit of attention herself. And there's the local lover boy Jake Dickson playing up to them both at the bar of the *Twa Tups*.'

DS Leyton nods, but it is plain he appears somewhat nonplussed. Is his boss testing on him the hypothesis that Megan Nicolson has changed her tune to switch the spotlight to Aidan Wilson? That she is now downplaying the notion that Mary Wilson might have had an affair – to deflect attention from the man with whom she did? But surely that man was not Jake Dickson, but Megan's own husband, Sean Nicolson?

He feels decidedly at a loss.

'I suppose we can only ask them, Guv.'

Skelgill hoots – although it is a sound that is not so much disparaging as sympathetic.

'And you reckon they'll tell us?'

DS Leyton puffs out his cheeks.

'It depends how we put the questions. Like you say, Guv, if people think they'll incriminate themselves, they'll go into their shell. But there might be a way. Let them think they're helping us catch someone else.'

Skelgill has finished eating and now he leans back and stretches his arms behind his head. He intones musingly.

'There's folk I'd like to interview that are no longer with us, Leyton. Mary Wilson, obviously – the last landlord of the *Twa Tups* – Winston Skipton-James – and old Walter Dickson, to name a few.'

DS Leyton suddenly brightens.

'We've got Walter Dickson's statement, Guv.' He leafs through his notes. 'Come to think of it, I was going to mention that. Here we go. Now, his account corresponds with the other two – Megan Nicolson and Patrick Pearson, those that last saw

Mary Wilson alive – but one thing that did strike me, you having told me about Jake Dickson not running – it was what he said about the race.'

For some reason DS Leyton's inflection seems to request permission to continue. Skelgill obliges.

'Aye?'

'Yeah, Guv – he said they left the *Twa Tups* to see the finish, because his nephew was running, and was the record-holder.'

It is Skelgill's turn to look perplexed – though there is a glint of interest in his eyes.

DS Leyton, thus encouraged, continues.

'I mean, Guv – I might be splitting hairs – but he was interviewed the day *after* the race. If he'd watched the finish he'd have known Jake Dickson didn't run – and that he wasn't the record-holder any more.'

'So, what are you saying, Leyton?'

DS Leyton shrugs somewhat fearfully.

'Well, Guv – what if he never went straight back to the shepherds' meet?'

There is a pause before Skelgill responds; he jumps ahead in the sequencing of the algorithm.

'What age was Walter Dickson?'

'Er – he was seventy-two, right enough.'

Skelgill makes a sound of exasperation – though it is not aimed at his colleague. It seems unlikely, in Walter Dickson's case – but if there does eventually prove to be a local perpetrator, he really doesn't want it to be a dead one. But now he states a point of fact, which unexpectedly offers support to his colleague's logic.

'The race went off at 12.30pm. The record was around the forty-two-minute mark. So if you wanted to see the finish you'd need to get across by ten-past-one sharp.'

DS Leyton holds out a petitioning palm.

'So they must have left the pub not long after they saw Mary Wilson, Guv?'

But Skelgill produces something of a Machiavellian grin.

'How exactly does this help your Aidan Wilson theory?'

DS Leyton huffs and puffs before producing an answer.

'I'm just taking a leaf out of your book, Guv. Keeping an open mind.'

When he might object, instead Skelgill asks a pertinent question.

'Was there anything in either of Megan Nicolson's or Patrick Pearson's statements about the time they left?'

But DS Leyton is shaking his head.

'Like I say – I reckon our only option is to interview them all again. See what they can remember about the detailed timings.'

Beneath the artificial lights of the barn café Skelgill's features seem suddenly lined with fatigue. He gazes rather wanly into his empty mug and then cranes his neck to stare interrogatively at the counter, specifically the glass cabinet that displays the cakes and scones.

16. THE CUMBRIAN KITCHEN

Tuesday midday, Police HQ

Skelgill is alone in his office. He sips tea contemplatively. Before him on his desk are the two shepherds' meet leaflets, over twenty years apart, but with little to separate them in looks. He has the back pages side by side, the lists of winners of mainly sheep classes. And how little the names have changed. Edmondsons, Fergusons, Harrisons, Hoseasons, Jacksons, Richardsons, Robinsons, Sibsons. The progeny of invaders who settled more than a millennium ago. Viking farmers that brought their Herdwick sheep. They named the fells. They cleared the oaks to make their 'thwaites'. Balder- for Baldr. Slatter- for slaughter.

DS Leyton arrives at the open door to see his boss looking strained.

'We need a break, Guv.'

Skelgill looks up rather vacantly.

'You've got holidays left, Leyton – just put in the form and I'll sign it.' He lands a palm heavily on this year's leaflet. 'Take tomorrow off – go to the shepherds' meet – I'll probably see you there.'

DS Leyton laughs nervously. His boss's reaction is a concoction of sarcasm and bloody-mindedness.

'I meant the other kind of break, Guv – *breakthrough*.'

DS Leyton supports with one hand a small round tray with two mugs of tea upon it. He slides it onto the desk and then shifts the larger receptacle to within Skelgill's reach. It is one custom never in danger of the risk of rejection.

'Cheers.'

Skelgill drains his own mug and immediately reaches for the fresh brew. It is a wonder to DS Leyton that his superior is ever out of the gents', but he rarely seems to go – other than as an excuse to poke around people's homes.

'No bother, Guv.' Now he displays something of what he holds in his other hand. 'Couple of bits of news – though not what I'd call a breakthrough.'

He passes over a clear plastic envelope – it contains what Skelgill recognises as the Ordnance Survey map he somewhat illicitly switched during their visit to Nick Wilson's caravan.

'Didn't realise you'd put this into the lab, Guv. Gave me a bit of ribbing they did – saying you were up to your tricks again.'

Skelgill makes a face that reveals his indifference to any such criticism.

'The boffins have drawn a blank on that fingerprint, Guv. Apparently it's a clear impression but there's no match on the system.' Now DS Leyton produces a wry grin. 'At least we know it's not DI Smart's serial killer. Although I suppose that were never likely. It could just be Nick Wilson's, Guv. Easy enough to verify if he's willing.'

Skelgill makes a scoffing sound that for once might contain a hint of remorse.

'The poor donnat'll be convinced we're trying to pin it on him, Leyton. First we want his DNA, then his dabs. He already asked me if he were a suspect – despite how ridiculous that is. Shows what folk think the police might get up to.'

DS Leyton grins empathetically.

'Still, Guv – if it ever turns out to be material, at least we know it's a restricted circle of people who could have come into contact with it at the caravan.'

Skelgill looks irked by his colleague's downgrading of the evidence – but rather than gainsay him he offers a constructive alternative.

'The age of this map, Leyton – Nick Wilson would have been a kid when it was new. It's more likely he got them second hand.'

DS Leyton looks a little bewildered.

'Cor blimey, Guv – where will it end?'

'Probably with Smart getting his man.' Skelgill takes a gulp of tea and twists his lips as though there is a deficit of sugar. His tone is sour. 'We're running out of time, Leyton.'

DS Leyton also has with him a printout, two copies, in fact, but he does not bother passing the spare to his boss. Instead he indicates he has something to convey.

'Aidan Wilson's "fancy woman", Guv.' Skelgill raises an eyebrow over his mug. 'We've got details of the B&B – and the proprietor at the time – although she's not in the district any more. You were right that DS Jones was onto it.'

This seems to stir some emotion in Skelgill, though in the event his response is prosaic.

'What's the story?'

'The woman's name is Nancy Wheeler. Age sixty-nine. The reason we've had a job tracing her is that she's in a retirement home over on the coast – *Sunset Haven*, at Maryport.'

'Aye – it's beside the marina.'

DS Leyton bows to superior local knowledge.

'We found her through the tourist information office. They have a record of her as landlady of a B&B at Grange, called *Derwent View*. She was a widow; she ran it for about six years in all, roughly three either side of when Aidan Wilson would have been there.'

Skelgill is looking interrogatively at his sergeant. He seems to sense there is a shortcoming on the horizon, and he is proved correct.

'Unfortunately she's got some kind of dementia, Guv.'

Skelgill appears pained by this information – though his colleague cannot fathom his underlying motive, and continues with his narrative.

'I mean – that don't say she can't help us – folk who are suffering often have decent long-term memory – it's more what they did in the last ten minutes that they struggle with. The missus's old man, he's in a care facility down in Walthamstow – every time we phone to make sure he's okay, he asks me what's an app. Then he'll ask me again a couple of minutes later. "What's an app, squire?" Maybe four or five times during the course of a call. But try asking him which dog won the Grand Prix in 1966 – he'll tell you in a flash. And what it cost him!'

Skelgill makes an effort to seem interested, but evidently it is not convincing. And now his colleague begins to sound less hopeful.

'I realise it's not someone you could stand as a witness – but she still might be able to help us with some information, Guv?'

'Has she got relatives?'

DS Leyton nods.

'We've got contact details – the team are getting onto that today.'

Skelgill rakes the fingers of one hand through his hair; he seems to realise it has not been properly attended to since its soaking yesterday.

'Remind me – what age is Aidan Wilson?'

DS Leyton glances at his crib-sheet – there are handwritten notes to this effect – the same question and its concomitant calculation has occurred to him.

'He's fifty-eight. He was thirty-six at the time Mary Wilson disappeared. And this Nancy Wheeler would have been forty-seven or forty-eight. Bit of a big age gap, really.'

DS Leyton glances up to see Skelgill glaring at him; thankfully it is an empty stare that he recognises as not personal – just that he has raised a troubling notion for Skelgill.

'I mean, Guv – obviously, it ain't nothing as adults – look at half the presidents around the world with their dolly b– ' He stops, realising he is digging a hole for himself. He hits the heel of one hand against his forehead and reverts to his original vein. 'Anyway, Guv – I gave *Sunset Haven* a call – they said we can just drop by any time, no appointment needed.'

Skelgill nods grimly. But he does not answer. He stares at his mobile phone – he had glanced at it involuntarily when DS Leyton mentioned the age discrepancy – and now he looks again, as though he is willing it to ring, or for a message to appear. After a period of silence, DS Leyton offers a prompt.

'Want to give it a go, Guv?'

Skelgill makes resigned noise; indeterminate, it lacks enthusiasm.

'It's either that or Borrowdale.'

He gives no indication of which he considers to be the greater drudge. DS Leyton is about to make a suggestion when there comes a sharp rap and the simultaneous opening of the door. The distinctive glossy pate and grinning visage of George the desk sergeant insinuates itself into the crack. It is a moment that calls to mind a scene from *The Shining*.

But for George to have sought him out, Skelgill anticipates a fishing enquiry.

'We have a specimen at reception insisting he must see Inspector Skelgill.' George now smiles even more broadly, exhibiting a prominent gap between his front teeth. 'One Kendall Minto.'

Skelgill makes an exclamation of disgust.

'Ordinarily, Skelly lad, I would have put me boot where t' sun don't shine – but I reckon he might have just played his joker.'

George steps forward and hands over a printed calling card – it is a style familiar to Skelgill – indeed it bears the contact details of DS Jones.

Skelgill is momentarily nonplussed, which becomes consternation as he flips the card over to reveal his colleague's familiar script, and her flowing monogram: *"Guv, if you are reading this, it is a genuine lead! E.J."*

While Skelgill stares at the card, George begins to exhibit signs of impatience.

'I'd better be gannin' back to the shop front – what shall I tell him, lad?'

Skelgill's expression is forbidding.

'Stick him in an interview room. One without a view.'

George raises a finger to show his understanding. He steps away but hesitates at the door.

'Skelly, lad – got any size twelve hooks-to-nylon in your motor?'

Secretly vindicated, Skelgill smirks. He grabs his car keys from the stack of documents in his creaking in-tray and tosses them across his desk. George makes a neat one-handed catch and departs with another broad gap-toothed smile.

'It looks like Maryport can wait, then, Guv?'

Skelgill is turning DS Jones's card round on his desk. He nods.

'Aye.'

'What do you reckon it is, Guv? That's a bit irregular of DS Jones.'

'Aye.'

'Maybe that's the both of us taking a leaf out of your book, Guv?'

This remark finally elicits a meaningful response from Skelgill, albeit he looks up reproachfully.

'Some things can't be taught, Leyton.'

In equal measure there is a mixture of the cryptic and the devious in his tone. As to the fact of the matter, on the whole DS Leyton is probably relieved about it.

*

In a bare windowless room they find Kendall Minto seemingly contentedly seated at a table with two empty chairs opposite him. As usual he is trendily dressed. He looks up with anticipation as the detectives enter, and is about to rise when Skelgill speaks.

'Don't get up.'

Skelgill eschews any attempt at handshakes. He regards the young journalist critically; he seems no worse for his punch on the nose and Skelgill proffers no words of concern. The detectives take their seats; Skelgill folds his arms somewhat belligerently; DS Leyton's manner appears a little more forgiving.

Kendall Minto can see he should get to the point. He has been browsing on his phone, which lies on the desk in front of him. He makes a small hand gesture towards it.

'I couldn't use your Wi-Fi, could I? It's asking for a password.'

It looks like DS Leyton is ready to oblige when his move is quashed by a glare from Skelgill.

'Ah – no matter – I'll stick with my mobile provider. It might be a tad clunky.'

205

He taps the fingers of both hands lightly on the surface of the table; Skelgill is thinking they are unaccustomed to manual labour. The reporter composes himself.

'You may be aware – I've been writing a series of articles – about the Mary Wilson case – and Operation Double Helix?'

DS Leyton nods amenably; but Skelgill gives the distinct impression that he disapproves of the act of trespass into their territorial waters; worse: that the young man is like a lamprey to a salmon. The journalist might reasonably argue that it is not parasitism that is at play, but symbiosis. Receiving no other response, he continues.

'They've been serialised on our website – the *Gazette* – and of course that has a far wider reach than the printed newspaper. Global.'

He casts about expectantly; perhaps it is a pause for dramatic effect.

'I've been contacted by a fellow from Illinois – I'm talking the USA. He emailed yesterday – and I spoke with him late last night. I think you ought to hear what he has to say.'

Now he regards Skelgill earnestly. Skelgill makes a contortion of his face that suggests Kendall Minto needs to explain more fully before his consent will be forthcoming.

'His name is Tom Roland. I suppose he's what you would call an expat. He says he was born in Windermere but moved with his family to The States aged ten. He must be in his fifties now. He runs a small-town catering business called *The Cumbrian Kitchen* – it appears to be a kind of café-takeaway specialising in provincial pastries, sweet and savoury. I've had a look at their website – it's bona fide – there are photographs of him and his wife proudly displaying their wares.'

DS Leyton cannot resist a quip.

'Wonder if he sells Bowder Scones, Guv?'

Kendall Minto appears unsure how to react, as if this is something he should take seriously, but Skelgill merely glowers and DS Leyton looks rather sheepish. The journalist regards him sympathetically; it is a small moment of affinity, perhaps. He picks up the thread of his proposition.

'I could tell you myself – but I think it's better if you hear it directly from the horse's mouth. He's agreed we may contact him. Okay?'

He reaches to place a palm on his mobile and looks questioningly at Skelgill.

'What time is it there?'

'Inspector, they're six hours behind – but it's fine – he says he rises at five to bake – he'll be expecting the call.'

Skelgill now gives a grudging nod.

Kendall Minto manipulates his black leather phone case to form it into a display stand and positions the handset at the end of the table for communal viewing. He taps away at the screen.

'I'll use the *FaceTime* app – you might need to lean in so he can see us all.'

Skelgill glances at DS Leyton and they adjust their positions accordingly.

In just a few seconds the screen responds and the florid face of an apparently rotund middle-aged man wearing a white catering hat and smock fills the picture. They have interrupted him munching a mouthful of food. He wipes rubbery lips leaving a smudge of flour on the end of his bulbous nose.

'Hey, Kendo – how's it going?'

DS Leyton is unable to suppress a smirk. But Kendall Minto remains unperturbed.

'Tom, hi – I'm with two British police officers – Detective Inspector Skelgill and Detective Sergeant Leyton. Cumbria Constabulary.'

'Hey. Honour to speak to you, gentlemen.' His accent sounds entirely American.

The detectives mutter greetings accordingly. The journalist, however, is keen to keep things moving.

'Tom – I can see you're up to your eyes in pies – but if you could repeat to the officers what you told me?'

'You bet. Just a minute.' The man's image disappears from the screen and is replaced by a shot of a bright ceiling light – he must have put his handset down. They hear his voice. 'Hey – Jessie – take over mixing these patties will you, honey? What?

207

Sure they're good – curry and cheese! Hey – don't knock it till you try it.'

Skelgill frowns. *Curry-and-cheese patties?* He knows exactly where he can buy them!

The face reappears and it seems the man sits down and props his handset up. He leans closer. Skelgill thinks he sees something of the Lakeland farmer in his broad honest face.

'Okay. As I was telling young Kendo there, it will be eleven years ago, come November. Jessie and I took a fact-finding vacation. We'd had the *Kitchen* running for a couple of years and we wanted to shake up our menu. So we toured two weeks around the Lake District – a busman's holiday, right?' He chuckles, as though nonetheless remembering it fondly. 'We must have blitzed a hundred eateries, from bakers to bars – testing all the local pastries. *Hah* – I landed at Willard twenty pounds heavier than I took off – and that wasn't the mint cake in my luggage! Sure – it was a bit sneaky – we'd act the dumb Yanks, just being curious about the eccentric British diet – and we'd pinch their recipes! But – hey – we're not in competition across the pond!'

Perhaps he realises he is beginning to digress. He raises a finger as if to admonish himself.

'So this one evening – for information, it was actually the day after Bonfire Night, because Jessie pointed out we'd missed a fireworks display that was advertised – we dined in a little *olde worlde* pub in Grasmere – I don't recall its name – but it had a well or something out front.'

'*The Bell?*' Skelgill is quick to interject. 'That's got the village pump.'

'I believe you might be right, sir. That name strikes a chord. It had a traditional four-ale bar and live music in one corner – an older guy on a guitar and younger woman vocalist. It was jazz – right up our street, so we stuck around. We were lodging in a B&B in the village – just walking distance. The night went on and the drink flowed – it became what my grandpa used to call a "stoppy back" – know what I mean?'

'A lock-in, aye.' Again it is Skelgill that replies.

'Thank you, officer.' Tom Roland clears his throat. 'At this point I should mention we knew nothing of your Mary Wilson case – we have enough home-grown homicides to keep the media busy, 24/7. Anyway – it was only yesterday – I was checking out the *Westmorland Gazette* website – they sometimes feature traditional recipes – and I came across young Kendo's article.'

Kendall Minto turns to the detectives.

'It was a piece to coincide with the funeral – it was written respectfully – but I hoped it might jog a memory – by highlighting the unsatisfactory outcome of the DNA screening programme.'

'Well, it sure jogged mine!'

This is Tom Roland who speaks again. He seems to know he is reaching the crux of his evidence. They see him remove his hat and mop his brow with a length of paper towel.

'Sorry, boys – if you can't stand the heat, eh?' He regroups. 'So it must have been around midnight – the musicians had finished but there was still a lively crowd. I went up to ask if they'd serve a nightcap – Jessie here likes her *Drambuie* – who doesn't, *huh?* Close to where I stood the guitarist and some other guy were perched on barstools, lining up shots – and that's when I overheard it, right, Kendo?'

'Sure.'

'Yeah – the musician, he said to the other guy – and he spoke with an American accent, though I'd swear he was a local, but it made my ears prick up – and his words as near as I recall were: "About ten years ago I took a DNA test for this cat – because *he'd* already submitted one to get a buddy off a traffic violation – so I did the cat a favour, right? Else they'd both have been charged – obstruction of justice."'

There is a silence. Perhaps thinking his revelation has fallen flat, Tom Roland is prompted to speak again.

'That's about the length of it, officers. How does that sound, Kendo? Same dope as yesterday?'

Kendall Minto is nodding – but he is staring at the dumfounded detectives.

For his part, Skelgill is experiencing one of those psychedelic moments when reality and fantasy become one – a giddiness when a hormone responsible for euphoria floods the arteries and rushes to discombobulate the brain. The image that flashes into his mind's eye concerns the first time he caught a fish – sea-angling with a static line; his father had put his hand in his pocket to pay for him to go out in a pleasure boat from Whitehaven – a seven-year-old boy with a crowd of holidaymaking adults. Nothing was doing for ages. Then, maybe the twentieth time he lifted the gear – it felt no different because of the heavy lump of lead tied to the end – but there, an explosion of vitality, glistening in the morning sunshine a flapping zebra-striped mackerel in metallic blue and silver, glinting like the world's most precious gem drawn from the blue depths; a moment beyond his wildest dreams.

'Mr Roland – did the musician identify the man that he claims he impersonated?'

The baker is quick to respond.

'No, sir. You can imagine – I've been racking my brains since my first conversation with Kendo. But that's all I heard him say. At the time I had no idea it was of such potential significance – it just sounded like two drunken guys swapping misdemeanours. You see – before the guitarist spoke, the other guy had bragged that his wife took points on her licence for his speeding violations. My liqueurs were served and I paid and took them back to our table. I mentioned it to Jessie – she remembers – but we'd had quite a few ourselves and I guess we just let it pass and got onto other things. Next day I reckon we'd both forgotten – we had hangovers to deal with – and at breakfast we resumed our mission collecting recipes!'

Skelgill is nodding, his features taut.

'How about the musician – or his female partner – do you recall their names – or the name of their act?'

Tom Roland lets out a disappointed sigh. 'No, sir – it just said "Live Music" on a board outside the pub. Of course – it may have stated the name of their duo, but I guess it wouldn't have meant much to us. But I was thinking – a bit of gumshoe work? It struck me as the sort of joint where the locals prop up the bar for decades. Maybe it's still the same innkeeper?'

Skelgill is nodding. Of course these thoughts have already several times traversed his mind and no doubt that of his colleague. He is itching to move on this lead. But he has a couple more key questions.

'The guitarist and the singer. Are you able to give any description?'

'He was – I would say, in his early sixties. I don't remember too much – not pretty, maybe creepy, even. Long thinning hair in a ponytail – mean face – with teeth – I remember that, snaggled and sticking out. Kind of thing we Yanks notice – except I'm a bit of a fraud on that front!' He pauses, but his audience does not interrupt. 'The female – she was more like forty. Too good looking for the guy, really. Thin and dark, long hair – she sort of hid behind it. Sultry. They didn't seem all that connected. I think she bailed on him as it got late.'

Skelgill offers a suggestion.

'Could they have been father and daughter?'

'That wouldn't be my guess, officer.'

Now DS Leyton suddenly chips in. He leans closer to the handset.

'Mr Roland – DS Leyton here, sir. Can you remember what they played?'

'Officer – that's a good point. Like I said – Jessie and me, we both appreciate a bit of jazz. *As Time Goes By*. *Autumn Leaves*. *Makin' Whoopee*. Popular numbers, of course. Oh – and – what's that? – yeah, Jessie here's saying *Ain't Misbehavin'* – that's less common, if you know what I mean?'

Skelgill glances doubtingly at DS Leyton; but his deputy, in noting down these titles seems to be miming along with a tune that he evidently hears inside his gently bobbing head. Skelgill, meanwhile, treats the man's question as rhetorical and intervenes decisively.

'Listen, Mr Roland – we may need to take a formal statement from you – but, if you'll excuse us – we should put some wheels

211

into motion. We appreciate your time – you're obviously a busy man.'

'Inspector Skeldale – it's been a pleasure. For real.'

*

'Reckon he's reliable, Guv? He ain't too hot with names – he just called you *Skeldale* and he's rechristened Minto as *Kendo!*'

Skelgill, having rather peremptorily – even a little cruelly, DS Leyton felt – dismissed the said journalist from their presence with only a modicum of grudging thanks and no hint of a promise to keep him in the loop, has been brooding for a good minute while DS Leyton amended and made additions to his notes. As an aside, DS Leyton had judged Kendall Minto to be surprisingly chipper.

'What about the jazz stuff – was that accurate?'

DS Leyton scans the page he holds open with spread fingers.

'Yeah – pretty much, Guv. Sounds like he knows what he's talking about.'

Skelgill exhales heavily; his thoughts have been on something of a rollercoaster ride.

'Let's hope this Tom Roland's like your missus's old man, Leyton – got a better long-term memory than short.'

DS Leyton nods pensively. Then he is overcome by a burst of enthusiasm. He pats his notebook energetically.

'This is flippin' gold dust, Guv.' There follow a couple more superlatives, of Anglo-Saxon extraction. 'Only a *faked* DNA test. The Chief will self-combust!'

Skelgill's expression suggests he does not quite share his sergeant's exuberance.

'Don't count your chickens, Leyton – we could still end up looking for a needle in a haystack.'

Despite the gratuitously conflated idioms, DS Leyton manages to keep his thoughts on track.

'But if the worst comes to the worst, it's only five hundred blokes, Guv. At least we know their names. And re-testing, it's much quicker these days. We're sure to find the blood sample that was substituted.'

Skelgill remains circumspect.

'But how many of them are no longer in the area – emigrated, even – or dead? It only takes two to be missing to stop us from identifying the cheat. I'll bet you a good quarter of them are gone, one way or another.'

'There's always relatives, Guv.'

But this argument is more tenuous, and DS Leyton's tone lacks conviction. And Skelgill still has some cold water to pour on matters.

'And don't forget – finding a DNA match alone won't solve the case. What does it actually prove – a connection between a person and a key fob? Any defence barrister worth their salt would rip us to shreds.'

But DS Leyton digs in his heels.

'It proves a fraud, Guv. Who would perpetrate that kind of scam? Why else but to avoid detection – they all knew what the tests were for. Whoever it is, that story about covering for a mate that he's spun to the musician – what a load of cock and bull! They weren't DNA testing drivers back then. You'd be unlucky if they smelt your breath for gin.'

Skelgill, who is listening more closely than he reveals, cannot argue with this logic. Rather irritably he stands up and reaches for his jacket.

'It might be cock and bull, Leyton, but it sounds like the guitarist fell for it. We need to find him – he's the shortcut to the suspect. Come on – you can drive. George is probably still guddling about in the back of my motor.'

DS Leyton looks happy to oblige.

'How long to Grasmere, Guv? About forty minutes, ain't it?'

'Forty-five if we pick up some bait – I've got a taste for a pattie or two.'

17. ALL THAT JAZZ

Tuesday early afternoon, Grasmere

'Looks like a half-decent boozer, Guv.'

Skelgill, squinting through the rain-splashed windshield, nods pensively. Despite the hostelry's ostensible 'olde worlde' appeal (as Tom Roland put it) he has never been more than an occasional patron. On reflection, the vicinity is short of the kind of climbs or runs that he prefers – and Grasmere is not a lake that he has ever favoured for fishing; despite its hefty pike the chatter of walkers tripping around its modest three-and-a-half mile perimeter is too invasive for his liking. That said, its picturesque backdrop is one of breathtaking beauty. The inn, too, nestled in the heart of the toponymous settlement of Grasmere has its bucolic charm; slate built like much of the village it is draped in tangled bottle-green ivy. Skelgill is unsure if it has escaped the clutches of one of the pub chains – mock hand-bashed chalkboards advertise 'Real Ales', 'Bar Meals' and 'Live Music'.

'Live music, Guv.'

'Aye.'

Skelgill says no more and DS Leyton swings into the car park at the rear of premises. It is empty but for a couple of vehicles that look like budget staff cars, and a tour coach with an Ayrshire address and telephone number.

They enter to find a similar layout to the *Twa Tups*, in that there is a modern extension at the rear, and in here a mediocre lunch is being served to a subdued party of pensioners. Skelgill follows his nose to the bar, which – as Tom Roland described – has retained its traditional qualities, though is a much larger room than its equivalent at the Balderthwaite tavern. This being a weekday in late September, the bar is sparsely populated. A young man of about twenty puts down his mobile and slides off a stool at the end of the long polished oak counter. He greets them with a pleasant smile.

'What can I get you, gents?'

'I'd like to say two pints of *Jennings* bitter – but you don't appear to have it.'

The young man makes the beginnings of an apology, together with a gesture at the alternative range of hand pumps – but Skelgill pre-empts any further debate by displaying his warrant card.

The young man grins.

'You're heavy grade mystery callers.'

Skelgill frowns.

'Come again, son?'

For a second the lad looks slightly unnerved.

'Oh – just a joke – I meant as if the brewery have sent you. We get mystery callers – to make sure we dispense according to recommendations, fill to the line, use the correct branded glasses – that sort of thing?'

His manner is pleasant, and he sounds educated, and Skelgill refrains from being any more obstructive; after all, he started it.

'It's a man we're looking for, not ale.'

'Oh.'

Now Skelgill cuts to the chase.

'Musician. Guitarist. Jazz. Could be aged around seventy. Known to have played here about eleven years ago. Possibly thereafter.'

'Ah.' The bartender creases his brow. 'I've just been here since January – and I'm afraid the present tenants only took over the summer before.' But then he raises an index finger. 'Have you talked to Mary?'

It takes some effort for both Skelgill and DS Leyton to appear to respond blandly; they shake their heads in unison. The young man now indicates a signboard on the wall behind them; it is similar to those outside, although genuinely handwritten, and its chalk smudged. It reads: "Jazz with Mary – every Tuesday and Friday, eight 'til late."

Skelgill turns inquiringly to the bartender.

'I believe she's been singing here for donkey's years – she would surely know, if anyone does. She lives in the village – she doesn't drive – so I expect she's around.' The detectives must betray some urgency in their body language, for he continues swiftly. 'It's the cottage immediately on the left of the post office. Two minutes' walk. You'll see the cat ornaments.'

*

'Think it's an omen, Guv – her being called Mary?'
'How many Marys are there, Leyton?'
'She'd be about the same age as our one, Guv.'

Skelgill does not answer, for their quick strides – he setting the pace – have brought them to the post office and, just past it, the address they seek. It is a narrow dwelling, just a door-and-window's width, its stonework lime-rendered and distempered in cream to achieve a uniformity of the terrace to which it belongs. There is a yard or so of herbaceous border protruding to the pavement either side of the front door; beds of pale blue hydrangeas are retained by perpendicular slates; among the plants lurk several stone cats, of a battle-scarred condition which is surely testament to regular walkabouts after pub closing time. Skelgill vaguely registers the presence of another such ornament on the broad slate windowsill – until it, the most realistic looking ginger, suddenly ducks beneath the partially open lower sash and disappears with serpentine elegance. From within there emanate the strains of a guitar, and a female vocalist. It is a curious rendition; his colleague could tell him it is scat singing. In the absence of a bell or a knocker he raps twice with the knuckles of his left hand. Immediately the singing ceases but the music continues.

The woman – she answers to 'Mary' – rather in keeping with the cats has the appearance of the caricature Halloween witch. Her cheeks are hollow and her nose quite prominent and aquiline. Skelgill guesses her age to be around the fifty mark, which complies with Tom Roland's description. She is tall and slim, and wears an ankle length dress in clingy black velveteen. Her long hair, raven and dip-dyed with tips of magenta, falls in unkempt tresses across her face, such that she regards them disconcertingly with one dark brown eye. A hand holds the door half open; the other nurses a tumbler of amber liquor.

She seems unruffled by Skelgill's introduction; they are invited inside. The front door gives on directly to a small cosy lounge; a slightly shabby suite draped in patterned throws surrounds a traditional stone hearth in which a log fire smoulders, producing a pleasant aroma of wood smoke. There are wall hangings, such as the Tree of Life, and a magnificent peacock, and half a dozen church candles flicker on a sideboard. The room, however, is dimly lit, the curtains partially drawn, and Skelgill senses that the ginger cat is lurking in some shadowy recess.

On a low table before the hearth stands a bottle of *Jack Daniel's*, its cap lying beside it. The woman moves ahead of them, turning down the music by means of a voice command directed at what Skelgill considers to be a sinister eavesdropping device; however she leaves it running quietly in the background. Her movements have a certain feline quality, and her voice is throaty and purring, unusually deep for so slender a person. She sinks into the armchair nearest to the bottle, and indicates loosely with her glass that they should join her. Rather listlessly she offers them a drink, but then seems disappointed when they decline. She seems amused when the cat – the ginger – materialises upon the arm beside Skelgill and steps purposefully down onto his lap. There was a time when he would have flinched – for no good reason – but, after many years of decrying cats as mercenary and unresponsive, he is a recent convert, and harbours a secret admiration for their ability consistently to outwit supposedly more intelligent dogs (and to take obvious pleasure in so doing). As the creature settles down, Skelgill indicates with a jerk of his head that his colleague – assigned to ask questions, as best qualified in the genre of jazz – ought to commence.

DS Leyton clears his throat.

'Madam, is Mary your real name? I mean – as opposed to a stage name.'

She smiles dreamily.

'Mary Elizabeth Jane de Boinville.'

DS Leyton glances at his colleague; Skelgill, however, knows of de Boinvilles from Westmorland, and is unperturbed. The sergeant makes a stab at the spelling, and then rather self-consciously requests her date of birth. She is unfazed by the question; it confirms her age to be fifty-one.

'Madam – we understand you've been singing at *The Bell* for some time. We're trying to trace a man we believe you may have performed alongside. In particular on an occasion approximately eleven years ago. Jazz guitarist. His estimated age at the time was sixty.' DS Leyton quickly flips back through his notes to their earlier conversation with Tom Roland. 'He is described as having long, thinning hair in a ponytail and distinctive protruding teeth.'

She has listened without revealing any trace of recognition, her breathing steady, blinking occasionally. But now she replies without equivocation.

'That would be *The Viscount* – Harry Nelson.'

DS Leyton senses a stiffening in the demeanour his superior, that they have so swiftly reached an identification. Before he can speak again, the woman continues.

'I sang with him maybe a dozen times. He wasn't especially pleasant. It was a purely commercial relationship.'

DS Leyton is nodding.

'And when did you last see him?'

'It would be five or six years ago – I think he began to travel about less.'

'Do you know where he lives?'

She raises her glass and sips slowly, regarding DS Leyton and then Skelgill contemplatively through her favoured eye. There seems to be a hint of amusement, as though she senses she is the cat and they are mice. Gently she flicks her glass to and fro.

'He *lived* in Aspatria. That's where he was from.'

It must be her intonation – but Skelgill is suddenly possessed by that 'fishing feeling', of an unsatisfactory bite in progress, when eventually he is forced to strike against his better judgement. Thus his interjection carries a hint of desperation.

'Do you know his address now?'

'Try the churchyard.'

'What?'

'He was killed outside *The Victory* – in Aspatria. Late one night after he'd performed – they say he was blind drunk. It was a hit-and-run. They never caught the driver.' Again she looks languorously from one detective to the other. 'Roughly two years ago. You would know that?'

Skelgill, though momentarily reeling, is wondering that he ought to. But Aspatria, outwith the National Park, is off his regular beat. Nonetheless, he feels disturbed by his lack of such basic knowledge.

DS Leyton, too, has been knocked off his stride by Skelgill's intervention and the disturbing twist in the tale. Meanwhile the woman reaches for the bottle, but finds it empty. She rises and passes behind them to the sideboard on which the smart speaker nestles innocuously amidst the candles. She opens a cupboard door and there is the clink of glassware. She returns with a fresh bottle of whiskey, and two clean tumblers, these items balanced on a wide book for a tray. She hands the bottle to Skelgill.

'May I borrow your strength?'

He senses his sergeant is watching his reaction, and is implacable as he cracks open the cap. He hands the bottle over – she pours a couple of fingers into a glass and offers it to him – but he leans back, his palms raised.

'We're both driving. It wouldn't go down well. Sorry.'

The woman gives a slight shrug, and instead simply sips from the new glass herself. She puts it down and removes the third glass from the book and lifts and opens it. They realise it is some kind of album.

'I have a picture of him – not for sentimental reasons.'

It takes her a few moments – but she finds what she is looking for and extracts a cutting from a local newspaper. It is a colour photograph. She stands in the foreground holding a microphone to her lips – the trademark tresses cover one eye. Behind her, seated, and in clear focus though not the intended subject of the shot, is a guitarist who brings to life Tom Roland's verbal photo-fit.

'What was with *The Viscount?*'

She shrugs.

'Oh – nicknames are a thing in jazz circles. And I suppose *The Count* was taken.'

Skelgill sees that DS Leyton is nodding; he must know whom she means. Accordingly he indicates that his deputy should resume the questioning.

'What was his connection to *The Bell?*'

Now she shakes her head lightly, although not sufficiently to dislodge the tresses that stubbornly cling to one side of her face.

'None, as such. He played the county circuit. There must have been a hundred or more venues back then. He was good, so he could pick and choose. And there's more money to be made when you're something of a locum – that's when he came to Grasmere – when one of my regular musicians called off.'

DS Leyton looks lost for what to say next. He reverts to the comfort blanket of his notebook and reads out the list of songs supplied by Tom Roland. The woman nods.

'They are exactly the numbers we used to do. *Ain't Misbehavin'* was his signature tune – not many could play it so well. I have to give him that – he was good. Anything from the Great American Songbook. He fancied himself as a bit of a transatlantic dude.'

DS Leyton regards her interrogatively.

'These songs, the report that we're following up – it was a specific night – the sixth of November, coming up for eleven years ago?'

The woman lifts her glass and smiles sympathetically.

'Sergeant, can you remember what you were doing?'

DS Leyton grins phlegmatically. They have agreed en route how much they can safely reveal, and now he puts this plan into action.

'Madam – the man we believe to be your associate – Harry Nelson – was overheard to tell another male – to boast to him – that he had impersonated a friend or acquaintance in order to get him off a road traffic offence. It was couched as a favour between mates.'

The woman is listening implacably. That they have now shown their hand – and that she is clearly not regarded as some kind of co-conspirator – does not seem to affect her demeanour. Her response comes evenly.

'It's hard to imagine Harry impersonating somebody. He was quite distinctive.' She casts a hand towards the photograph, which Skelgill has laid on top of the album on the table.

DS Leyton glances at his superior – perhaps concerned that their story has herein a flaw that requires further explanation. But Skelgill is unconcerned, and now he takes over.

'Can you think of anyone he would have shielded – presumably a person he knew well?'

'No to the first. And no to the second – I wouldn't have put it past him to act for a complete stranger if there were a few quid in it. Going dutch on the tips was not his forte.'

Yet she seems not to resent this fact.

'And he never mentioned this story to you?'

'Why would he?' Her words are somewhat abrupt, though her tone remains mild.

Skelgill is forced to try another avenue of approach.

'There may be a Borrowdale connection.'

'Just remind me, Inspector.'

Skelgill is always a little surprised when local folk do not know their topography. He is forever berating DS Leyton for learning next to nothing, in seven years or more. But now he responds patiently.

'Roughly speaking, the vale south of Keswick – beyond Derwentwater and about as far as you can go up into the fells.'

'That's quite an expanse.'

Skelgill is nodding.

'But not a massive population.'

But again she shakes her head – this time it is a clear indication of being unable to help.

'I'm sorry – there's nothing that comes to mind. Like I say – he played all over the county.'

Skelgill is silent for a moment – he has reached the end of the road, for the time being. He watches as she pours more drink – he notices that she fills the remaining unused glass. And then she offers it to him.

'Sure I can't tempt you?'

Skelgill jerks forward – he means to rise – but he realises he cannot move for the ginger cat is firmly secured upon his lap.

'Thanks – but we need to go. You've been very helpful. Mind if we borrow your press cutting?'

'Be my guest.'

He looks at her a little helplessly.

'Happen I'll leave the cat.'

The woman reaches and slides her long hands with their delicate fingers beneath its form and prises it persuasively from his thighs. As she rises she cradles it in one arm against her shoulder. Skelgill rather staggers to his feet.

'It's a pity you're not staying around – you could boost my audience tonight. I was rehearsing when you arrived.'

Skelgill grins rather sheepishly.

'It sounded impressive.'

She looks at him like she knows she is being fobbed off – that it is even something she might be accustomed to. But with her free hand she reaches forward and, as if to steady him – though he is now stable – she places her palm against his side.

'Friday, maybe?'

'You never know.'

*

'Reckon he's Tom Roland's man, Guv?'

Skelgill grunts as he shuts the door of DS Leyton's car. He glares at the clipping that rests on the console between them. DS Leyton has taken and transmitted a photograph.

'It all fits. He matches the description. She seems straight enough. Attractive woman.'

DS Leyton flashes a sideways glance at his superior – it is unusual for him to make such a remark. Skelgill must sense his sergeant's attention and begins vigorously to beat raindrops from the shoulders of his jacket. While DS Leyton has radioed through a series of requests for information, Skelgill has insisted on prowling around the village of Grasmere. But DS Leyton puts aside his misgivings; Skelgill operates at depths that cannot often be fathomed by the application of regular logic. If the woman has charmed him, then so be it. He turns on the ignition, but makes no attempt to set off. Instead he cranks up to maximum the heater and the fan, and engages the wipers, for the car is misted inside and out.

'I got an immediate answer on the hit-and-run, Guv.'

'Aye?'

'Just like she said. Two years ago this month. Killed outright. Perpetrator never identified. The only witness was an old geezer walking his dog. Vehicle believed to be a battered black pick-up, make unknown.'

Skelgill grinds his teeth.

'There's a lot of them about.'

'May not even have been registered, Guv – apparently we inspected all the licensed vehicles in the district for accident damage, contacted repair shops, garages. Diddly-squat.'

Skelgill is silent for a few moments. DS Leyton ventures an idea.

'Reckon he was taken out, Guv?'

Skelgill does not immediately answer. When he does, his question is profoundly intoned.

'Why wait twenty years?'

DS Leyton rocks his head from side to side.

'Well – something could have prompted it, Guv.'

'Aye – I could see that now – if Mary Wilson's killer got wind that we're poking about. Silence the one person who could put the finger on him.'

'What about Minto's original article, Guv – the one that DS Jones started with? The twentieth anniversary of the disappearance. That came out a couple of years ago.'

Skelgill is nodding; he has had the same thought. Though in characteristic fashion he cautions against it.

223

'Let's not jump to too many conclusions, eh, Leyton?'

'I suppose not, Guv.'

'Think about it – what do we actually know for certain? One – that he's called Harry Nelson.' Skelgill begins throwing out fingers. 'Two – he's from Aspatria. Three – he lived there when he was killed.'

DS Leyton is nodding.

'One way of looking at it, Guv – is that if he did a mate a favour, then there's a fair chance the mate was from Aspatria, too. We're cross-checking all the five-hundred-odd records for an address match. Maybe someone from Aspatria who was working down at Borrowdale at the time? And we're trying to identify any local relatives and acquaintances – in case that cove in *The Bell* wasn't the only person Harry Nelson spilled the beans to.'

But Skelgill is sceptical.

'Happen it would have come out before now – if he were that glib. I reckon that were a drunken one-off. Do we know if he was married?'

DS Leyton shakes his head, and then clarifies the ambiguity.

'A bachelor.'

Skelgill waits a moment, as if to signify the concluding of this particular query.

'So what's the other way?'

'Come again, Guv?'

It is apparent to Skelgill that his sergeant is being a mite disingenuous in skirting around the intimation he made half a minute earlier. Nonetheless, he spells it out.

'You just said "one way of looking at it" like you've got another up your sleeve.'

DS Leyton makes a face that admits to procrastination.

'It's more along the lines of what if it had been Harry Nelson that was working in Borrowdale?'

Skelgill scowls.

'You need to make yourself clearer, Leyton.'

'Well – I was thinking, while you were having a wander. About – well, cats.'

'Cats.'

Skelgill's tone conveys this is not a good time for a wind-up.

'Not actual cats, Guv – I mean, the *word* cat.'

'Leyton, which part of "make yourself clearer" don't you understand?'

DS Leyton raises his hands appealingly.

'Guv – going back to my uncle Kenny – the trumpeter, right?' (Skelgill nods reluctantly.) 'If he referred to some geezer he'd just performed with, he called him a cat. It's jazz-speak. One jazz player talking about another.'

'Aye, I've heard that.'

'So – I was going over what Tom Roland told us. When we listened to him, I assumed he was dropping his own Americanisms into his story. But, *cat* – that's not a regular thing. I reckon he quoted Harry Nelson verbatim. And I reckon Harry Nelson was talking about another musician.'

DS Leyton folds his hands together and waits for his superior's response. Skelgill's reply is forthcoming with surprising swiftness.

'Fair enough.'

DS Leyton is unsure of how seriously Skelgill is taking his theory – whether he is humouring him – or whether the other extreme possibility holds, that he has had the same notion but is letting his subordinate take the impending fall. He folds his arms and shrugs obstinately.

'Thing is, Guv – when we went to that caravan? That acoustic guitar of Nick Wilson's – it's a *Maccaferri* – well, a copy, anyway. That was Django Rheinhart's favourite – remember I said the kid was playing one of his numbers? It's got a strong sound – it suits jazz players.'

He turns his head to peer questioningly at Skelgill, as though he anticipates that his musical knowledge might prompt a degree of bloody-mindedness.

But Skelgill's response is pleasingly neutral.

'So, what are you saying, Leyton?'

DS Leyton swallows apprehensively. Then he blurts out the remainder of his conjecture.

'It's a jazz connection. It's a Borrowdale connection. And it's a connection with Mary Wilson. Guv, think about it – *Nick Wilson got the guitar from Aidan Wilson.*'

Skelgill begins to bite at the corner of a thumbnail. If 'The Viscount' Harry Nelson played gigs around the pubs of Lakeland, and Aidan Wilson shared an interest in jazz – it is likely they will have come into contact. For many years the *Twa Tups* in Balderthwaite hosted a thriving music scene. He stares unblinking through the rain-spattered screen at the distorted writing on the back of the bus parked opposite them; then there is the murmur of the wipers and the text clears. Then gradually it blurs again. Then it clears. Then it blurs. His sergeant's logic is persuasive – so why is he suffering reservations?

He is about to speak when his mobile phone rings. It is DS Jones's ringtone. He digs rather frantically into his jacket, as though he thinks she will hang up if he does not answer immediately. As he succeeds in connecting the call, DS Leyton's mobile rings, and Skelgill spills out of the car and slams the door.

'Jones.'

'Hi, Guv – I just caught up on the latest case notes. That's amazing – about Harry Nelson?'

She has obviously been monitoring their online reporting system that has logged DS Leyton's request for details of the deceased musician.

Skelgill has many pressing questions – some he cannot bring himself to ask – but he settles for one concerning the Manchester investigation.

'Does Smart know?'

'No, Guv – I don't think he's interested in what you're up to. He's convinced we've got the answer. That's the other reason I wanted to reach you – he's scheduled a press conference for 5pm tomorrow – to announce the name of the suspect and the charges.'

Skelgill curses disparagingly and does not apologise for his language.

'What about the Chief?'

DS Jones knows not to take personally his occasional indiscretions.

'She's going along with it, as far as I know, Guv. DI Smart's been liaising with her.'

Now he grimaces, but holds his tongue. Just when the trail might be warming up. But he determines not to show he is deflated by the continuing prospect of DI Smart's stitch-up succeeding; or of the associated risk that the Chief will close down the operation. Instead he resorts to one of his more controversial niggles.

'That business with Minto. How did you pull that off?'

'Oh, I er – I just suggested he should work with us – not to try for a private scoop and mess it up. He wants there to be a local solution as much as we do, Guv.'

Skelgill doubts that this explanation alone will have persuaded the pushy young journalist to turn his story over to them. But he finds himself unable to ask what other incentive he may have been offered. And now he suspects she is anticipating such an inquisition, for she suddenly makes her apologies.

'Guv – I have to go. I just wanted to let you know – about the press conference. I'll stay logged on to keep up with developments. I guess we'll be back late on Wednesday night.'

'Aye.'

They both seem to hang up without completing the expected formalities. But before he can analyse their exchange, the electric passenger window slides down.

'Guv – a bit of news on that woman Nancy Wheeler – from the care home?'

Skelgill clambers inside and glares rather irascibly at his colleague.

'We organised for a local WPC to go in and have a chat. Seems she remembers something of Aidan Wilson. And get this – she accused him of trying to strangle her.'

'What?'

'Yeah – but the thing is, Guv – the WPC had a word with a couple of the carers. Apparently she's done it before – accused other patients, and some of the staff, the visiting hairdresser and

227

chiropodist. Always the same story, crept up on her with a towel.'

'A towel?'

DS Leyton shrugs rather hopelessly. Skelgill slumps back into the seat. He lets loose a long sigh of frustration. After a while, however, he makes a more considered pronouncement.

'Look, Leyton – before we were interrupted – I agree that whoever got Harry Nelson to take his test for him is the prime suspect. And I want to find him, fast. But, like I said, we need some kind of corroborating evidence – DNA on a key fob won't convict the killer.'

There ensue a few moments' silence before DS Leyton makes a suggestion.

'Maybe if we released that information, it'll flush him out, Guv – he'll make a mistake.'

Skelgill is working on the thumbnail again. He turns away from his colleague and spits into the wind.

'Aye – but if you're right about what happened to Harry Nelson it could be the sort of mistake we'd regret.'

'Suppose so, Guv.'

DS Leyton inhales heavily. Skelgill begins to punch his left fist into his right palm.

'Leyton, I don't reckon there's anyone we've spoken to that's given us the full story. Aye, I get it – when there's stuff gone on that we don't need to know about – why tell us? But the mainly innocent create a smokescreen for the entirely guilty to hide behind.'

After a while DS Leyton ventures a suggestion.

'Think we should go along to the shepherds' meet, tomorrow, Guv? The location and whatnot – it might jog a memory or two. Treat it like a reconstruction?'

Skelgill is nodding pensively.

'Aye – there's a couple of folk we could usefully speak to. Megan Nicolson. And I reckon we need to try something of your music theory on Jean Tyson, without letting on what we know.'

DS Leyton is pleased.

'Seems like a plan, Guv. You ready to roll? There's probably quite a bit of info stacking up for us back at base.'

Skelgill grunts and his colleague shifts the car into gear and performs a rather over-exuberant U-turn on the gravel of the car park. The passenger window is still down and they hear strains of big band music and exuberant cheers as they pass the steamed-up glass of the pub conservatory. The pensioners' lunch seems to have become some kind of lock-in-cum-knees-up. The Scots know how to get their money's worth.

Skelgill is evidently prompted by the acoustic stimulus.

'How come you're a jazz buff on the quiet, Leyton?'

DS Leyton shrugs self-effacingly.

'Like I say, Guv – it kind of runs in the family – what with me old uncle Kenny being a bit of a player. Don't get me wrong – I ain't got a musical bone in me body – I wouldn't know a middle C from a middle finger. There's more chance I'd play centre forward for England than for an audience at *Ronnie Scott's* – and that tells you something – *hah!*'

Skelgill grins rather more maliciously than is merited.

'How come you don't have it on in the car?'

Now DS Leyton snatches a glance at his superior.

'I do, when I'm on me Tod – there's a Stan Getz CD in there now.' He indicates to the music console. *'The Girl from Ipanema* – you've heard that one, Guv?'

Skelgill continues to smile but more inanely.

'Aye, maybe.'

'I just know you prefer it quiet, Guv.'

'Leyton, I've got enough voices going round in my head as it is. I'll stick with the lass from Cummacatta.'

18. THE MEET

Wednesday 12.40pm

It is not a bad day for one with a mountain to climb.

Skelgill stands with his hands on his hips. Through a gap in the oaks he can see the line of runners making their way up Scawdale Fell. Tiny coloured figures in white and red and fluorescent yellow and green; they seem to make only the most painful progress. Was it so, back in the day? Back in *his* day – not easy to get his head round, twenty-two years that will not come again. Across the dale the sun is shining, but a shower over Grange Fell is clipping Cummacatta, and it seems to prompt Skelgill to resolve that about the woodlands he will go. He has been along to the Bowder Stone – he chatted with members of a local group that is putting on bouldering lessons for charity donations, and there is sponsored abseiling off Devil's Lowp. He had joked that they had better not think of calling out the rescue.

They will be packing up for lunch shortly, and Skelgill is additionally pressed by the notion that the *Twa Tups* will be besieged once the free buffet is unfurled, and he wants to time it right to get a quiet word with Megan Nicolson.

Had he continued south past the Bowder Stone he would have been almost as quick to go on foot. But his reflective ramblings have brought him back close to his car at the Cummacatta end of the woods – and, besides, he has left his mobile tucked above the sun visor; striking a small blow for solitude. Now he sees he has three missed calls from DS Leyton. Rather than drive off, he raises the tailgate as a rain shield and settles on the end of the flatbed. His sergeant answers.

'Guv – I got hold of Jean Tyson.'

Skelgill momentarily closes his eyes, as though he is striving to read any nuances in his colleague's voice; does he detect a hint of excitement?

'And?'

'Well – I think there's something, Guv – but I'm not sure what.'

Skelgill gives a small involuntary groan. It encourages his deputy to be more forthcoming.

'Like we agreed, I began asking casually about the guitar – that her young Nick had mentioned to us that he'd been given it by his dad – by Aidan Wilson – as a Christmas present.'

'Aye.'

'Thing is, Guv – she's a cagey old bird, ain't she? There's a dirty great copper in your kitchen asking you about family trivia. Either it's to soften you up for some punch line, or the trivia ain't actually so trivial. If you get my drift?'

'That might have been the mention of Nick. She'd be like a tigress with a cub.'

'Yeah – I get that, Guv – but I didn't dwell on Nick. I moved straight on to Aidan Wilson – asked her if he played much – was he into his music – did he do any performing? That kind of thing.'

'And?'

'She mainly pleaded ignorance. She said, yeah, he played his music upstairs when he lived at hers – but it was twenty-odd years ago, and he wasn't really at her place for all that long in the scale of things – she didn't really know what his interests were – he always kept out of her way and barely did more than pass the time of day.'

'We know that probably suited her.'

'Then I asked did he ever stay away, on account of his repping job – I was thinking of him lodging at country inns where Harry Nelson might have been doing a gig. But she reckoned once in a blue moon – if they had a sales conference, that kind of thing.'

Skelgill is frowning, worrying with the toe of his left boot at a loose stone that protrudes from the ground like a carnivore's premolar.

'This all sounds pretty negative to me, Leyton. What's the 'something' that you're on to?'

A prolonged clearing of the throat proves to be a species of hemming and hawing.

'Hard to put your finger on, Guv. But what you were saying about a limpet – touch it and it tightens up – and then you ain't gonna get nowhere until you try again later. I reckon from the off – the second I mentioned the guitar – she was clinging onto the rocks for dear life – even if she didn't want me to know it.'

Albeit this degree of abstraction is not his sergeant's regular modus operandi, for once he is speaking a language that chimes with Skelgill's own experience of the world, in which the sixth sense subconsciously synthesises the misguided efforts of the other five, and sometimes comes up with a result, *Excalibur* thrust glistening from beneath the placid surface of Bassenthwaite Lake. Naturally, he would have preferred it had his sergeant reported back that Aidan Wilson was a regular jazz buff and had hobnobbed with the musicians on the county circuit. But somehow he was not expecting anything so definitive; perhaps in turn he has absorbed some of his colleague's stoicism.

'How did you leave it?'

'I asked if she wanted a lift along to the shepherds' meet – she had her coat and boots on when I pitched up. But she said she was taking the dog and she'd need to keep him in the car some of the time, in case of him spooking the sheep – if you remember he's a bit of a live wire? *Hah* – tough little beggar, for the size of him.' This latter observation is suggestive of some unfortunate aspect of the encounter that has gone unreported. 'I got the impression she might be waiting for a lift – I didn't realise she still drives. In fact I half-wondered if there was someone else at the house. I went in round the back, into the kitchen, like we did last time, and the connecting door through to the front room was closed. A couple of times the dog was scrabbling at it, and she was telling it off for being silly.'

Skelgill scowls. The rock at his foot is proving to have deeper roots than he expected.

'Was there a car outside?'

'Thing is, Guv – there must have been about a dozen roundabout, maybe more, maybe twenty. I reckon visitors are driving on to Slatterthwaite to park and then walking back to the shepherds' meet.'

'Aye, they do that.' Skelgill gives up on the extraction and sits upright, raising his eyes to scan the skies. 'There's normally a field set aside in Balderthwaite, the paddock that runs down to Slatterdale Beck.'

'That's where I am, Guv. I thought I'd wait for you here, being as it's raining on and off.'

Skelgill ponders for a moment. Then he offers a suggestion.

'Maybe go and have a mooch around, Leyton – see who's there that we know – what they're up to. Keep an eye on Jean Tyson.'

He says no more about this last specific request – though there is the suggestion that he considers her a bellwether that will draw into the open something about the rest of the flock. DS Leyton seems content to follow his superior's instructions, and reverts with a more pragmatic question.

'What about you, Guv?'

'I'll duck into the *Twa Tups* – see if I can get a word with Megan Nicolson while it's still quiet. Most folk stay over at the meet until the runners come back down. It's mobbed silly after that.'

'Righto, Guv – as it happens I've brought my deerstalker – birthday present from the nippers. I'll tie down the flaps – that should do nicely to keep me incognito.'

Skelgill finds himself grinning – whether it is at Mrs Leyton's sense of humour, or her husband's so often artless nature – though a more cruel interpretation would be his assessment that there is no amount of apparel that could disguise his sergeant's provenance. He ends the call and gives the recalcitrant rock one final futile kick before slamming down the tailgate.

The route to Balderthwaite sees him cross paths with a road-hogging peloton, a glistening giant *Lycra*-clad arthropod snaking down the dale, and it perhaps is just as well that he is driving in a reflective mode, for there is little time to adjust in the limited confines of the winding lane. He is reminded it was on the same bend that a dashing Mary Wilson in her little red *Fiat* almost took out a touring member of the same two-wheeled fraternity. If only she had clipped him she probably would never have made it to Cummacatta Wood.

The near miss troubles him. Though he cannot get further than a general sense of discomfort – or even whether it is the antisocial behaviour of today's riders or something more specifically to do with his recalling of Mary Wilson's last hour. But nothing will come to him, and such is the short distance that before he knows it Balderthwaite is upon him. Now the bends become sharp and angular, between properties without pavements, and aimlessly dawdling visitors impede his progress. From an opening just ahead emerges a stout character in an ill-fitting mackintosh, shiny black wellingtons and a too-small deerstalker – he does not notice Skelgill as he lurches head down towards the nearest entrance of the shepherds' meet. Skelgill lets out a strangled cry of amusement, but he swerves away to his left, into the same gap from which his partner has just emerged, for it is a shared thoroughfare that leads both to the parking paddock and the *Twa Tups*.

There is limited availability in the pub car park, and a lad who looks like he is sagging school has been posted on the gate. Skelgill uses his warrant card to pull rank. Wide-eyed, the youth is only too pleased to let Skelgill pass – here is something to impress his pals as soon as he can get a charge on his phone.

Skelgill pushes open the door from the passage into the snug bar. It is busier than he expected; perhaps the rain has chased in a few of the softer tourists. He hesitates for a moment; perhaps he is trying to conjure the image, twenty-two years back, at this time of day when the two judges and Megan Nicolson were the only inhabitants. He finds it hard to picture now – though there are two people on stools at the bar – *the* stools – and there is a barmaid – though not *the* barmaid. Not Megan Nicolson. Skelgill recognises her, however, as one of the women drafted in on the day of the funeral to serve in Debs' farm café – and, while she is not an immediate local (from Keswick, he recalls) she seems to recognise him.

He must reveal a trace of disappointment – for he is sure he detects in her countenance a corresponding flash of self-doubt, a reaction he would not wish to elicit; besides, she would hold her own in a beauty contest. But his intention to dig into the detailed timings on the day of Mary Wilson's disappearance is thwarted, and his temper momentarily gets the better of him. Of course, she might have seen him dog walking, ignoring his fellow cynophilists – or he may once have arrested a relative – but she seems to bear no grudges, and asks what he would like to drink. As usual the *Twa Tups* offers an intriguing selection of cask ales. And, truth be told he could murder a couple of pints – but realistically a half is all he could risk, and about as useful as a candle in the wind.

He decides to come to the point.

'I was hoping to get a word with Megan – I assumed she'd be on.'

'You just missed her – she got a text message. She said she needed to nip across the road for a few minutes.'

'What – to the meet?'

'Aye – I assumed that's what she meant. I don't think she'll be long, love. Why don't you have a drink and wait?'

Skelgill is tempted to go after his quarry. But some competing instinct makes him yield. He forces himself to say the words "half pint" and orders a cask conditioned Nordic-style lager that threatens damage to the cranium.

The young woman is obliged to serve another queuing customer, and Skelgill has to step away from the small bar to make room. The tables are taken, save for squeezing in next to some stranger. But it offends his ingrained sense of masculinity to stand with his long fingers wrapped around such an inadequate vessel, so he carries his beer across to the fireplace and rests it on the mantelpiece. The wall above, and indeed most of the walls in the small shadowy room are crammed with pictures, mainly photographs. Taken as a whole, it is merely a form of decoration, it adds to the *olde worlde* charm – something that modern pub designers try to replicate knowing that today's generation of patrons, obsessed with their selfies and their social media will never bend close to interrogate; they will never see through the thin veneer of authenticity. But in real village pubs like the *Twa Tups* such an ad-hoc decades-old accumulation would be a goldmine to the social historian wishing to understand the evolution of its community. There is probably a PhD on the wall facing Skelgill alone. Gnarled farmers wrestle fearsome tups; there is actual Cumberland wrestling; huntsmen hold up trophies that leave little to the imagination; there is a gasping fell-runner from the 1950s who reminds Skelgill of the famous image of an exhausted Sir David Bannister; the pub darts team in the days of the Kevin Keegan perm; a cricket match – grandiloquently titled "Borrowdale v The Rest of the World"; there is a shot he recognises as the premises of Walter Dickson & Co before the advent of the internal combustion engine – the cracked paintwork above the lintel seems to say "Cartwright" – it could be the then-proprietor, or maybe just the occupation; there are antique images of the *Twa Tups* – it doesn't look so different, just the barefooted kids who have been ordered to line up – the Victorian poor always seemed to have bags under their knowing eyes, old before their time; and – right at one end of the mantelpiece – small and insignificant and offering no reason to catch Skelgill's eye (other than it has – that his subconscious has already processed its content and noted it might be worth his while) is a photograph that is taken inside the pub. It *is* worth his while, for it provides another 'mackerel moment' for Skelgill.

Significant, but not most extraordinary, is the hand-printed caption. It says, "After the Meet" – and the date it was taken, one year before Mary Wilson disappeared. The higher grade of extraordinary is reserved for the subject matter – actually banal, unless you are a detective in search of one vital clue that could turn a murder investigation. The composition of the faded polaroid is typically amateur. The two intended subjects in the foreground are cut off just around their midriffs and two-thirds of the image is the wall above them – the corner in fact, to Skelgill's left, rising up to the ceiling. The duo are seated, and holding instruments. Skelgill waits for his head spin to clear. He pulls out his mobile phone and redials the last number.

'Leyton, get over here.'

'Where's *here*, Guv?'

'The pub, you donnat.'

DS Leyton starts to ask questions, and in fact goes on to protest that things are just getting interesting, but all this goes unheard. When he enters the snug bar only a minute or so later Skelgill is standing proprietorially before the fireplace cradling a half-drunk *pint* of beer. In his free hand he holds a shepherds' meet brochure, at which he is squinting at arm's length.

'Having a bevvy, Guv?'

'You can drive, Leyton.'

'Where are we going?'

'Never mind that. Look.' Now Skelgill swings his left arm in a wide arc and indicates with his glass that DS Leyton should inspect the small photograph above the end of the mantelpiece. Puzzled, but knowing better than to ask why, he shuffles around the raised stone flags of the hearth and bends at the waist with a small grunt.

'Struth – that's Harry Nelson!'

But now he makes an even more strangled exclamation, subsuming what would otherwise be an unprintable outburst beneath an indeterminate splutter.

'And that's – cor blimey, Guv! It's –'

'Leyton – I can do the ID – but what about the guitar?'

DS Leyton makes an effort to compose himself. He tugs off his ridiculous looking deerstalker and mops a palm across his brow. Again he leans forward.

'You can't see it all, Guv – but it looks like a possible *Maccaferri* – whether it's the same one – maybe if we enlarged the photo?'

'And look at this.'

DS Leyton turns to see his superior holding out the leaflet. He takes it.

'What am I looking for, Guv?'

'Right-hand side – last item on the programme of events – where it says *entertainment.*'

DS Leyton tilts the pamphlet towards the pub window to enhance its legibility.

'Wait a minute – this is *what?*'

'It's the brochure for the year after Mary Wilson disappeared. Me Ma kept it for the family album – it's got the results of the previous year's fell race.'

DS Leyton is nodding as he stares intensely at the page.

'Fingerpicking.'

Skelgill does not reply, but he takes the leaflet back from his colleague and folds it into his jacket. He downs the remainder of his pint in one and places the glass on the mantelpiece beside his other empty. He wipes his mouth with a cuff, and rocks back on one heel like a high jumper about to commence his run-up.

'What do you want to do, Guv?'

Skelgill regards his colleague with alarm, as though he has missed some key point.

'Find Jean Tyson.'

'Ah – that's what I was trying to say, Guv – about what was going on over at the meet.'

'Like what?'

'Well – like you said – keep an eye on Jean Tyson. She was there, right enough – with that there Lakeland terror on its lead. She seemed to be doing the rounds. I saw her talking with her grandson, Nick Wilson – he was helping Jake Dickson with some display of old farm equipment – a working steam engine. Then she had a chinwag with Sean Nicolson – he was just finishing off shearing a sheep – and by the way his missus appeared to speak to him an' all. Thing that caught my eye was that Aidan Wilson was knocking about – if you ask me, he was trying to get a word with Jean Tyson – seemed to be biding his time. I reckon he was going to intercept her – but she went into the judges' tent – and that was when you just rang me.'

Skelgill is nodding, though his arms are folded and his gaze fixed on the door as a growing stream of patrons is beginning to enter what is fast becoming a crowded little bar.

'Come on – we'll go over.'

They work against a small human tide, both inside the pub and out, for by the time they cross to the shepherds' meet enclosure the men's fell race has finished. Competitors are milling around, taking on fluids, and dousing themselves with buckets intended for sheep to drink from. But the general drift is now firmly in the direction of the *Twa Tups*.

Skelgill marches directly to the judging tent. The door flap is zipped and a card hangs from the awning informing them that judging will resume after lunch. Skelgill checks inside, but there are just a table and two chairs and a stack of papers, and the trophies all crowded into a couple of wooden milk crates.

Meanwhile DS Leyton is scanning around the field.

'I don't see anyone I saw earlier, Guv – that was only ten minutes ago.'

Skelgill pulls up the zip of the tent.

'Nick Wilson's there.'

They stalk across to the exhibit, a clanking smoking miniature steam traction engine. It appears to be operating on the principle that to keep it going is the best strategy, and thus Nick Wilson has drawn the short straw and has been left in charge. Like a Brobdingnagian he perches on the tiny trailer and tinkers with the valves.

Skelgill hails him.

'Have you seen your gran?'

Nick Wilson cowers anxiously.

'Aye – but she's just took dog down t' woods.'

Skelgill spins on his heel – but then he turns back.

'Does she drive?'

The young man shakes his head – he seems surprised that Skelgill would think this.

'She said she were getting a lift.'

Skelgill stares at him for a second.

'From?'

He looks worried; that he ought to know and will be in trouble.

'She didn't say.'

239

Now Skelgill gives a nod of finality and sets off towards the closest exit to the *Twa Tups*.

'My motor's nearest, Leyton.'

He pulls out his keys and passes them to his colleague, who in his well-intentioned choice of wellington boots is finding the slippery ground hard going.

Now they have to force their way out of the pub car park – cutting a swathe through the oncoming crowd in a manner that gives the boy on the gate more material for his social media feed. And likewise DS Leyton has to honk and hoot at stragglers who meander blithely in the lane as if it were a pedestrianised zone – visitors giving no thought to the fact that a tractor fitted with forks or a dozer bucket might at any moment swing around a building and make mincemeat out of them.

Finally he can put his foot down.

'*Whoa* – she shifts, don't she, Guv? Deceptive for an old jam jar.'

'Cheers, Leyton.'

After a couple of minutes they approach a layby and Skelgill orders his deputy to pull in. As he bales out he instructs his sergeant to drive on to the Cummacatta Wood parking area and work his way back along the public path. His own point of ingress – although not apparent to the uninitiated – is close to the Bowder Stone, the latter hidden by the trees and the landform. He crashes into the undergrowth to emerge only a minute or so later close to the great rock, on the opposite side to where he had chatted a little earlier to the bouldering crew.

They have packed up and gone for lunch. All that remains are smudges of chalk on the overhangs, where their poor guinea pigs were dangling for dear life. He notices that someone has left an extendable bouldering brush; a bit of a Heath Robinson affair, it would not look amiss amongst his fishing gear.

At the parking area there is only one vehicle; it is a somewhat dilapidated *Volvo* that he does not recognise. It is locked. Peering in – the windows need a good clean, and the interior, by the look of it – there is nothing to provide an indication of to whom it belongs. He pulls out his phone – a vehicle registration check can take as little as thirty seconds – but he has no signal.

He thinks about calling out, but as quickly dismisses the idea; despite that his voice could warn off a predator some deeper instinct preaches stealth. And now he takes the same path along which just nine days ago he led his colleagues; that felt more like a sightseeing expedition; today his heart is racing. He is acutely aware of sounds and movements – and yet simultaneously oblivious to the myriad small sensory pleasures of his previous visits – the delightful damp musty smell of the woods, the cool rain on his face, the elegant understated poise of enchanter's nightshade at his feet.

He has built up to a steady jog when he rounds a bend in the path and stops dead in his tracks.

Coming towards him, not twenty feet away is Jean Tyson. Archie, the Lakeland Terrier – or *terror* as his colleague has inadvertently renamed it – is straining at a leash that Skelgill recognises to be the same green twine that ties up the fading runner beans in the Slatterthwaite cottage garden.

The woman does not seem fazed by his presence. But to his surprise she drops her gaze and continues purposefully as if to pass him.

Skelgill steps sideways to block her path.

'Jean – are you alright?'

She looks up – there is the most curious expression in her small grey gimlet eyes – if he could put it into words it would be some incompatible amalgam of disbelief and jubilation. Her narrow-lipped mouth does not respond, perhaps other than a slight twitch at its corners.

'Where is he?'

She stares at him unblinking, and only after a few moments does she give the slightest disdainful jerk of her head. He reads this to mean behind her.

He hesitates for a second. But he knows there to be no threat from where he has come – indeed that it might be her car she is returning to.

Skelgill runs off.

241

Barely two more minutes pass before he finds himself skidding to a halt for a second time. Now there is genuine alarm in his reaction.

'Leyton! Are you tapped?'

His bellowed warning is delivered as he reaches at a canter the little offshoot of the path that leads to the abseiling point above Devil's Lowp. All that is visible is the broad beam of his sergeant who, down on his knees near the edge of the cliff, is apparently bracing himself to obtain the slightest peep over the edge.

Despite Skelgill's fiery if well intended outburst DS Leyton for a few seconds neither moves nor speaks.

'You'd better see this, Guv.'

'You mean you're not praying?'

DS Leyton inhales as though to reply, but evidently thinks the better of it.

Skelgill, exhibiting none of his sergeant's tendencies towards vertigo, strides up to stand beside his prone colleague and peer down into the abyss.

Now he refrains from speaking.

Many thoughts cross his mind; it is like a stone has been cast into a small tarn, and the ripples, upon reaching the banks, try to return to the centre, interfering with one another, creating a pattern of confusion. But eventually they cancel out, and all is calm.

'Looks like he went over backwards.'

*

'This place gives me the willies, Guv.'

'Aye, you said, Leyton.'

'I keep expecting to see him come lumbering out from behind a wall like some whacking great zombie.'

Skelgill makes an indeterminate noise in his throat. His sergeant's manoeuvring of his precious 'old jam jar' up the rising and rutted track towards Slatterdale Rigg in part distracts him. But now he produces a response.

'Least we won't need his permission to re-test his DNA.'

DS Leyton glances across at his superior but then makes a face of apology as they instantly hit a pothole. Skelgill issues an expletive that requires a plea of mitigation before his sergeant can return to the thread of their conversation.

'You reckon it'll match, Guv?'

'I'm struggling to doubt it – let's see what we find here. Wait – stop!'

They are just passing the car graveyard. The sun has emerged from behind a band of cloud, highlighting more obviously the different colours of the abandoned vehicles.

They get out. The wrecks are arranged in two rows, and the detectives fan out, like merchants searching for particular items of scrap.

Skelgill stalks over to a black pick-up, wheels removed, on piles of rocks. He examines the registration plate – it is about ten years old – but it looks to be the vehicle most recently dumped here. He squeezes around to the front – and his features crease in alarm. In the bonnet is a sizable indentation.

'Leyton – come and see this.'

But DS Leyton responds in kind.

'Guv – come and see *this.*'

There is something in his colleague's intonation that prompts Skelgill to allow DS Leyton's request to countermand his own.

His sergeant has dragged a rotten tarpaulin off a vehicle that is half sunken in what looks like a slurry pit.

Revealed is a small red car, severely rusted and coated in grime and the accumulation of the activities of farmyard vermin.

Skelgill is shocked, such that he makes a statement that he knows cannot be correct.

'It's Mary Wilson's.'

But DS Leyton is shaking his head.

'It's a different reg, Guv. But it could have been the car that was seen being driven like crazy on the day she went missing.' He stretches out an arm. 'Look – the old tax disc – it's the right year.'

Skelgill grimaces and jerks a thumb over his shoulder.

243

'And I reckon that's our black pick-up.'

DS Leyton follows his superior's indication to stare at the other vehicle. After a moment he speaks.

'Where do you want to look, Guv? In the house?'

Skelgill shakes his head.

'In time, aye. But while it's still light I want to see what's in that barn.'

'Think we'll find his keys?'

'Probably not.'

When DS Leyton offers to stop for this reason, for a search of the farmhouse, Skelgill ushers him past and directs him to reverse up to the barn entrance. He takes a rope from his flatbed and clips one hook onto the chain that secures the double door and the other onto his tow bar. He calls out.

'There you go, Leyton. Have fun.'

DS Leyton has his window down.

'I better take it steady, eh – build up the pressure?'

But Skelgill seems to think otherwise.

'Remember the limpet, Leyton.'

DS Leyton nods phlegmatically – and with a sudden roar of the engine he lets out the clutch and Skelgill's car leaps forward, not breaking the iron shackle, but explosively ripping the two sides of the barn door off its hinges.

Skelgill wastes no time in pulling a powerful *Lenser* torch from his jacket and marching into the newly exposed void.

He has to admit that his first reaction is one of relief. On the face of it, at least, there is nothing amiss – this ancient stone building, for centuries the local slaughterhouse, bears no signs of recent horrors, neither animal nor, as was his worst fear, human.

But after a search amongst the dust and the dumped equipment he does find something of an eye-catching nature. Flashing red and white and metallic, on the sill of a boarded-up slit window, stands a *Peak Freans* biscuit tin, the sort of thing that would be seen on a table of bric-a-brac in an antiques shop. Modest as such, it is distinctive for its lack of dust. Skelgill pulls on a pair of nitrile gloves and with his lock-knife prises up the hinged lid, avoiding any unnecessary contact. He flips back the lid – and raises his torch.

And there is the magenta scarf.

Skelgill is still holding it up, staring with wonderment in the torchlight, like he has some holy grail as his sergeant shuffles tentatively alongside him. They do not speak for a while, and when they do, DS Leyton makes an altogether different conversation, as though the scarf is simply too sacred to refer to.

'Those dogs are going ape, Guv. They didn't like us ripping the doors off. That's why I hung back – I've phoned the RSPCA to get someone up here who knows what they're doing.'

Skelgill does not answer. He directs his torch back into the tin and peers inside.

'There's *Fiat* keys an' all, Leyton – her missing keys.'

DS Leyton now leans forward.

'And what else is that, Guv?'

'Looks like ladies' underwear. Quite a few pieces.'

DS Leyton seems now for the first time to become possessed by the fear that has secretly haunted Skelgill for the past fortnight.

'Jeez, Guv – what if there's more victims?'

'Leyton – I'm hoping Jean Tyson will be able to identify these. I'd rather think that at the moment.'

245

19. CASTING OFF

Friday noon, Debs' Farm Cafe

'That's the DNA test results in – they confirm the match between Patrick Pearson and the original sample from Mary Wilson's knitted key fob. Also there are traces of his DNA on the scarf – it would seem he recently handled it. They're still testing the other items.'

DS Jones seems a little breathless; the fresh air – the breeze and the rain – has brought an extra flush of colour to her cheeks and the tip of her nose. She gives an involuntarily shiver as she slips off her jacket and wraps it around the back of her chair. Skelgill notices her sylphlike elegance as she resumes her seat. They had all but finished their scones before she left – but she has a corner remaining and she pops it into her mouth. He watches reflectively as she flicks her tongue over her top lip to catch a dab of clotted cream.

He is relieved to have her back in his fold. She must be drained from her trip to Manchester – and it cannot have been easy travelling north with a cranky DI Smart, his press conference abandoned, his guns spiked by dramatic events in 'sleepy Borrowdale'. Now his sergeant is in her element, multi-tasking, coordinating various operations and already sketching out the skeleton of the report they must submit to the Public Prosecutor. On this account, he can see that DS Leyton shares his relief.

The constabulary has commandeered the lounge bar of the *Twa Tups* as an incident room and convenient location for interviewing the locals; but Skelgill has led his colleagues to take elevenses at the nearby rustic café. He thinks the pub should stick to what it does best, serving ale. But their change of venue has necessitated that DS Jones escape the thick walls of the old converted barn to get sufficient of a phone signal to pick up this latest news, the final confirmation that they have awaited.

'Also very interesting – we've identified where 'Patrick Pearson' took his original DNA test.' DS Jones makes quotation marks in mid air with her fingertips to bracket the man's name. 'It was at the testing unit at Keswick. Why would he drive past the one in the village to go to another seven miles away?'

The two males are nodding – for this is a rhetorical question to which they all know the answer. DS Leyton anyway supplies it.

'Less chance that the local bobby on the door would recognise his stooge Harry Nelson. If the nurses had called out "Patrick Pearson" and that squirt had got up to give a blood sample instead of the seven-foot hulk – he'd have stood out like a sore thumb to anyone who vaguely knew Pearson.'

DS Jones is nodding.

'We've retrieved the ID documents from the archives. Apparently it's quite clear from the photocopy of Patrick Pearson's passport that it had been tampered with. The photograph of Harry Nelson that had been inserted was crooked, and the film that covers it was creased.'

There are raised eyebrows, but no one offers recriminations. It was most likely a nurse drafted in from outside the area that was given the job of registering the men volunteering their samples. Who would have imagined that one of them was an imposter?

Skelgill is at this very moment berating himself for a not dissimilar oversight. He has the shepherds' meet leaflet borrowed from his mother's album spread out on the table before him, and now he stares at it ruefully. What at first glance was an innocuous line of type subsumed by the rest of the densely printed page now seems to shine out like the neon lights of Soho: *'For your evening's entertainment in the Twa Tups, back by popular demand – Fingerpicking Jazz with local maestro Patrick 'Pick' Pearson."*

DS Jones sees that he is discomfited.

'What's bothering you, Guv?'

Skelgill looks up sharply. He gestures with a backhanded flick of frustration at the sheet.

'His nickname – Pick Pearson – I heard enough people call him Pick. I should have sussed out the music connection. To think I've been walking round with this clue in my pocket. And all along there's been a photograph on the pub wall crying out for attention.'

DS Leyton is listening apprehensively – wondering why his superior is not tarring him with this same brush, as instigator of the jazz theory.

'But, Guv – we weren't on that track in the first place. There was no indication when we visited his farm – he looked like the last person you can imagine with a guitar in his hands. I thought they called him Pick because it maybe had something to do with a pickaxe or a pitchfork, or he picked his nose – or maybe nothing at all. I was at school with a kid we all called 'Panner' – no connection to pans that anyone knew of, old man wasn't an ironmonger, old lady wasn't a cook – but his surname was Parker, so it just sounded neat.'

And now DS Jones joins to further mitigate her superior's self-reproach.

'It didn't cost anything. I mean – maybe Jean Tyson was at a small risk – but at least you kept her safe. No one else was harmed by you not acting faster.'

Skelgill scowls belligerently.

It is not strictly true that no one else was harmed. Pick Pearson died. And, though the evidence that would surely have convicted him has since swept like an avalanche from the cliffs of Great End, he feels a pang of regret that he won't see that particular job done in a court of law. In some respects, via his one-hundred-foot descent from Devil's Lowp, Patrick Pearson had evaded justice.

Neither is it strictly true to suggest that the risk to Jean Tyson was merely 'small'. For his colleague to make this assessment seems to him one massive understatement. In her defence, DS Jones was not there at the time. She cannot have appreciated the sudden unravelling of events, the escalation of tension – indeed recalling it with hindsight makes Skelgill all the more fearful. Though Jean Tyson has denied it, he is now convinced that the person DS Leyton had suspected to be loitering in the front room at her cottage was Pick Pearson. He would have overheard her being questioned about the guitar, and Aidan Wilson's proclivities with regard to jazz. He probably gave her a lift to the shepherds' meet. Certainly he drove her to walk the dog in Cummacatta – the old *Volvo* belonged to him, not her. And thus Skelgill doubts the other aspects of her statement. That it was Pick Pearson's suggestion to go down in the woods. *What if it had been hers?* The natural assumption is that it became plain to the eavesdropping Pick Pearson that the police were closing in upon him – and that, for the time being, out of some misguided loyalty Jean Tyson was covering for him; but for how long could she be trusted? However, what if it the penny had not so much dropped for him, *as for her?* That the facts implicit in DS Leyton's questions were the final confirmation she needed of a suspicion she had long harboured? And even if it had not been her suggestion to go to the woods, perhaps she willingly went along with it – understanding she was at risk, but also knowing that she could take him by surprise.

Skelgill has not elaborated upon his fleeting encounter with Jean Tyson – or, at least, his *reading* of her dogged silence: a scene now etched in his mind – a picture that speaks ten thousand words. It tells a tale at odds with her subsequent statement: that Pick Pearson asked her at the shepherds' meet if they could talk in private about something; that he suggested they use the excuse of taking the dog down to the Bowder Stone; that they had done this; that they had reached Devil's Lowp; that the gate had been left open, as was often the case; that he had gone through – she had cautioned against it – and the dog had tripped him!

Skelgill is reminded of her words on their first meeting at her cottage, she diminutive and dour, finally coming to terms with what had happened to her beloved Mary. *"A mother can bide her time."* He realises now he has accepted the controversial conclusion to which his instincts jumped on the shadowy path so close to where Mary Wilson disappeared – that village justice had been served in Cummacatta Wood. There is no proof – and perhaps it does not matter – for the case against Pick Pearson is

249

becoming incontrovertible. With a visible effort, he pulls himself together.

'What else have we got, then? Let's recap before we commit this to paper.'

He directs this question to DS Leyton.

'Ah, well, Guv – the vehicle inspection unit have produced a preliminary assessment of that black pick-up. The first indications are that it is most likely human impact damage – the dents rarely stretch so far up the bonnet if it's an animal, even a big deer. They'll be able to compare the pattern to the recorded injuries suffered by Harry Nelson. And they're hopeful they might get some DNA – they're doing a blood spatter analysis on the grille and the radiator, where it could have become baked on.'

Skelgill is nodding earnestly; DS Leyton continues.

'Nick Wilson's guitar appears to be the one that Patrick Pearson was holding in the photograph in the *Twa Tups*. Forensics are doing some enlargements to confirm – there'll be a unique pattern of markings on the scratch plate. And they found a good fingerprint just inside the sound hole where it's never been cleaned – a match for Patrick Pearson.'

DS Jones is eager to understand the background to this aspect of the case.

'So what happened – how did Nick Wilson end up with the guitar?'

DS Leyton looks to Skelgill to elaborate. He raises his hands in an attitude of prayer, resting his elbows on the table and pressing his index fingers to his lips. It is almost as though he is debating with himself whether it is an opinion he wishes to divulge. Then he takes a deep breath and begins to speak, his gaze directed between his two colleagues.

'As far as the guitar's concerned, maybe when he couldn't play any more – when his arthritis got too bad – I reckon Pick Pearson gave it to young Nick – but not directly, not in person. Perhaps it was to impress Jean Tyson. But I reckon she told the kid it was a Christmas present from his dad – to make the poor devil feel better. And maybe Pick Pearson went along with it because he was playing a long hand.'

Skelgill's colleagues nod in unison, their expressions those of concern. DS Leyton puts into words perhaps what they are both thinking.

'That gives me the creeps, Guv – the thought of that monster prowling about in the dark – peeping Tom – half-inching their underwear.'

DS Jones is quick to interject.

'What do you think about that, Guv?'

Now Skelgill stares broodingly at his empty tea plate. Jean Tyson has identified the magenta scarf found at Slatterdale Rigg as identical to the one Mary Wilson wore on the day of her disappearance. As far as she is concerned, it is Mary's scarf. The underwear that was with it, she has grudgingly admitted probably belonged to Mary, and that, yes, they had suffered occasional losses from their washing line. But she has pointedly refused to be drawn on any speculation concerning Pick Pearson, such as that he harboured some kind of obsession for Mary – or indeed herself. Skelgill finds himself curiously predisposed towards her reticence – he can only put it down to his local roots – despite his niggling scepticism of the dog's reported role in Pick Pearson's downfall.

'Guv?'

Skelgill starts from his reverie.

'Aye – I shouldn't be surprised if he were trying to get his feet under the table at one time. There's Jean Tyson – a widow – and Mary, growing up to be an attractive young woman. He lives just up the dale, passing by regularly; there's always an excuse to drop in.'

DS Jones is nodding, and she has a contribution to make.

'When you think about Mary – Mary Tyson as she was – that she got herself hitched so young with Aidan Wilson. Maybe there was an element of self-protection – that she felt uncomfortable with Patrick Pearson's neighbourliness.'

Skelgill recalls the reaction of Jean Tyson – when on their first meeting he asked her what must have seemed a crazy question – who could have murdered Mary? And yet she had involuntarily glanced at the open top half of her back door – was

251

it often darkened by the unwelcome shadow of Pick Pearson? Even if this were something that Jean Tyson tried to discourage (or perhaps she had made the mistake of not doing so), it would have been difficult having a giant of a man passing and no husband present to deter such attention. And maybe she was flattered – until such times as he began to show an unhealthy interest in Mary. And then later when Mary was gone – at his hands – did he continue to hang around – to ingratiate himself by encouraging the boy? Jean Tyson had opined that the culprit might enact this very tactic.

DS Leyton has a further point to add.

'Guv – the print on the map. I reckon you were spot on. That was Patrick Pearson's an' all. Nick Wilson said he took the maps from his gran's house when he moved to the caravan.'

Skelgill can imagine Pick Pearson dropping in; waiting for Jean Tyson to bring him tea, casually browsing a map of the district taken from the sideboard – and finding it irresistible to trace with a grimy finger the spot where he had concealed Mary Wilson's body, the Kissing Cave above Cummacatta Wood.

'Do you reckon she was there all the time, Guv?'

DS Leyton's question recalls an earlier discussion – when Skelgill had somewhat facetiously suggested that the body was placed in the cave after the area had been searched. The old abattoir at Slatterdale Rigg could have served as a temporary morgue; moreover, the records have revealed that Pick Pearson coordinated the search party that covered his own land – just as Arthur Hope had done in the adjacent limb of the dale up at Seathwaite. He could easily have made sure that no one else looked in the barn. But Skelgill no longer subscribes to this theory. He shakes his head.

'Aye – it probably were. Bloke his size – he'd have had no difficulty carrying her. Happen he came back later, though, to shift all those rocks. Probably the same night, after he performed in the *Twa Tups*. If anyone had noticed his car, he'd have had reason to be down in Balderthwaite.'

After a few moments' silence it falls to DS Jones to pick up the conversation.

'What do you think actually happened at Devil's Lowp, Guv?'

She speaks with no special inflection, but her inclusion of the word *actually* in the question leaves Skelgill in no doubt as to what she is getting at. His response is terse.

'You've read her statement.'

But DS Jones does not give up so easily.

'Do you think he was going to throw Jean Tyson over the edge?'

DS Leyton looks rather alarmed; Skelgill glowers uncomfortably. It is a while before he replies.

'The trail had led us to him, Jones. We were within minutes – maybe a minute – of nicking him. The rest of the evidence would have followed. Him killing Jean Tyson wouldn't have saved him.'

'But he didn't know that – he might have thought that silencing her would suffice – if she'd 'fallen' over that cliff, apparently chasing after her dog?'

Skelgill plies his sergeant with a look of reproach. It lasts sufficiently for them each to be reminded of the other's distinctive eyes – hers rich hazel, his enigmatic grey-green; for once the more amenable green seems to be in ascendance. He makes a gesture with both hands raised in the air above his head, his fingers spread as if to represent the dale around them.

'Justice has been done. Don't you get it? – they've shut up shop.'

Now it is DS Leyton that is determined to know more.

'What are you saying, Guv?'

Skelgill sighs impatiently – but then he relents.

'Leyton, let me give you an example. It looks to me like Megan Nicolson and Jake Dickson were left alone in the *Twa Tups* around the time Mary Wilson disappeared, right?' (His sergeant nods.) 'Let's just say there'd been a little thing going on between them – no wonder they can't put together a story about what each of them was doing. They don't want to. What if Megan had suggested he popped down to give her a hand with a keg in the cellar? You know what I'm saying?' (More nods from DS Leyton.) 'At the time especially, they wouldn't have wanted

253

anyone to know about them – but on top of that they missed out on being key witnesses to Pick Pearson leaving the pub – and that he didn't return to the meet, but instead that he followed Mary Wilson in his car.'

Skelgill's colleagues make no rejoinder, so he continues.

'Likewise Sean Nicolson. Given his relationship with Mary Wilson – he was never going to be forthcoming – about that, or about what happened on the day. He knew he hadn't killed her, so he just kept his head down, and has done ever since. When the DNA test results came back, it cleared him – it cleared them all – so they shrugged it off and got on with their lives.'

Skelgill turns to look at DS Jones.

'Like I've said – you were right, Jones. The investigating team should have treated folk as possible suspects, not witnesses. But there were hundreds of people in the area on the day of the meet. Happen they couldn't see the wood for the trees. Then the DNA plan was hatched, and they just sat on their hands thinking that would sort it. It didn't – it turned out more hindrance than help. By then it was too late.'

Skelgill's colleagues are still silent, ruminating on his analysis. He adds one final rider.

'There've been clouds over Borrowdale for enough years; we don't need to prolong it by unravelling every last twist and knot of what relationships folk have had. It's time to let sleeping dogs lie.'

DS Leyton remains a little troubled; shadows cast by the overhead spotlights exaggerate his heavy jowls.

'But we can't let sleeping dogs lie about the DNA – not about Nick Wilson's DNA – and Sean Nicolson being his father.'

Skelgill nods solemnly.

'Aye. We need to tell Nick. Then it's for him to decide. But you know what, Leyton – I'd wager Sean Nicolson's champing at the bit to have a heart to heart with the lad. And I don't reckon it's going to come as any surprise to Megan Nicolson. She's loyal to Sean because in his way he's stayed loyal to her. You noticed she changed her tune, I reckon that was all about protecting him – and their family. I expect she's had a hunch all along that

Nick's his son. How could you not, when you see the pair of them?'

DS Leyton is shaking his head ruefully.

'Whew – village life, eh?' He looks at DS Jones, more cheerfully. 'No wonder they never run out of plots for that there *Ennerdale!* And your young pal Minto – he's going to have a field day.'

DS Jones suddenly looks discomfited; she senses that Skelgill is watching her closely. But it is her nature to take the bull by the horns. She turns to face her superior.

'Guv – I, er – kind of promised him that if he happened to come up with something that helped us – well, then I would –' (she swallows and does a kind of *mea culpa* shrug) 'well – I said I'd get him a private interview with the Chief – I was hoping you could have a word? You must be in her good books at the moment?'

Skelgill's emotions seem to ride a rollercoaster that oscillates between consternation and relief.

'The Chief's good books have a shelf life of about five minutes – before she breathes on them and they turn to cinders.' This raises good-natured chuckles from his companions. 'But I don't see why she wouldn't meet him – she must already have a line of communication open. At least her office – if not her in person.'

DS Leyton is first to respond to Skelgill's rather puzzling suggestion.

'What do you mean, Guv – a line of communication?'

Skelgill gives his sergeant something of an old-fashioned look.

'Leyton – who do you think's behind the leaks?' DS Leyton splutters but before he can answer Skelgill continues. 'Was it you?' DS Leyton quickly shakes his head. Skelgill turns to DS Jones. 'You?' She responds likewise. 'Well – it weren't me – and it only queered Smart's pitch – beside he's not bright enough to do something that subtle.'

DS Leyton is looking entirely perplexed.

'But, Guv – why would the Chief's office have leaked the story about the Manchester connection?'

Skelgill stares at him for a moment and then transfers his gaze to DS Jones – but she is beginning to nod comprehendingly. Skelgill makes a circling gesture with one hand.

'Apart from keeping us lot on our toes,' (they understand he means the competing teams of detectives) 'maybe it didn't do us any harm with the public – folk in the dale thinking the police had got it sewn up – they weren't quite as much on their guard as they could have been – and inch by inch we were working our way through their defences. When the break came, we knew which direction to move in.'

Skelgill is looking at DS Jones – but now he produces a wry grin and cocks his head pointedly in the direction of DS Leyton.

'Credit due on that score to our very own *Fats Waller*, here.'

DS Leyton recoils with mock surprise, though there is pleasure upon his face, perhaps only slightly tarnished by the small underlying prospect that his superior is cruelly taking the mickey – given that he could do with shedding a few pounds. But DS Jones is quick to confirm the compliment – she reaches across the table to press his forearm in congratulation. He responds rather sheepishly.

'You've been doing your research, Guv.'

'How come?'

'Fats Waller – he wrote *Ain't Misbehavin'* – remember, Mary de Boinville said it was Harry Nelson's signature tune?'

When there is an opportunity to accept the kudos for what is in fact pure fluke, Skelgill reacts in an altogether more self-effacing manner. He leans back in his chair and folds his arms, his gaze lowered, and he intones almost wistfully.

'I was thinking of ducking in to see her tonight. Friday's one of her days, isn't it? They've got some decent guest ales on at *The Bell* – and there's a new little curry place in Grasmere I wouldn't mind trying.' Skelgill glances up to see his colleagues both looking amused. He offers a further explanation, though it sounds no more convincing. 'Happen I ought to learn a bit about jazz.'

DS Leyton flashes a sideways glance at DS Jones – there is a curious light in her eyes and with a barely perceptible nod she appears to encourage her colleague to respond.

'Guv – I'd offer to come with you – so you're not on your Tod – but I've only gone and promised the missus a carryout from her favourite Chinese – after all these late nights when I ain't been much use around the place.'

Skelgill regards DS Leyton somewhat vacantly. Then he transfers his gaze to DS Jones, to see she is smiling quizzically. She gives him no time to speak.

'I like jazz. In fact far better than the hip hop DI Smart wa.. ~d me to listen to.'

She ¹ds his gaze and there is perhaps a sudden colouring of his promin. ~heekbones. He averts his eyes.

'Fair enough.

DS Jones looks . ~S Leyton who gives her a wink unseen by their boss. Then she ~ks the time on her mobile phone, and begins to rise.

'Er – if that's not until tonight – and we're going to be busy with reports this afternoon – hadn't I better order us another round of scones to keep us going?'

***

257

Next in the series...

CAT AMONG THE PIGEONS

Virile; handsome; ruthless. When maverick gamekeeper Lawrence Melling takes over at traditional Lakeland sporting estate Shuteham Hall he soon ruffles the feathers of not only elderly Lord Edward Bullingdon and his younger model wife Miranda, but also their adult offspring and fellow estate workers.

Meanwhile local conservationists perceive an existential threat to rare hen harriers nesting on nearby Over Moor. And when Miranda's jewellery worth a six-figure sum goes missing, and a trusted employee inexplicably disappears, DI Skelgill and his team lift the lid on a plot that simmers with envy, greed, lust and revenge.

Just as a simple solution beckons, in a further diabolical twist it seems the prey turn the tables on the predator. But is it an audacious murder or an innocent accident? Is this the work of a lone actor or a conspiracy? To fathom the mystery Skelgill finds himself in the firing line, whichever way he turns.

'Murder on the Moor' by Bruce Beckham is available from Amazon